LOVE BITTEN

VAMPIRE BLOOD ROYALS BOOK 1

SABRINA C ROSE

LOVE BITTEN

Copyright © 2020 by Sabrina C Rose.

For information visit: www.sabrinacrose.com

Book Cover design by Moore Book Designs

Editing by: Clockwork Cactus

First E-Book Edition: December 2019

Paperback Edition: June 2020

ISBN: 978-1-7350488-0-2

For my web serial fam!

Thank you for casting your votes and reading every week. You have honestly made writing this the best experience ever!

You da best!
-Sabrina

Hello Gorgeous!

This is my first official "dear fabulous reader" letter and it gives me chills! I'm so, so, so, so, glad you're here. Thank-you for your interest in my work. It truly means everything to me.

In your hands, you have a copy of Love Bitten: The Special Edition.

Whoop, whoop!

The reason why it's so special? It includes goodies that are not found anywhere else, like an exclusive prologue, deleted scenes, author q&a, and other bonus content. And! You'll get a sneak preview of Book 2 in the Vampire Royals Series, Love Game.

I'm not going to lie; I'm obsessed with watching behind the scenes videos on how things are made. I've always believed the creative process is fascinating and thought maybe you might like to see mine.

So, I've poured over some of my old documents and thought I'd share some of the behind-the-scenes with you. I'd love to know what you think about them.

I won't take up any more of your time.

Enjoy,
Sabrina

LOVE BITTEN
VAMPIRE BLOOD ROYALS BOOK 1

Special Paperback Edition

PROLOGUE

A Text Message between Julius and Evan
Sent Thu, Nov 3, 8:48 PM

Julius: Ha! I am the master of the alter realm!

Evan: Let's not get ahead of ourselves...

Julius: But I finally got texting to work.

Julius: AND I leaned a new word. It's fuck.

Julius: Spelled F-U-C-K. It's universal

Evan: You're writing it to me. I can see you how you spell...

Evan: Aren't you supposed to be getting the car?

Julius: I am. It's not... ready yet.

Evan: What do you mean, it's not ready yet?

Julius: Sometimes, humans are geniuses. It's a noun, a verb, an adjective... Fuck, their language is so colorful.

Evan: Julius... The car.

Julius: What about it? It's almost done.

Evan: ~~Done with what, exactly.~~ It's a rental, you just pick it up.

Julius: Nothing really, just a few minor modifications.

Evan: Modifications? Julius what did you think it meant when the king said to LAY LOW!

Julius: Just a suggestion.

Evan: Are you fucking kidding me?

Julius: See, that word is handy. Right?

Evan: I'm going to break your neck. I swear, if you jeopardize this deal...

Julius: And they say you're the fun one. Calm down, it's almost done.

Evan: How long? We have to be there at 9.

Julius: He does know we aren't really creatures of the night, right?

Evan: Julius...

Julius: It's coming out now. It's so beautiful.

Julius: [*sending failure.*]

Julius: [*message send failure*]

Evan: What the hell are you doing?

Julius: Trying to send you a picture of it. It's so beautiful!

Julius: We definitely need to mod one of these at home.

Evan: Seriously? We're going to be late.

Julius: I'll be there in five.

1

ERICA

WHY DID MARIE INSIST on driving like she was carting around Miss Daisy? Annoyed, Erica clenched her fists in her lap and stared at the speedometer from the passenger seat of her best friend's car in annoyance. "Can this thing go any faster?"

"It's a bag of bolts!" Marie cried, motioning to her dashboard. "Any faster, and it'll fall apart. Calm your tits, we're almost there."

Marie made a right turn toward the sleek high-rise building on 5th Avenue that Erica's soon-to-be ex-fiancé, Max, owned. Past midnight, the Financial District was light on cars and people. The fewer people she saw, the angrier she'd gotten.

That bastard said he was working late. And if he wasn't at the office, she was going to wring Max's neck.

It was their anniversary for goodness' sake.

And to think, she'd been fretting over his well-being

when he didn't show up for dinner. She'd waited for two hours at a candle-lit table—thinking progressively worse thoughts. Maybe Max had gotten into an accident on his way home. Or worse—lay dead in the street someplace.

He should be so lucky.

Not five minutes after she called his brother Cav, worry pitted deep in her stomach, her phone beeped with a single message.

Working Late.

Working late? Max was so full of hot air, she wondered how he didn't burst. He was the one who'd begged her to cook for him in the first place. He said it would be like old times. Back when she'd fix him dinner in nothing but an apron, red lacy panties, and a pair of matching thigh-high stiletto boots. Heck, she'd even cooked his favorite plate— rare as hell steak with mashed potatoes. Not a green bean in sight.

The worst part? He didn't even bother to call her to let her know he wasn't coming.

If he'd been working, then why didn't he answer any of her hundred phone calls?

She knew why.

Her shoulders slumped as her mind flitted to the string of messages she'd received from his ex-secretary two months ago, telling her that Max had been having an affair. With her. That, in fact, on all the nights he'd "worked late," he'd had her spread-eagled across his desk. Erica's breath quickened as the image of Max banging his secretary gained traction in her mind.

She'd confronted him. And of course, Max told her

not to believe a word of it. According to him, his ex-secretary was on a revenge plot because he fired her. It was plausible, but her gut told her something was off. But when Cav, Max's brother, told her she'd tried it with him too, she put the nagging unsettling feeling away and forced it from her mind.

Now, Max was working late. Again. And the nagging feeling was back. She folded her arms over her chest and fought tears.

Gosh, she was such an idiot.

"He'd better be at work," she mumbled as her best friend, who sat silently in the driver's seat beside her, turned up the street adjacent to Max's company's high-rise. "I swear, he'd better not be cheating on me. To think, he made me feel like I was crazy for even asking. After three years, how could he do this to us?"

"Maybe it's a misunderstanding," Marie shrugged, keeping her eyes meticulously on the road. Wow, that was nice of her. Frick, Max was probably cheating. Marie would have never sided with Max. Ever. She hated his stinking guts for reasons she'd never explained. She just said he wasn't worth her time.

But Marie didn't get to see the same side of Max that she had. He was loving and sweet and affectionate.

"What?" Marie said defensively, tucking her dark, almost midnight black, hair behind her ear.

She sighed instead of answering, watching Marie's stacked piercings gleamed in the flickering street lights as they drove past.

She used to have her ears pierced like that. Until Max

made her get rid of them. He said they no longer fit with their new image. Over the past year, not much she wore, said, or did fit with their new image. So, she'd changed herself for him. She'd given up so much for Max.

Marie continued softly. "All we know right now is that he's working late."

"What if he isn't?" Her voice cracked, fear overshadowing her anger. "What if he's... with someone?"

"Then, we'll kill him. But we don't know anything yet."

Her friend's deadly serious tone made her want to smile. Only, it never made it to her lips. "I know he won't answer my calls."

To illustrate her point, she pulled out her phone and called Max again. Still, it rang out. Her previous hesitation, vanished. Anger bubbled inside of her. The coward wouldn't even talk to her now. Well, that was too bad. She was going to be face to face with him soon. He wouldn't be able to avoid her then.

The car came to a stop just around the corner from Max's building. Before she could ask why they weren't parked out front, Marie was already getting out of the car. Erica fumbled with her seat belt and scrambled after her. She should have been nervous, but too many glasses of wine at her non-existent anniversary dinner had forced out any good sense she had left. Every piece of her itched to get to Max's despicable face.

When they turned the corner, she froze.

There, curbside, sat Max's stupid gleaming black Mercedes. She deflated. Well, he wasn't lying. He *was* working late. Marie was right, it was a misunderstanding.

"He's here. Maybe we should..." Erica took a step backward, but a pair of headlights flashed behind them as a white SUV came to a stop beside them.

A woman with cherry red lips rolled the car window down. "Hey, excuse me. Do you know where the Shift International Building is?"

Her breath caught in her throat as she watched the girl with blonde hair like her own give them an expectant stare. Maybe it was a coincidence. There were tons of other companies that leased space from Max. She could've been there for someone else.

She stood immobile, unable to think. Marie moved first.

"It's right here." Her friend pointed at the high-rise.

"Oh good! See, I told you we wouldn't get lost," the girl said to her passenger and swung the sleek SUV around and parked neatly in front of Max's car.

She could only watch in morbid fascination as the two glamazons spilled out onto the sidewalk. The blonde wore a faux fur coat that barely covered her, and neither did the cherry-red skirt she wore underneath it. Her red-headed friend was dressed similar, in a short floral dress, that she tugged on as the autumn wind briskly blew around them.

"Look at you two all glammed up. Hot date?" Marie asked from beside her, her bartender training kicking in hard. She was all charm and easiness. At least one of them could remain friendly and press for the information they needed. She, on the other hand, was gaping like a fish.

"Yeah, I know the owner." The blonde gave them a

knowing wink, then turned to her friend. "I can't wait for you to meet his brother Cav. Can you say hawt!"

Erica nearly choked.

"Let's go, it's freezing out here," the passenger said to the blonde, tucking her arm under her friend's.

"Don't let us keep you. You two have fun!" Marie said brightly, but as soon as the girls walked up to the after-hours button and pressed it with a buzz, her face flattened into a scowl. "Can you believe that asshole?"

"It might not be him." The denial revved tenfold, but she couldn't peel her eyes away. He had five brothers, two of which were partners in his commercial venture. They very well could be there for him. Even still, her fingers tightened into a fist as the two scantily clad women pressed the after-hours button a second time and waited for a response.

Please, let it be Ryrden. Please, let it be Ryrden.

"Who?" The speaker crackled at first, the word slightly mangled.

"Heather and Mel. We're here for Max."

Erica's nails dug into her palms so hard, they almost bled. There was a long pause.

"You're right on time ladies," Max said from the intercom. "Come on up."

The girls were buzzed into the building. Anger coiled inside of her when the door closed with a click. Puffs of air left her in streams like a raging bull in a cartoon. She was going to burst a vein. Erica stalked toward the building. "That two-timing, rotten bastard."

"Whoa there." Marie tugged her back, but she

resisted.

"Let me go, you said we could kill him."

"Or..." Marie splayed her arms out to Max's shiny black Mercedes like Vanna White showing a new letter. "We can kill *it* instead."

That was the best idea of the night.

"Let's." Erica nodded in agreement. She bounded over to the car and kicked it with the heel of her boot.

Loser. She kicked it again.

"Hey!" Marie called, holding her hands out to calm her down. "You're going to break your ankle if you keep it up. Come on."

Marie began to retreat to her car.

"Where are you going?" she asked. "You said we could kill his car."

"Yeah, but not with our feet." Marie smirked, leading her to where they'd parked around the corner. The back door let out a harsh screech that echoed across the brick building sides. Marie's lithe body bent in half as she dug around on the floor. When she finally emerged, she held up a crinkled yoga mat.

"We're going to beat his car with a yoga mat?" Her eyebrows disappeared into her hairline, then crinkled as she frowned.

"Of course not," Marie unwrapped the bunched-up mat on the pavement. A well-worn metal bat rolled out onto the sidewalk with a clink.

"Why do you keep a bat in your car?" She looked at her strange friend.

"You mean you don't have one?" She sputtered. "We

work late nights at a bar for crying out loud. It's for protection."

"In a yoga mat?"

"Of course! No one expects for it to hit with a bang," Marie pulled a second mat out of her car.

"Two?" Erica asked with a questioning look.

"Two is batting practice. One is assault with a deadly weapon," Marie said, tossing it to her.

"You're my soul mate." Erica gave her friend a wry smile before turning back to the main street.

Her feet faltered as she looked at the shiny oil slick car under the street lights. She couldn't take another step, like the car had a forcefield repelling her from it. Her liquid courage seemed spent. Erica's heart pounded in her ears as she looked at Max's precious car.

"I-I don't think I can do this," Erica stammered, her palms grew sweaty against the handle of the bat.

"Oh yes you can. You want revenge." Marie nudged her forward, pointing her bat at the white SUV in front of Max's car. "It's your anniversary and this is who he's spending it with. He doesn't deserve you."

Marie was right.

She'd spent so much time throwing herself into Max's vanity projects like his brand-new Mercedes and his flashy new commercial building, and his business fancy dinners, where the wives and girlfriends only wanted to talk about their latest luxury vacations. She threw herself into Max's dreams because all she ever wanted was for him to be happy. Even if that meant leaving herself behind and changing the way she dressed or what she ate.

Over the past year, she hardly recognized them anymore. She'd become quieter and more reserved. And, Max... Max had become less of the guy who brought her flowers just because and more of the jackass who was working late to spend their anniversary with the two bimbos upstairs. Her courage came back in full force.

Max didn't deserve her. Now, it was time to show him.

"Come on Marie, let's give this jackass what he deserves."

"Let's do this." Her friend raised the bat over her head.

Let's. Erica stared at the car, pictured Max's face—his chiseled jaw, dark eyes, his perfect bone structure—and swung.

"I gave you everything!" The bat crashed down onto the hood with a thud, chipping his pretty little custom paint job. She felt light as air seeing the damage.

The car blipped, then the alarm went off. Its piercing wail threatened to split her ear drums. She didn't care. Without a second thought, she swung the bat at the passenger side window. Flecks of glass shattered into pieces, falling into the car and onto the pavement.

"I loved you," she said to his car as if it were him.

She swung the bat again, hitting the windshield with a hard thunk. Cracks splayed all over it like spiderwebs. She swung again. It folded in and cracked, but it didn't break. Marie took up the other side, and together they dropped the bats with all their might. This time, the window gave way.

Giddy, she giggled hysterically. Max was going to

weep when he saw his precious baby. Right down to the very much dented, dumb as sin, red pinstripe he had detailed to outline the front hood. Only, when she looked for the telltale stripe, it wasn't there.

Oh no.

"Marie, stop!" She rushed out as her friend shattered one of the headlights. "I don't think this is—"

Her words were drowned out by a booming, "What the fuck are you doing!"

Dropping the bat, Erica spun toward the thundering voice. Two figures emerged from the building. She found herself face to face with a very beautiful, very intimidating, and very, very, furious face. His emerald green eyes darkened as the bat nudged at her shoes, goading her to pick it back up. His face curled into a snarl as he took in the scene behind her.

Frick.

It was as if everyone at the same moment realized what they'd just done. She took an involuntary step back, looking from the tall man in front of her to the car they'd just destroyed.

"That's my car!"

Marie gasped. "Oh god."

She squeaked in agreement; her eyes wide with shock.

"Erica," Marie called to her just as she locked eyes with the stranger's vicious gaze. "Run!"

She tried, but her feet refused to move.

2

JULIUS

J ULIUS'S FACE BURNED HOT as he took in the scene in front of him. He tried to breathe through it, but the beast inside of him rose higher to the surface with every inhale. His fangs elongated and sharpened. Two stupid humans were destroying his brand new, top of the line, custom designed car with pristine leather seats so soft that every baby butt in the alter realm would weep in shame.

He was going to kill them.

Calm, brother. Evan's mutinous voice squeezed between his thoughts of breaking one girl in half before draining the other.

Stop reading my mind. Julius seethed.

Your fangs are down.

He forced them to recede as he closed the distance between him and the two girls.

"What the fuck are you doing?" He roared. The sudden sound sent them both jolting up right.

A sharp gasp escaped one as she whipped around, dropping the bat in her hands with a clink at her feet. Her heart beat like a battering ram inside of her chest. Its quick pace formed a hypnotic beat that revved the beast inside of him. Her blood pumped up her neck and settled in her cheeks, making him wet his lips in hunger. He wondered what she tasted like. His fangs threatened to drop again.

Julius, you need to think of something else.

Get out of my head.

Focus on something else. You're losing it.

Evan's words flitted from his mind as his gaze reluctantly traveled from her throat to her face.

The universe blinked. Everything peeled away, then refocused solely on her. She. Was. Gorgeous.

Her face was so striking. Round, innocent cheeks, big doe eyes, and a near perfect symmetry he wanted to study for an eternity. Her hazel eyes were wild with emotion. When they found his, a jolt of electricity shot straight to his groin.

Julius sucked in a slow breath as his gaze trailed down the length of her. Golden wavy hair fell down to the small of her back, while fuck-me curves and legs that belonged tightly wrapped around his waist called to him. One singular thought repeated in his mind: Claim her.

Come, let's go back upstairs. Evan encouraged.

Back upstairs? He would not go back up there now. Not when the most delectable creature he'd ever laid eyes on was in front of him.

When the girl's full lips trembled, an image of the brunette upstairs going down on Cav as they were leaving made him want the girl in front of him to wrap those pretty pink lips around *him.*

"Oh god." Her companion's voice thrust him back to reality, breaking his trance.

For a moment, he thought she'd read his filthy thoughts, but realized she was looking at his car—his very much desecrated car. He regained himself.

"That's my car!" he pointed at the car.

The girl squeaked; her eyes widened with shock.

"Erica," her dark-haired friend urged. "Run!"

Yes, Erica. Run so I can chase you, the beast inside of him mused. Julius agreed to let him claim her as soon as they caught up to them.

Stop! Evan's voice hardened in his mind.

Erica stalled, watching him with a curious glint in her eyes. Or was it a challenge? The beast inside of him appreciated that.

Erica's companion moved fast. She dashed around the smashed car, boots crunching against the glass in the street, she knocked into Erica and yanked her away. They broke out into a run.

I'm a hunter, and this is my favorite game. The beast inside of Julius seized control and took off after them.

Don't. They're human. Evan followed him. His heavy footfalls propelled Julius to run faster. Harder.

She's mine. A vicious thought ripped through him. *Back off Evan.*

The two girls dashed around the corner. Erica's sweet delicious scent wafted in his direction. She smelled of lilac, honeysuckle, and fresh blood. A potent mix. His fangs dropped. She was his.

Julius, stop!

No. Not when he was so close that if he reached out his fingers could graze her soft golden hair. *You're mine now, Erica.*

A sudden boulder of pain smashed through his skull, as if the gods themselves hit him with a lightning rod causing its white-hot heat to sear into his brain. Julius fell to his knees and grabbed the sides of his head.

Sorry, brother. Evan was doing this—making his brain hurt as if he'd squeezed it between his fingers and yanked it backward.

"Let go of me," he grunted, clutching at the back of his skull is if he could pry off Evan's hold on his mind with his hands.

No. Not until you calm down. Evan's iron grip tightened, but he was focused on fleeing.

"She's getting away." He tried to wrench himself toward her. Evan refused to let go.

He helplessly watched Erica shove herself into the passenger seat of a rusted-out black sedan. Her friend was already putting the keys into the ignition.

"Wait," he shouted.

They didn't wait. Her friend pressed the gas hard. The tires screeched as the car launched from its space and sped off.

"No," he cried out as he watched the car run several

red lights as they fled.

Immediately, the tension on his brain was gone. Evan let go of his mind.

Julius rose to his feet, then launched himself at his brother. "How dare you let them get away?"

"Are you kidding me?" Evan asked. His long skinny fingers wrapped around Julius's wrists and yanked his hands away from his shirt collar. He poked him square in the chest. "You went full vampire in front of two humans, and you're asking me why I let them get away?"

"So, what would you have me do? Nothing?"

"The King sent us with one mission, Julius. So yes, you do nothing."

"They can't just destroy my car and get away with it. Damian would understand." He pointed down the street where they were last seen. "Their scent is still fresh. I'm going to track them."

"You're not going anywhere."

"Watch me."

Then, he felt it again. A tingling feeling slid up the back of his neck and into his skull and took hold of his brain.

"Stop it!"

"Calm down."

Julius moved anyway. Only, his skull didn't comply.

"Breathe with me." Evan's breaths were slow and methodical.

"No."

"Breathe with me, and I'll let you go," he amended.

He didn't have time for this. Their scent grew weaker

by the second. He narrowed his eyes at his brother and took a long spiteful breath. "Happy? Now, let me go."

"Five more."

Evan's grip held firm.

"Fine," he bit out and breathed with his brother. They must have looked like a pair of idiots in the middle of a vacant street expelling large puffs of air. He swore to all the gods across all the realms, he would never go with Evan to the alter realm again. Even if breathing like a fool did calm his agitation.

"We're here to lay low. Not risk exposure."

"I know what we're here to do."

"Then, act like it. You lost yourself back there."

Julius clamped his mouth shut and wrenched himself away from his brother, thoughts duplicitous. Evan was right, and that fact grated on his nerves. He'd completely lost himself. Letting his beast control him was dangerous for everyone, not just the humans he ran after. He hoped they hadn't seen his fangs. Or how his irises darkened into black pools and expanded across the whites of his eyes.

"They didn't," Evan answered his train of thought as they finished their final deep exhale. "Alright, let's get back."

Nodding, he walked back to the parked car. It was completely ruined. His earlier anger curled inside of him and settled on his shoulders as he assessed the damage. The car was riddled with dents. Every window it used to have was smashed cubes of safety glass on the ground. They'd even smashed the headlights out. A defeated growl escaped him as he gently grazed fingertips along the once-glossy paint.

"I'll call for a cab," Evan said quickly. "Maybe you should wait inside."

"I don't want to wait inside. I want to track them right now."

"We've discussed this." The tingling came back.

"I'm just saying, I want to. Not that I will." He gave Evan a scathing look. It was Evan's fault he wasn't allowed. His brother pulled his phone out of his pocket. Evan's nimble fingers dashed across the screen before he pressed it to his ear.

He returned his attention to the car. A look of pity scrunched his face into a frown. "Look at what they did to you." He whined, petting the car before resting his head against the dented door frame. "You were so beautiful."

"No one told you to get a custom car." Evan shrugged. "Next time, get a rental."

TWO NIGHTS LATER

"Are you still sulking?" Evan pushed behind the bar in their hotel suite, grabbing a highball glass and a bottle of dark liquor before pouring himself a drink.

"Fuck off."

"Ooh. Looks like someone is testy."

"I said: fuck off."

Evan snickered. "Well, lighten up buttercup. We have

another prospect to check out tonight."

His brother's overly cheerful disposition made him want to munch someone. Instead, his shoulders slumped as he took another swig of tequila. Of all the liquors in the alter realm, this one tasted less like sucking on ass and more like liquor should. The bite of it warmed the back of his throat, but it didn't quench the thirst that had lingered there ever since his car was smashed to bits. Her scent had long since dissipated, but its memory was still fresh.

"You've got it bad." Evan tsked and put the glass to his lips and emptied it. He made a face as he gulped it down. Apparently, he didn't like the dark liquor either. Served him right.

"What's the prospect?" He changed the subject, sliding his now empty glass back and forth between his hands against the shiny mahogany bar top.

"A night club called Savu."

"Smoke?" Julius asked and prayed for a coincidence. Then he thought of the wolf shifters with a growing conglomerate of commercial buildings across the city, and knew not to believe in coincidences. He grabbed the bottle and poured another shot. "Please don't tell me it's another shifter. Or worse, a mage."

"Money is money." Evan pulled the bottle away from him and capped it.

"Hey!" Julius protested, but it was already tucked underneath the bar and out of his reach. "Are you trying to incite a turf war?"

"It's business. Even though they're hot headed, the wolves will understand that. No matter which clan we deal with."

"Clan? So, it's not a mage. Thank the all gods. You can never trust a mage. They always have their own agenda." Then, a burning question popped into his head. "I thought there were only wolf clans in this city?"

Evan shrugged. "They're not all that's out there."

"So, this prospect isn't a wolf?"

Evan shook his head and grabbed their coats from a closet in the hall. He was playing coy. There were only two coats inside of it, but he rifled through them as if he were sorting through several in a department store.

"Out with it. Who's the owner?"

"His name is Stick. He's a loner." Evan tossed him his black leather jacket. "He hails from no clan."

"What is he? A bear? A skin walker? What?"

His lanky brother shrugged nonchalantly. "A fire serpent."

Julius stopped breathing for a moment. His woes from a minute ago had completely vanished. "You found a dragon? I thought their kind fell into legend."

It'd been at least a century since the last dragon had been sighted in any of the known realms. For a while, a rumor circulated that dragon shifters had found another portal, one that led to a realm they'd called their own. He'd figured it was merely a story told to young children. Not even Gustav, his older brother, the explorer, had found it on any of his adventures.

"So, they exist? How many of them?"

"No one knows about him and neither do we," Evan said firmly. Ah. It was a secret Evan had plucked from the dragon's mind.

"You know, I'm beginning to hate this realm. First, my car gets destroyed. Now, there's an actual dragon in our midst and I can't make anything of it. What good is it being a prince if I get run over like this?"

"To serve, on your honor to the King. Our brother needs investments with quick cash to stave off the blood shortages. And since we show the most promise for not exposing vampire kind in this realm, we get the privilege of being in a place that doesn't fawn over us." Evan bared his teeth in a wide fake smile.

He frowned. "I hate being a Prince."

"Said no one, ever. Let's go. There will be plenty of free booze and women to drown your princely sorrows in after we secure this deal." Evan wagged his eyebrows, knowing his weaknesses well. "You know the legend of dragons. They have a way of attracting the pretty ones."

"So, it's true then?"

Evan returned a look of mischief. "Brother, if we secure this deal, you'll be drowning in more pretty women you can handle."

Now, that was more like it, he grinned. Finally, their trip was taking a turn for the better. He followed Evan to their private elevator and into the parking garage, where a car service waited to take them to the night club called Savu.

The best part of being in a city was the fact that it hardly took long to get anywhere. Sure, the parking left a lot to be desired, but they didn't have to worry about parking at Savu. Stick held a spot for them roped off at curbside. At least the dragon knew hospitality. This was the only joy of the alter realm.

From the outside, Savu was an ordinary two-story brick building filled with large blacked-out windows and an unassuming staircase that led up to a plain blood red door. At street level, the club extended to a small restaurant littered with couples and groups holding solo cups and eating pizza.

So, this was the potential investment. He might have gotten his hopes up.

"Don't judge a book, brother." Evan smirked, then nodded over to the entrance line that snaked down the block and wrapped around the corner. Julius's eyes widened.

His brother was no liar. Hordes of the most beautiful people he'd ever seen gathered in line like Stick was handing out gold bars and free tickets to the next world.

"It's even better inside." Evan clasped a large hand against his back and wiggled his eyebrows before leading him to the guard near the stairs. "We're here to see Stick."

The guard, tall like himself but bulkier like he carried boulders under his shirt, touched a small device in his ear and called for his boss. The communication device was much different than the one in Julius's pocket. He stared at the black plastic that wrapped around the bald man's ear and wondered how it worked. It barely took a second to hear Stick's voice inside of the man's ear, "Let them in."

The line shifted as the bouncers held the crowd back to make way for them. Now, this was the service he was used to. He climbed the stairs behind Evan and through the doorway of the nightclub. As expected, it was filled with people. From the look of it, anyone left outside would be just that: left outside. A rhythmic beat muscled its way through the club. Flickering lights sprayed the crowd with flecks of colorful lights, shining over the dancing bodies that shifted around the club in earnest. On the inside, Savu was everything he imagined it to be.

He could definitely drown his sorrows in this. He'd already seen a few women that caught his eye. A girl in a skin-tight black dress that barely touched her thighs eyed him from across the room. She smiled at him. Yes, tonight was going to be glorious.

"Welcome." A man in dark blue jeans and a plain navy button-down shirt diverted his attention. The man was tattooed to the gills. A scaly pattern laced its way from his neck down to his hands. Even in his human form, he looked like a dragon.

"Stick." Evan thrust his hand out. "This is my brother, Julius."

Stick swiped a hand through his hair, then down the sides of his jeans before offering it to him. Julius took it. The man ran hot and his grasp remained firm. Good. They needed someone worth his salt in this venture.

"Please, come this way. Tonight, you'll be afforded the VIP package, which includes..." The dragon talked about the ins and outs of his club and the night he promised they'd have, but it was hard to focus on his words.

His mind was trained elsewhere. Just beneath the scent of fresh sweat, blood, and booze, something sweet, like fresh flowers after the morning dew caught him by surprise. A scent he'd memorized.

Erica.

He couldn't believe his luck. He smiled inwardly. Dragons had a way of attracting the pretty ones. And Erica was definitely one of the pretty ones.

His head whipped around, gaze dashing back and forth through the club, looking for her. He scanned every face, looking past every dancing body in his search.

Where is she?

He moved. Evan stiffened but made no move to grab him when he excused himself from the club owner. He flossed through the crowd to the dance floor. No. The scent was weaker there. He turned around and moved back toward the entrance.

Julius. Evan's voice whispered inside his skull even though he looked to be engrossed in what the club owner was saying. *Calm, brother.*

He was calm. Calmer than he'd been all night. He focused on her scent, the one that smelled like spring after a rainstorm.

There.

Just behind the bar, Erica poured several shots for a group of college guys who looked no older than her. Her eyes sparkled when one of them said something she found funny.

"Salud." He read from her gorgeous lips. She toasted with them and drew a shot to her lips and downed it back.

"We'll get you settled in the VIP area," Stick said from behind him and pressed a hand to the device in his ear to call a name, but he stopped him.

"Them," Julius pointed to the collection of people behind the bar. "Do they work for you?"

Stick nodded. "Everyone behind the bar does."

A mischievous smirk brightened his face. He never believed in luck. But tonight, was the exception.

"Do you want one of them to tend your section?" Stick asked, releasing the button on the communication device in his ear. Julius set his gaze on his prize. Her hazel eyes were still sparkling as another set of people found their they way in front of her.

"I'm going to stay down in the pit, Julius—" Evan began, but Julius cut him off.

"I want the blonde," he demanded.

"As you wish." The dragon shifted and pressed the communication device again. "Erica, you're on VIP. Come set your station."

Stick guided him up a set of stairs to a VIP section that boasted a bird's-eye view of the night club, but he wasn't interested in watching the club. Not when there was someone more interesting that had his attention.

He studied the girl with the long wavy blonde hair as she filled up a tray of liquor and hoisted it on her shoulder. She hadn't noticed him yet.

Good.

It would be sweeter. He leaned back into the booth and stretched his arms wide, watching her walk from the bar toward him. Erica's stride was graceful and fluid like a deer unaware of the lion.

She didn't know what was in store for her. If he had it his way, he'd punish her for destroying his beautiful car. A flood of naughty images blipped through his mind as he stared at the short hem of her shorts that revealed the most delicious set of legs he'd ever laid eyes on. It was decided. He needed them around his waist. His mouth watered.

J Erica climbed the stairs to the VIP area. She wore a dazzling smile, which quickly turned into a flat line before rounding out in shock. Her doe eyes flew open. Gasping, she nearly dropped the tray of alcohol.

Oh, yes. The beast inside of him purred when her sweet honeysuckle and lilac scent became stronger. *I've got you cornered now.*

Erica sputtered and her heart barreled inside of her ribcage. Her hazel eyes danced a thousand miles like she was trying to think of what to do next.

A mischievous smirk settled on his lips.

"Hello, Vandal."

3

ERICA

CRAP.

No. This was bigger than crap. This was definitely worthy of an f-bomb.

Fuck.

This wasn't happening.

He wasn't in front of her, Erica reasoned with herself. There was no way she was staring into the same pair of striking green eyes she'd fled from two days ago after she'd taken a bat to the glossy black exterior of his car. The odds were too great. Mathematically, in a city this size, she should have never crossed paths with him again.

Yet, there he was, sitting comfortably in the VIP booth, dressed in a tailored suit that fit his muscle-laden body to perfection. His arms were splayed across the booth like he owned it. His gaze raked up her frame with an intensity that almost made her drop her tray.

God, she wished the floor would open up and swallow

her whole. The one time she sought revenge, karma's bullcrap knocked her square in the teeth.

It was the guilt, she reasoned with herself. She'd felt so bad for destroying his car that she'd expected the police to show up at her doorstep at any moment to cart her off to jail. This was her penance.

Closing her eyes, she tried to calm herself. This was nothing more than a hallucination. It had to be. A patron must have slipped something in her drink. There was no other rational explanation for *him* being ten feet away from her.

When she opened her eyes, every strobe light in the room found him at once. Slack jawed, she stared at the gorgeous face of the man whose car she'd beaten to smithereens. It was clear that this was real. He was there.

Her stomach turned inside out and lodged in her throat.

She needed to run. She glanced at the VIP section's stairs. Big Rig, the VIP's private bouncer for the night, blocked the entrance at the top of the stairs. The only way past him would be to either make a scene or hoist herself over the balcony and risk plummeting to her death on the dance floor below. She'd rather do the latter if she had to explain to Stick why she couldn't serve his VIP.

There had to be a way out of this.

Think, Erica, think.

Her thoughts raced. She glanced behind the bar to her best friend's vacant station; Marie would know exactly what to do. She could talk her way out of anything. Like that time they were caught street racing on the highway.

While she hyperventilated in the passenger seat, her friend remained calm.

"There's a three-step process to this," Marie had reassured her as the cop's red and blue lights whirled behind them. "First, act clueless. Next, deny everything. And when all else fails, come up with a plausible excuse to explain it away."

If her friend could convince a police officer that they were merely driving fast to move out of the way of some crazy fool who was weaving in and out of traffic, then she could convince the VIP in front of her that she had nothing to do with the shiny car she'd beaten into oblivion. Easy.

She gulped.

"Hello Vandal," he said. His deep voice had no trouble finding her ears over the harsh synth beat playing from the speakers. A smirk played against his full lips as he stared at her like a lion who'd sunk his claws into a gazelle. Erica gathered as much courage as she could.

Step One: Act clueless.

"Vandal? I'm sorry?" She laughed nervously and looked directly into his eyes and gave him a sweet smile. Her heart thudded hard inside of her chest. "My name is Erica."

His eyebrows set into a hard line. "Oh, I know what your name is, Vandal."

"Vandal? Is that some kind of thing they say where you're from?" She tried to keep a saccharine smile plastered on her face as she put the drink tray down on the table in front of her. Taking a deep breath, she tried to calm her nerves. "Can I get you a drink?"

"So, this is the kind of game you want to play?"

"Game?" A thick lump formed in the back of her throat. "I'm sorry, I don't know what you're talking about."

"I'm sure the fingerprints on the bat that destroyed my car knows exactly what I'm talking about."

Her hand faltered when she grabbed for a bottle of chilled vodka to set it on the bottom rack of the à la carte service table in front of him. The man let out a noise that sounded like triumph as he rested his thick forearms against his knees and leaned in closer to talk to her.

"So, we can drop the pretense, *Erica,*" he finished, his breath hot against her ear.

Her heart threatened to explode. Frick, why didn't some divine act save her? Was it too much to ask to have the roof cave in? A sinkhole to open up? Something?

Then, her best friend's advice skyrocketed from her memory. *Deny everything... again.*

"I-I don't know what you mean," she stammered, hoping the music dwarfed her voice.

When his eyes narrowed, it was clear he'd heard and wasn't pleased. Her instincts to flee kicked in.

She stood, but he was quicker. A large hand grasped her wrist and kept her pinned in place. A jolt—one that felt suspiciously like desire instead of fear—shot through her at the heat of his touch.

"I am not one to be trifled with." His voice as hard as he was intimidating. A nervous flutter of butterflies erupted in her gut.

33

Don't let him get to you. Get yourself together, Erica.

When he leaned in, the scent of his cologne clouded her mind in a foggy haze. He smelled like the crisp morning air. It was intoxicating. He even *smelled* expensive. His cologne must have cost more than her whole life. Like his car.

"Do you want to try that again, Vandal?"

She tried to search for something—anything—to say but, her head emptied of everything except cobwebs and pocket lint.

Biting the inside of her cheek, she glanced over her shoulder, trying to locate her boss. Stick was invisible within the sea of partiers. She glanced at Big Rig again. With his back facing them, the oversized bouncer was focused on keeping unwanted guests out of the VIP area and oblivious to what was happening inside of it.

"I-I don't want any trouble," she stammered.

"That's funny. Neither did I, but my car was destroyed all the same."

"It was an accident."

"Which part?" he asked. "The part where you shattered my windows or the part where you cost me forty-seven thousand dollars in damage?"

The air left the room.

Forty-seven thousand? Her chin dropped to her chest. Karma hated the hell out of her. How did teaching Max a lesson turn into causing nearly fifty thousand dollars in damage to a stranger's car?

"Um. Wow."

"Yeah, wow," he mocked. "And someone has to pay

for that."

Pay for it?

She didn't have that kind of money. After forking over her life savings to enroll in art school, there was barely enough in her account to cover her half of the rent for next month. "I-I can't."

"Then, it looks like we're at an impasse, Vandal."

"W-what do you mean?" Her legs wobbled when she took a step back. He stood in one fluid motion of his own, recapturing her wrist like he was afraid she'd bolt away again if he let go. When he reached his full height, her jaw dropped a second time.

Whoa. He was tall. Next to her five-foot-six frame, he seemed like a giant. She licked her dry lips as she watched him with curiosity. Sure, he was intimidating as all heck. But there was something else. Something alluring.

The shadows of the VIP area bounced off his angular face. The light found him in all sorts of interesting ways. It shadowed his eyes and laced around his chiseled jaw and full lips. Everything about him was virtually flawless. Heck, even his teeth seemed polished to perfection. It was as if God had hand-carved the man in front of her himself before delicately placing him on Earth with the rest of the poor mortals. It made her want to paint his likeness.

He moved into her personal space. At first, she thought he might crush her. Instead, he grabbed a glass from his à la carte station and poured himself a drink one-handed while holding on to her wrist with the other.

He wasn't hurting her, she realized, staring at his hand in wonderment at how large it was. His fingers overlapped around her tiny wrist. His piercing gaze traveled down her arm, as if he were curious to see what caught her eye. He dropped her wrist like she'd burned him. A chill fanned across her skin at the loss of contact.

He cleared his throat. "Someone needs to pay for the damages. Whether it's monetary or penitentiary, it makes no difference to me."

Immediately, she stopped thinking of the multitude of color swatches she'd need to capture the beauty that resonated in his eyes when the club's multicolored strobe lights flickered in them and focused on his words.

"Penitentiary... As in jail?"

He shrugged his broad shoulders and cocked his head to one side as if to say 'if it must come to that.' She couldn't go to jail. Not when she had a career defining showcase to prepare for.

"That's extreme isn't it?" she asked.

"You know, I spoke to an officer who gave me his card and, funnily enough, he asked that I call if anything else came up." He plucked a business card from his pocket and let it dance between his fingers. "I'd planned to throw this away, but I'm glad I kept it."

"I'm sure w-we can come to some sort of arrangement," Erica pleaded, eyes darting over to Big Rig, who'd probably hold her until the police showed if the VIP demanded it. "I-I'll make it up to you."

"You're going to make it up to me?" He chuckled. At least he was no longer furious. "I thought you didn't have that kind of money."

"Money isn't the only currency. I can pay another

way."

A smirk settled on his lips. "I have to hear this."

From the look on the man's face, she realized what he must've thought she was insinuating. "Oh my God, not that!"

"Not what?" He asked, his smirk growing wider.

"I mean—" She cleared her throat before turning to the only possible way out of this. "I'm an artist."

"How does that help me?"

"I do—" her voice caught. "Custom originals. Of anything."

"It will take a lot more than a custom original to ease the hurt of that car." He looked amused.

"Picassos sell for millions."

"You're comparing yourself to one of the masters?" he asked incredulously.

"I can rival him."

"Cocky?"

"Confident," she said, even though her rolling gut said otherwise.

"Now, I have to see this. Show me."

"I can't now, my paint—"

"It was said that Picasso could sketch something exceptional in twenty minutes. Do it in ten, and I'll consider your offer."

"R-right now?" The heavy bass of the music pounded in her ears.

"Right now." His brow lifted in challenge. He dug into his breast pocket, found a pen, and held it out to her. "Surely his rival wouldn't take issue with it."

Erica bit the side of her cheek and studied him. The man in front of her made her want to please him—to prove to him that she could rise to any challenge he set. By the time the strobe lights dashed into their corner again, she plucked the pen from his hand and moved over to sit in the booth. He followed.

"What do you want me to draw?"

"Anything that delights you. Whatever you're strongest at. I'll play fair."

That wasn't playing fair. It was harder to work to a blank canvas with infinite possibilities. She shrugged and thought of what she could draw in ten minutes that wouldn't look like a fourth grader drew it. Once she settled on an idea, she rolled up his sleeve.

"What are you doing?" he asked, but made no move to stop her.

"I need a canvas," she studied the smooth skin of his forearm, then his hand. Thankfully, not a hair was in sight. "This will do."

"I'm glad I'm to your liking," he mused wryly.

"Remember, you asked for this." Her grip tightened on his hand as she examined it before glancing back at him. "So, if I draw something, and you like it, you'll book me for a commission. The commission sets us clear."

"If I'm impressed." He nodded in agreement, an encouraging smile gracing his lips. Even smiling, the man was devastating. Why was she always attracted to his type? The domineering, strong-willed, always-knew-their-power-and-went-after-it types. Like Max.

Max. Her heart deflated.

"Everything alright?" The VIP asked, his dark brows collapsed together in concern. Probably because she was staring at his hand longer than necessary.

"O-of course," she said quickly, pushing the thoughts of Max and why he still hadn't called her out of her mind. Instead, she focused on the ridges of his hand and examined the bone structure. When her fingers grazed over his knuckles, he cleared his throat and shifted.

"What do you have in mind?" He took a long swig of his drink before settling back into the booth.

"I can't give away all my secrets." She smiled, hoping it exuded more confidence than she felt. His large hand would provide plenty of space to draw, but skin was tricky. It didn't always behave. She prayed for the muscle memory of her high school days when she'd draw patterns all over her arms at school.

"Good. I like surprises." He settled back into the booth. "Ready?"

"I'll set a timer." She pulled out of phone.

"I'll keep time also," he said with a quirked brow. "I don't want you to cheat."

She tossed him a playful wink. "I don't need to."

"I like your confidence." His deep voice, rich with approval, reverberated just over the music.

As he fiddled with his own phone, she set several alarms to buzz in her pocket to keep her on track. The last thing she needed was to run out of time.

When she was finished, she guided his hand to lay flat on the thick meat of his thigh and pulled the man's warm hand into her lap and ran the black ink pen over his smooth skin to test the ink fluidity. The ink glided over his skin effortlessly and stayed exactly where she put it. She smiled inwardly. Thank goodness for small miracles.

"Ready?" she asked.

"Always," he purred. They set the timer.

Using large strokes, she got to work.

The club faded away as she held the man's strong hand in her lap and drew on the back of it. After a few minutes, her creation took shape. The line work was effortless, but the heat of his gaze on her every movement was intense. A flush crept into her cheeks as he watched her work.

The first buzz went off on her phone. She was halfway through. Her nerves ignited. Having only ten minutes to extinguish a fifty-thousand-dollar debt was the hardest thing she'd ever done.

"A raven," he mused softly next to her ear. A shiver of relief cascaded down her spine when his deep voice vibrated beside her. At least he could make out the blob on the back of his hand as she shaded in what would have to pass for feathers.

Her phone buzzed again. Two minutes left.

Her nerves spiked, and adrenaline soaked her hands. With her hands shaking, Erica forced the pen to dash across his smooth skin, hoping her vision would come to life.

In no time, her phone buzzed again.

One minute.

Her breath caught in her throat as she gripped his forearm in a white-knuckled grip and willed her hand faster. She wasn't nearly finished with her rendition of a raven.

"That's time," he said too soon, just as the final buzz went off in her pocket.

"Five more seconds."

"I see what you're trying to do." He made no move to stop her as the pen slid over his hand.

His words forced her away from him. Sighing deeply, she looked at the slashes of black ink across his hand. This raven wouldn't even rival something a kindergartener could produce, let alone one of the great masters of art. What was she even thinking, talking herself up like that?

She looked up at the VIP in trepidation. She'd never failed so badly at something before. A sick feeling, rough like gravel in her gut, made her sink back into the booth.

Absently, she rubbed the back of her neck and fought tears. Waiting for him to show any hint of his feelings felt like an eternity.

She tugged at the hem of her shirt and bit the inside of her cheek, watching his jawline flex. He made no other movement, just stared at the splotch of ink on the back of his hand. Her heart bounced in her ribcage and threatened to tear a hole in her throat.

Nerves thrust her back out of the booth and over to the balcony. But she didn't look down at the pit. No. She may have been at the balcony, but she was completely focused on the VIP. He was unreadable. Did he like it? Was he going to call the police?

There was no way to know if she didn't ask. Swallowing a thick lump, Erica steeled her courage and stepped toward the VIP. He was too focused on his hand to notice.

"So," she fished for his attention. "Do we have a deal?"

4

ERICA

A S SOON AS THE QUESTION was out of her mouth, his striking green eyes didn't leave hers. The intensity of them rooted him. Maybe he hadn't heard her.

"So," she began, but was cut off by footsteps bounding up the metal stairs to the VIP. When she caught sight of her boss's spiky coal black hair, she to an unsteady step away from the VIP and made herself busy straightening the bottles at his drink station. Her boss would kill her if he saw her fraternizing. A gesture, she could surely use right now.

"Mr. Craul," Stick greeted the VIP.

"Please, call me Julius." He turned to her employer with a smile.

"Julius." Stick moved between them and motioned

toward the pit. "Come, let me show you the wares of the club. We have several music areas, six bars, two performance stages..."

Show him the club? That meant she'd have to wait to hear his answer. Intently, she watched Julius's body language, determined to soak up even a single clue as to which way he swayed. When he tugged at the crisp hem of his pristine white shirt like he was trying to force the cuff over his hand to hide her drawing, his verdict was clear.

He hated it.

Frick.

She was going to jail. She needed to get out of there.

"Erica, reset your station," Stick ordered as they headed for the stairs. Julius never once glanced back.

For that one moment, her most of the time prickly boss was a godsend. His relentless need for perfection would provide her with the perfect opportunity to escape. While he was giving Julius the grand tour of Savu, she would sneak out of the club unnoticed. After that, she'd quit the place cold turkey, walk away and never come back.

Stick's spiky hair bobbled through the crowd with Julius in tow. Now, was her chance.

She beelined straight to the coat check and didn't pass go.

"Eri! You're headed out early tonight?" Barbie asked when she forked over her pink ticket in a rush.

"Yeah, not feeling well," she replied, glancing over her shoulder. Julius and her boss were lost in the sea of partiers. Hopefully, it would remain that way.

"Too much booze." The coat attendant nodded in understanding as she looked her over. "It happens to us all eventually."

Did she look drunk? She palmed her hair for a moment, wondering if she looked disheveled, but quickly decided it didn't matter now.

"So, what did you in? My first time was Jose Cuervo. I haven't touched the stuff since. Need me to call you a cab?" Barbie leaned against the counter and readied herself to chat. Why did Stick require them to check their coats at the door instead of throwing them in the back like she did at every other bar she worked? Most nights, it was a perk. Tonight, when she was in a rush, Barbie's chattiness was a hindrance.

"No, I just need my coat," she replied abruptly, hoping to hurry the skinny dark-skinned woman along. She didn't have time to talk.

Barbie gave her a startled look before disappearing into the back room.

She drummed her fingers against the coat check counter.

What was taking Barbie so long back there? Usually, she would zip in and out with a coat in hand faster than any other coat check person that was ever employed at Stick's club. Tonight, she seemed to drag.

She didn't have time. Sooner or later, Stick would notice she was gone.

Finally, Barbie returned. Her long skinny fingers were pressed against the comms in her ear.

"Yeah, I see her. She's, uh... right here. Hold on a sec,"

Barbie tossed her a confused look as she laid her coat between them.

Erica snatched it away and turned on her heel, but Barbie had already removed her earpiece and stuffed it into her hand. Why did she have such rotten luck?

Erica held the device up to her ear. "Yeah? It's Erica."

"Where's your phone?" Stick asked, his tone reaching several levels of over it.

"I, um, must have left it in the VIP area."

"Then why aren't you back at your set to retrieve it?"

"I-I had to use the bathroom."

"At the coat check?" The impatience in his voice exploded. Erica whirled around, looking for her boss's angry face. He wasn't in sight.

"I...I thought I left something in my jacket."

"What? Your brains?" Stick roared over the comms before clearing his throat. Apparently, Julius was nearby, or her hotheaded boss would have laid into her. His next words barely passed for the professional club owner he was going for. "Hurry up and get back to your station. Our patrons are never to be kept waiting."

"I'll be there in a second," she said, even while shrugging her coat on.

The line silenced. She returned the comm to Barbie, who's wide dark brown eyes stared at her with incredulous shock. The waifish girl tsked and shook her head. "You're skipping out? Stick's not going to be happy."

Yeah, well, she had bigger fish to fry right now. Erica shrugged and made her way toward the exit. Several bouncers were still at the entrance, checking people in and out of the club. Her heart fluttered in her chest as she settled in the shortest line, praying like heck she'd make it out before she was caught.

Please let Harmon check me out. She prayed to every god she could think of. With any luck, oblivious Harmon would let her pass without question. He never paid attention to conversations over the comms. Every bouncer except him would have noticed she'd promised Stick she was going back to the VIP area and not to the exit.

"Hey. You with the blonde hair. Hold up a second." A stranger weaved through the crowd toward her. Immediately, she tensed up. He could be talking to anyone, but the way it seemed his voice traveled over the crowd, it was meant for her.

What now?

Please let it be some drunk trying to get her phone number. At least then she could ignore him. That was generally how those interactions went. She'd pretend he didn't exist, and he would grumble some obscenity under his breath and move on.

"Hey, blondie!"

Ignoring how grating that term was, she continued her pretense and willed the line to move faster. It was only a matter of time before Stick realized she wasn't going back to her station. Time was running out.

For once, she hoped that karma would just stop with her bull crap already. No such luck. The guy in front of her paused to make small talk to Harmon who blocked the exit.

What did I ever do to deserve this? She tilted her

head to the sky and frowned.

Tapping her foot impatiently, she tried to ignore the voice still calling after her. After a moment, Harmon turned his attention onto her. By divine luck, he motioned for her to step on the yellow florescent feet painted on the floor in front of him. As she predicted, he didn't ask a single question.

"Hey!" The stranger caught up to her and tapped her shoulder. Of course, Harmon the Oblivious didn't sense her plight. The bouncers nearby did. Jay stood a little straighter and broadened his shoulders in a stark warning that he wouldn't hesitate to use every bulging muscle in his body to toss the stranger from the club if he messed with her.

"Is he bothering you, Eri?"

She should have said something. Or better still, she should have bolted to her car as fast as her legs could carry her. Neither happened. The bouncer stepped forward, partially shielding her from the stranger. The guy behind her threw up his hands in surrender.

"Hey, I don't want any trouble, alright," he said. The drawl of his deep city accent was apparent. "Some guy wanted me to give her this."

The man, whose dark hair was shellacked to his skull, thrust a gleaming white business card toward her. Erica took it and flipped it over in her hand. It was completely blank except for a phone number printed across one side. Her eyes searched the greaser in front of her for answers. "What's this?"

"I dunno. Some guy paid me fifty bucks to give you

this and say you have a deal."

5

JULIUS

JULIUS WANTED TO RIP HIS brother's throat out for not intercepting the club owner before he'd whisked him away from Erica. He watched her intently from his vantage point in the crowd and fought a smile. She'd returned her coat to the woman at the coat check and headed for the bar. Good. She was quickly becoming an addiction. Her touch left the beast inside of him unsettled and craving more.

We're here for the club, not the girl. Evan's voice crept up inside of his mind, even though he was across the room.

He was one to talk. He was dancing in a throng of them.

Unlike you, I'm tracking the cash exchange at the bar, Evan said. *Since we've been here, Stick's cleared nearly ten thousand at the bar by the entrance alone. Or did you forget we didn't just come to Savu for some skirt?*

Stick placed a hand on his shoulder and pointed out one of the performance stages where a couple of girls danced in unison.

I know what we're here to do, he replied.

Then act like it.

"This is the performance stage all of our artists like to use. Zena Shaun was here two weeks ago," Stick boasted.

From the way he said it, she must have been someone. Julius oohed appreciatively even though he had not the slightest idea who that was.

"Yeah," Stick continued, "She was here to promote her new single. To All the Boys. Have you heard it?"

"Not yet. I haven't kept abreast of the latest pop culture hits."

"Really? That song is everywhere. It hit the top 100 charts overnight." Stick looked startled and it was clear he'd said the wrong thing. Part of Stick's marketing model was built on entertaining celebrities in his nightclub when they came to town. As his investor, he should know the who's who of the human world.

She's a pop star.

"I don't usually listen to many pop stars," he said to Stick, who laughed in agreement.

"I didn't either until I started this club. I much prefer a metal band."

None of it made sense. Maybe he'd ask Erica to help him translate this. His eyes glanced through the crowd in search of her.

I'll be over in a minute. Even inserted. *When we're*

done scoping the place out, you can get back to your precious piece of ass.

He fought a growl. *Don't call her that.*

Oh, someone's touchy! Evan's sing-song voice grated on his nerves.

He grumbled. *Get out of my head, Evan.*

Do your job, your highness, and I won't have to be.

Fine. His teeth set in a hard line as he followed Stick around his club.

The owner prattled on about the sound systems, the max capacity, and every boring thing that was not Erica. Apparently, his brother was done counting the money exchange at the registers since he met up with them quickly. To his disappointment, his brother droned on about the business, asking questions that could easily be deduced by looking around. If he didn't know any better, he'd think his brother wanted to keep him away from Erica. But for the life of him, he didn't understand why Evan cared who he wanted in his bed.

"And how do you staff your establishment?" Evan asked, clearly ignoring his sour thoughts.

"Word of mouth mostly," Stick explained. "There's no dearth of paying clientele, and that tends to attract the best promoters and bartenders in the city. In the beginning, most of my staff were walk-ins. Funnily enough, I was fully staffed before the doors opened without having to rely on any of my contacts or placing an ad. And based on the applicants that have come in, I could probably staff bars at four more locations."

So, the dragon had thoughts of expansion. That

intrigued him. From the cover charge at the door, the line that snaked around the corner, and the turnover at his bar, Julius was quite certain the dragon's cash flowed like a river. His king needed that.

"Do you have the market to open more establishments?" Julius asked, turning his attention to the task at hand. The quicker they could secure a deal with the dragon, the faster he could get back to Erica.

For a moment, his eyes drifted up to the VIP overlook, searching for her. Still, it remained empty. He scanned the club until he spotted her near the bar, putting the final touches on a tray and readying her return to the VIP area.

"Of course. The city is growing exponentially," Stick replied. "The market is ripe for new business development."

He's telling the truth. Evan shot over to him, but his thoughts drifted again.

He watched Erica straighten her almost-too-short shorts before lifting the tray over her shoulder. The bare skin of her legs made him lick his lips. The beast inside of him let out a low growl as several partiers eyed his beauty while she made her way back to the VIP area. None of them were worth her time.

He was already aching from the loss of her velvety soft skin against his. Just the slightest touch from her drawing on his skin... Her sun-kissed warmth had set him ablaze, especially when her pulse raced, thrumming from her wrist and through his hand. It radiated in his body and throbbed in his chest as if her heart beat for his.

By the gods, he could only wonder what it felt like to

be inside of her.

Focus, Julius.

As much as he hated his brother's invasive thoughts, he was right. Now wasn't the time to launch himself at the girl across the room and fuck her into the floor. That would come later. He followed his brother's advice and focused on something else. He admired the ink on his pale hand.

With a blotchy pen and an impossible time constraint, he was still starstruck at her feat. It was amazing how much it looked like the insignia of his house. Right down to the feather's intricate crisscrossed pattern that beveled in elongated diamonds. Even unfinished, it would pass for a near perfect replica of what adorned the breastplate of the armor he wore back home.

It's just a coincidence. Evan said without pausing in his conversation with Stick.

Or instinct. Of course Erica drew his house insignia. Julius had never believed in fate, but glancing down at the bird on his hand, he knew that was what drew them together. He loved watching her work. She radiated like a fireball. In her singular focus, everything else seemed irrelevant to her. He wondered how that singular focus would perform when he finally got her into his bed.

By the all gods, he wanted to claim her.

The beast inside of him agreed and let his fangs drop for the third time that night.

For fuck's sake. If you blow this for us, let it be on your head.

Let it be on your head? You're even starting to sound

like them, he teased but was diverted when Erica ascended the stairs. She wore a small smile all to herself and seemed to bounce on her toes in excitement. He hoped their deal excited her as much as it did him.

His brother, however, had other plans. Evan purposefully found ways to keep Stick talking, thwarting his plan to get back to the VIP area. He even asked that they travel to the rooftop terrace that had been closed off for the coming winter. Despite its impressive view of the city, he was only enthralled by one thing at Savu. And it was abundantly clear that Evan didn't want him to get to her.

Well brother, that's too bad. She's mine now.

6

JULIUS

THE PHONE IN JULIUS'S POCKET buzzed for the tenth time in the past two days. He looked at the display and frowned. Not Erica.

"Answer it," Evan said, his voice competing with the faucet inside the adjoining master bathroom in their penthouse suite.

There was nothing to answer. A text message flashed on the screen.

There's a building on the avenues...

"Open the home screen," Evan turned off the faucet in the bathroom, clearly reading the message through his thoughts.

He thumbed several buttons to get his phone to respond, then hissed when it did nothing more than show the time and date.

"Hold your thumb on the button at the bottom," Evan coached from inside of the bathroom. This time, the noise of a fan whirled above him before the water turned back on.

"What the hell are you doing in there?"

"Cleaning my teeth. Humans are sensitive to the smell of synth blood. They don't even realize they're smelling it, but they find it off-putting."

"Good to know." Was that the reason Erica hadn't called him yet? Was she put off by him?

"They also seem to like toothpaste a great deal," Evan continued. "There are pictures of it everywhere. So, I figured I'd give it a try. You know, understand the culture a bit more. I don't care too much for the mint flavor. It burns the hell out of my mouth. But bubble gum is my jam."

He watched the silhouette of his brother put the tube to his mouth and squeezed. He lifted a brow. "I don't think you're supposed to eat it."

"Don't judge me." Evan poked his head out of the bathroom. Globs of foam circled his lips as he scraped what looked like a miniature white hair brush on the inside of his mouth. "It's called a toothbrush. Humans are so obvious, it's almost comical. Now read the message so I can see what the wolf wants."

Julius fought an eye roll.

There's a building on the avenues we should check out tomorrow. It's a beaut.

"Text him back. Tell him we'll go." Evan never once looked at Julius as he typed two letters: O. K.

"What's a beaut?"

"A beauty," Evan explained.

"Then why not say that? Is that a wolf thing?"

"No, it's a human thing."

"Humans are strange." Of all the creatures in his acquaintance, humans of the alter realm were by far the most eccentric. From their funny listening devices to how they spoke, he never quite kept up with how fast they changed. What he needed was a guide. His thoughts turned back to Erica. She'd be perfect. If only she'd call him. Because, unlike his brother, he didn't have the luxury of plucking relevant information from their minds. Evan never had to work to guess at what people were thinking.

"I do too have to work," Evan's forehead appeared in the doorway as he leaned over.

"Why do you insist on reading my thoughts?"

"Because it annoys you." Evan grinned, wiping the toothpaste from his mouth. "Besides, humans are easy to read. You're not paying enough attention."

"Says the mind reader. When's our next visit with the dragon?" Julius pushed off the door frame of the master suite and walked toward his brother who'd turned on the water a third time.

"We're not going back to Savu." Evan frowned as he looked at him in the mirror.

"Excuse me? We're cutting ties with the dragon? The same one who seems to attract riches and hordes of beautiful people as the legend suggests?"

"I didn't say we weren't going to invest with the dragon. I said we're not going back to Savu."

"Why not?"

"There's no need. I have all the paperwork on the desk." Evan pointed out the bathroom door toward a desk at the far end of the room. Three neat piles of paper were stacked on top. "Besides, you lack focus."

"I'm completely focused."

"...on the girl."

"Her name is Erica."

"I don't care what her name is, we're not going."

Julius didn't need Evan's permission to see someone he was interested in. When did his younger brother start caring when he got laid?

"I don't care," Evan replied.

"Then why are you fighting me so hard?" He asked before making his way to the common room and fishing his coat out of the closet near the elevator. He was going back to Savu to find Erica, but what Evan said next gave him pause.

"Why are you so desperate?"

The hair on the back of his neck stood at attention. "I am not desperate!"

"Says the vampire who lacks the patience to wait out a potential. It's been, what, a day and a half and you're already foaming at the mouth."

He eyed the bits of foam clinging to the corners of Evan's lips. He was one to talk.

Besides, he was hardly foaming. Not yet, anyway. Though, as the hours ticked by, a growing thirst settled at the base of his throat. One that nipped at the ache inside of him. Even though he'd fed that morning, the thirst hadn't been quenched.

At the time, he'd thought it was a bad batch of synthetic blood. An ill-formed batch would barely take the edge off. He thought of following it with the real thing. Blood was plentiful in the human realm. But it was dangerous to drink from the source right now. Real blood would only compel the beast in him to track Erica and claim her. A low rumble of approval erupted in his chest at the mere thought of it. His vampire was eager for her.

"*That* is why you shouldn't go back to Savu. You're barely keeping it together as it is." Evan's voice was heady with accusation.

Anger curled up his spine. If he remembered correctly, it was Evan who was the last of them to learn to control his vampire once he presented. How dare he talk to him as if he hadn't had a decade more practice at controlling his base self.

Thankfully, the phone in his pocket buzzed before he punched his brother in the face. He opened to a message from an unfamiliar number.

Hey, it's Erica.
Sorry it's been a while...
Want to meet up tonight? I don't have to work.

A smile broadened his lips into a curve. It was about time.

"By the gods." His brother groaned and turned back on the water.

Julius: Of course. Text me the time and place and I'll be there.

Erica: I get out of class at 8, want to meet at my studio around 8:30? I'll send you the address.

He would have screeched in excitement if cool-headed royals did that sort of thing. He stashed his coat back in the closet, then sat at the bar and stared at the phone screen with a goofy grin, then read her message again. Evan turned off the sink and strode into the common room. He leaned against the doorframe of the master with his lanky arms folded across his chest. His shoulders were stiff.

"You've got it so bad, it's ridiculous."

"What does that even mean? 'Got it bad.' Is that another one of those funny human euphemisms?"

"It means you're smitten with her."

"Lusting. I'm hardly smitten," he went back to his phone again, but the feeling of his brother's incessant stare never seemed to leave him. Annoyed, he tossed Evan a questioning look. "What?"

"I just haven't heard such singular thoughts since Damian found Giselle. And—"

"She's not my mate." Julius cut him off before he had a chance to speak about their brokenhearted king. He would never let anyone get that close to him. Not after seeing the devastation a shattered mate bond could do to a vampire.

"If you are certain." Evan's voice was tight with worry. What his brother failed to realize was that Erica was only a distraction—a temporary distraction. Hearing those thoughts, Evan looked relieved. "Then, you think I'm overreacting?"

"You have no need to worry, brother. This is what I do. For me, it's all about the chase. As soon as I get them, I release them back into the wild and move on to the next. Erica is no different."

Evan didn't look convinced, but there was no reason for his doubt. So, he conceded. "Humans in this realm are not like ours. They are not as strong."

"I'm no novice. This is not my first time in this realm," he reassured him.

"Remember, their kind doesn't know of vampires. We cannot risk exposure."

"Yes, I know."

"And—"

"Okay, Mother." He laid on the annoyance thick so his brother would get the hint.

"Sorry," Evan scratched his forehead sheepishly. "I'm overreacting again, aren't I?"

"Everything will be fine. Let me get her out of my system, and I'll be the good little prince our brother dispatched for the crown."

Evan sighed, but nodded. "For the all gods, just be careful."

———

JULIUS'S LIPS CURLED INTO A SNEER as the acrid scent of cigarette smoke, rotting garbage, and city sewer permeated his nose. A gust of cool late autumn air wisped around his coat as he walked up to a building that had more windows than bricks holding it up. It couldn't have been in a worse part of town.

At least on the inside, the building wasn't a complete dump. Old and not worth Erica's time, but it was serviceable, he supposed. He'd walked the hallway several times before he realized there was no elevator to bring him up to the fifth floor. He found the stairs behind a set of doors at the end of the hall and climbed them, wishing like hell he could use his vampiric speed to get there faster.

He sighed in frustration as he hit the third floor, tempted to take the stairs three at a time, but he couldn't risk exposure. From the murmurings, closing doors, and general life that was happening on the other side of the white-painted cinderblock walls in the stairwell, someone would likely happen upon him at the precise moment he'd done it. Despite the slow pace, it didn't take him long to reach the numbered door that matched the address Erica provided.

Though, what he heard on the other side prevented him from knocking. Erica's voice was raised in agitation.

He leaned in, anxious to hear what made her that way.

"So, three years means nothing to you then?" Her voice hitched.

No one responded. It took him a moment to realize she must have been speaking on the phone. He wished like hell he was on the opposite side of that door, close enough to hear who she was speaking with and what they were saying.

"Are you kidding me? We're supposed to be planning

our life together, not taking a break."

Planning their lives together? His vampire nearly ripped the door from its hinges and burst inside. They did not agree to her planning her life with someone else.

"If we're taking a break, then we're through. I'm not going to be benched on the sidelines while you get to star in the playoffs." Her voice was heavy with ultimatum.

Another brief pause, then she exploded.

"Fine? All you have to say is fine?" Her voice tightened. "You know, everyone was right about you. You don't deserve me."

Apparently, the conversation was at an end because he heard a cry of frustration, then a loud clack from inside before it settled into silence. He should have felt bad for eavesdropping on her conversation, but he couldn't help himself. Not when she was distressed.

He knocked on the door.

Abject silence followed before her delicate footsteps made their way toward him and she ripped the door open. A forceful gust of wind rushed past him.

"What?" The sound was harsh and said through gritted teeth. Her eyes were wild again, in the same way they were when she gleefully destroyed his car. Her cheeks flamed in a bright crimson that stretched across the sides of her face and down her neck. Her hair jostled out of the untidy blonde knot tied at the top of her head. She was pissed. And it made him want to fuck the anger out of her.

"You wanted me to swing by," he said, holding up his phone when she didn't move.

Her eyes widened and her face softened. "Jeez, I

completely forgot."

In truth, she didn't look like she was expecting anyone over, let alone him.

"If this is a bad time, I can always come back..." he offered, although he had no intention of leaving her. Not in this state. Not until he found out what idiot was playing games with her heart so he could kill him quickly and have her all to himself.

"No," she said in a rush, tucking a strand of blonde hair that had fallen from her bun behind her ear. "Come in, please."

Even in the low light, the inside of Erica's studio completely blew him away. All the walls were painted over. Stylized faces, graffiti text, and bold colors lined nearly every wall. He followed the line work up and around the large windows, and through to where there was a small kitchen on one side.

"This is your studio?" he asked with an appreciative nod as he looked around. This city was filled with hidden gems. He wasn't surprised that Erica found one of them.

"Yeah, for now. Until I..." Erica trailed off as she flitted around the studio clearing surfaces of paint-soiled napkins and plates of half-eaten sandwiches.

"Until?"

The soft glow of the studio lights on her face stole the air from him. She was gorgeous.

"Until I can afford to upgrade to the studio of my dreams. The art district downtown is filled with them. It's like they were built with the modern artist in mind. Galleries in the front and open space studios in the back.

They're amazing."

If Julius hadn't heard her shouting just a few minutes ago or seen the look that still settled in her eyes or the angry way she slammed the dishes as she moved them to her sink, he would have sworn they were having a pleasant conversation. He needed to know the reason for her anger.

"So... you're with someone?" he blurted out, staring at the phone in her pocket just as she dropped several more dishes in the sink with a loud clang.

For a moment she was silent before she rolled her eyes and threaded her fingers in her golden hair. A look of stress darkened the hazel of her eyes to brown. "I so can't deal with this right now. Please don't tell me you're *that guy*."

"What guy?" The accusation in her voice made his neck hairs raise.

Erica made some strange hissing sound with her teeth and stamped her foot. "You're all the same."

A blast of heat ran up his spine. Yes, she was upset, but the royal in him would not tolerate her tone much longer. "I'm not like anyone you've ever met."

"I bet you are. I bet the reason why you're here isn't because you wanted me to paint you something. I bet once you saw a flash of tits and creamy thighs, you thought you could hold this debt above my head and I'd sleep with you. Tell me, am I getting close?"

When he didn't answer, she stood incredibly still, pressing her fingers against the bridge of her nose the way he'd seen the King do when his patience had worn completely thin. She sighed.

"You weren't interested in my art, were you?" she asked, her voice snatching at the back of her throat.

"I admit that I was not," he answered truthfully.

A flash of hurt pierced her eyes, visibly pushing her back a step. Then, her eyebrows collapsed together; a look of fury engulfed her face. Apparently, that was not the response she was looking for.

He prepared for her balled fist to come hurtling at his face, but she didn't hit him. Instead, Erica gave one hard laugh, then weaved through the stacks of canvases and boxes past him to grab a cup of murky blue water with several paint brushes sticking out from it and moved toward the sink. Her nostrils flared.

"So, what are you here for Mr. Craul?"

"Besides your tits and creamy thighs?" He shot back the joke, hoping to break the tension with a laugh. Erica was having none of it. Her eyes narrowed.

"Get out," she cried, hurtling the cup of murky blue water at him. He dodged out of the way. It hit the floor behind him with a clack and the blue-tinged water sprayed at his feet.

"Whoa. What is your problem?" He flinched, dusting a few droplets from his pants.

"My problem is you and everyone like you," she said, her chest heaving. "You're all brawn. Never vulnerable. And here I am, the sensitive artist, always attracted to big stuffy jerks."

This wasn't about him. This was about the guy on the phone and who she thought he was. He became the manifestation of her deepest fear.

"I'm not like the others," Julius's voice crew calm against her storm.

"Fine, then. Prove me wrong," Erica's arms folded across her chest, her knee cocked out to one side as she waited expectantly for him to say something. "Tell me something you've never admit out loud."

Her posture and her words may have been defiant, but her eyes were pleading. At the moment, she needed someone to show her the difference. Her piercing hazel gaze landed on him. When she looked at him like that, all the thoughts emptied from his head.

"Well?" she asked, half-hopeful.

His mind churned and the beast inside of him paced. He couldn't think of anything. Except the one thing he should never say to a human in this realm. But he needed to prove to her that he was worthy.

He let out a breathy sigh before saying, "I'm a vampire."

7

ERICA

ERICA STARED AT JULIUS'S serious face for half a second before her lips turned down. Tension seized her shoulders.

"Of course, you are."

"Let me explain." Julius held out his hands as if to steady her.

"No need. It's clear that when you say you're a vampire, you mean you're a bloodthirsty leech." She layered on the sarcasm. She was really not in the mood for this. He was joking, or trying to be funny to loosen her nerves, but she was over it.

"Leech is not the term I'd use."

"You're wasting my time."

She shifted and readied herself toward the front door, but Julius's beautiful face softened into a pleading look. "Wait... I mean... Look, I'm not good at this."

No, he wasn't. The way he was white-knuckling his coat told her as much. He was going to have sore fingers in the morning if he kept that up. Julius looked like he was in pain just thinking of being open about any topic other than a frivolous one he controlled. One thing was certain: Julius Craul did not do serious.

"Clearly," she said.

"Second chance?"

"Last chance," Erica amended, her arms crossed in defiance.

Julius cleared his throat. "But first, I feel we need to have an understanding of terms before we proceed."

"You're stalling, Mr. Craul."

Just saying his formal name made her realize he was here for her benefit, she was the one who destroyed his car, not the other way around. She owed *him* a debt. But at that moment, as he fidgeted with the buttons on his lapel, Erica felt the balance of power teeter to neutral standing before starting to tip in her favor.

"I am not. I want to ensure that if I tell you my darkest secrets, Erica, that I am returned the same courtesy." His voice dipped low. The teetering balance of power tipped right back to him as his hands stilled against his lapels. He looked her in the eye, rooting her in place. His previous discomfort vanished, and he was in his element again. This was the businessman who was scoping out her boss's bar. Her heart started to thump in her chest at the power he exuded. "My honesty comes with a heavy price."

"I'm not afraid," she said, trying to keep her voice even. It seemed like his previous discomfort jumped from him and bled into her. "Do it, and you'll have my absolute honesty."

He cleared his throat again. For a brief moment, his bravado cracked. But Julius squared his shoulders, dropped his hands to his side, and looked her directly in the eyes. "Fine. I set a three-week time limit to all my relationships."

Whoa that was honest.

"I'm surprised it's that long," she murmured, thinking of her first real impression of the man in front of her. He looked like he knew his way around a bed very well and hardly committed to anything further than that.

"Excuse me, I'm pouring my heart out here," he said in mock offense.

She bit back a smile, trying desperately to keep a serious face. She was angry. But as much as she didn't want to admit it, her hard exterior was softening. Julius was actually making an effort. No one had ever made that kind of effort before. "Sorry. Go on. You were saying that you've never had a real girlfriend…"

Julius shook his head and stared at the ground. "If I'm being honest, most of the women in my acquaintance are not really attracted to me."

An incredulous snort burst from her throat. That was extremely hard to believe. Look at him, for crying out loud! His green eyes found hers and as if on cue, a lock of his dark sandy brown hair fell into his face, framing his chiseled jaw. He was model gorgeous. And even adorned in a suit, she could tell his abs were perfection. There was no way any woman, living or dead, would pass him up. He must have been pulling her leg.

"This, I have to hear."

"I come from a powerful family," he explained. "Because of that, the women in those circles only wanted me for my wealth or status. It took me a long time to realize that more times than not, she used my family's name to further her agenda. So, to avoid the snakes, I hid behind grandeur, money, and charm and made them all temporary. But, secretly, I've always wanted to know what it felt like for someone to truly love me for me."

He was contemplative. That was code for he'd had his heart miserably broken the first time he trusted someone else enough to offer it. Anger curled inside her.

"Who was she?" She wanted to know every detail about the person who broke Julius's heart so she could bitch slap her into last week, make her apologize, then forward slap her out of existence.

Julius paused, smirking as if he could read her thoughts. "No, no. I've told you one of my secrets. Now it's time for you to tell me one of yours."

"That's not fair."

"Those are our terms."

It was her turn to shift uneasily. How did she compete with that? When he shifted his weight, Erica realized they were both standing in the middle of her studio in an impasse state. Just a moment ago, she was ready to kick Julius out of her studio and onto the curb. Now, she was intrigued by him.

"Where are my manners? You can have a seat anywhere," she motioned to her sparsely furnished studio.

Outside of the half-dead chocolate brown leather couch she'd inherited from the previous tenants, where the seat was frayed and the stuffing protruded out, there was nowhere for him to sit. She bit her lip as she eyed the couch with disdain. Why hadn't she replaced it?

Julius didn't seem to mind. Like at Stick's club, his arms stretched across the back when he sat in it, perfectly at ease. The stark contrast of his fancy suit against the cracked leather of the sofa made it look like he was on set for a high fashion grunge photoshoot.

"And..." he continued with a smirk. His gaze raked down her frame, brow cocked in amusement. "You're stalling."

It was getting harder to think with Julius looking at her like that.

"Am not."

She *was* stalling. She leaned against her kitchen counter and faced him, folding her arms across her chest, she thought of the least invasive thing to say to Julius. It was a balancing act. If she came out with something too severe, she might scare him off. Too lame, and he was going to call her out. So, she settled on the safest thing she could think of.

"I've always felt like a disappointment to my parents."

"Get in line." Julius shrugged.

"Hey! I'm pouring my heart out here."

"Sorry, go on." Julius laughed, falling into their banter with ease.

"My mother is an engineer, my father is a businessman, and unfortunately, I'm an artist." She tried to shrug off the uneasiness that came with talking about her parents.

"Why is that unfortunate? You're amazing." The reverence in his voice was not lost on her. Her insides glowed at the compliment.

"My parents don't think so. I'm not exactly boasting material when it comes to their social soirees. Especially when their only child is an artist who can't even pay the bills with her art."

Crap. She shouldn't have said that. She would probably sell more paintings if she kept her big mouth closed about not selling them. Julius rose to his feet and navigated toward a few of her finished paintings and rifled through the canvases, thoughtfully studying them. In an instant, the businessman was back, and Erica was reminded of why he was in her studio in the first place.

"These should be flying off the shelves," he said as if he were trying to reconcile why she wasn't the runaway success she dreamed of being ever since her abstract clay sculpture won first prize in her elementary school's art competition. "It's clear that you have a solid product. What is your marketing plan?"

"I have an art showcase the Friday after next."

Julius didn't respond right away, like he was waiting for her to continue. A half a beat pulsed between them before he clarified. "How do you plan to get people to come to your showcase and buy your work?"

She stuttered. "Well, I hung up some flyers at school. People from my open studio are going to come and invite people they know."

He paused as he leaned one of her works against his thigh to look at a piece behind it.

"Do you want to know the absolute truth?" he asked.

"Let me have it." She sighed, fearing the worst.

"Your work is exceptional. However, you're never going to sell it if you're marketing to your classmates."

That was the last thing she wanted to hear two weeks before her art show. "Then, what should I do?"

"The right product needs the right buyers." He motioned for her to stand next to him as he thumbed through the stack of her most recent paintings. She did, very aware of her proximity to him. God, why did he have to wear that cologne again? It was even more intoxicating without the sweat-soaked humidity of Stick's nightclub clouding it. Erica leaned into it.

No.

What was she doing? She wrenched herself backwards and began straightening the blank canvases that needed filling before her art show. She needed to focus on her showcase. Not get sucked into another self-righteous jerk. Didn't she just call off her engagement five minutes ago?

She should have been a pile of weeping goo on the floor, not unraveling at the sight of Julius Craul practically worshipping her work and swooning over his cologne. But she didn't feel the devastation she was expecting. Maybe she hadn't given it enough time for the hurt to come. Maybe if she thought about the good times with Max, the pit of loss from breaking it off with him would consume her. Erica waited for it to come.

It didn't.

"Erica?"

She twisted toward him. Frick, she must have looked like a complete flake. Staring blankly at a stack of empty canvases, thinking about her ex, and wringing her hands together like a loon wasn't painting a picture of her sanity. Immediately, she loosened her arms.

"Yes?" She cleared her throat and focused her attention back on him. He'd asked her something or said something, but for the life of her she didn't know what.

"You seem... distracted," he said, studying her. "Are you well?"

"I'm fine... just a little thirsty. Would you like anything?"

"You're not offering what I want. So, I'm fine for now."

Was Julius insinuating that he wanted her? Or was that her hopeful, revenge-filled mind playing tricks on her? She sucked in a long breath and watched him. His face caught the light again in ways that made her heart leap. Her thoughts turned mutinous.

She was already craving a rebound. That must be a record of some kind. Gosh, Max had her so screwed up in the head. First, she didn't even mourn for the loss of their two years together. Now, as Julius looked at her like she was a milkshake he wanted to slurp down, she couldn't take her mind off of how wonderful a distraction it would be.

It wouldn't be so bad if she distracted herself with Julius. Give in to the temptation of just feeling wanted for once in her life. Her thoughts curved from the angry thoughts of Max and on to the welcome ones of Julius.

Being around him disorientated her, as if his cologne was some sort of love potion. The way he looked at her made her feel admired again. Wanted. A night of harmless flirting wouldn't be so bad. Would it?

Erica filled a glass with water from the tap and gulped it down. It went down thick.

My goodness, was she really going to go through with it? Flirt with Julius? Of course she was going to go through with it. Flirting was harmless. She deserved a little bit of flirting. So, yeah, for one night, she was going to flirt without shame.

Julius watched her the entire time. She could feel the heat of his gaze scan her movements, but when she finally looked over, he was rifling through her paintings again.

He paused on a portrait of two kids on a playscape at the park two blocks from her studio. Gently, Julius caressed the corner where she'd signed her name. He seemed to like this one better than the others. After studying it for several moments, he pulled it from the stack.

"It's clear you have a knack for realism. The textures that you get when painting skin are incredible. It's almost as if I could reach in and touch it. Your work will attract the kind of clientele that would pay handsomely for it."

"Well, how do I find them?"

"You said your parents host events?"

She nodded.

"When's the next one?"

"My father's 50th birthday party is Saturday." Erica held back a heavy sigh. "My mother usually throws a party for him and invites his business associates. I was hoping I was scheduled to work that night, that way I'd have an excuse for not going. But I'm guessing my mother got to Stick before I could because he didn't put me on the schedule."

"Then, that's perfect."

Erica doubted from the brightened look on Julius's face that he understood how awful those parties were.

"The misery that's sure to be the Wallace family party is perfect?"

Gone were the easygoing parties of her youth, where they were surrounded by family and friends. She couldn't remember how long it had been since she'd danced a cheesy line dance with her cousins. Ever since her father found that his rise in his business gained him equal political clout, their entire circle changed. It became more uptight, more exclusive, less friendly.

Less real.

"So, we go to that miserable dinner, invite the high rollers out to my showcase. And then what? Hope they show up on a prayer?"

Like that was going to happen. Those sharks took a cue from her mother and every chance she got she took the opportunity to make her feel inadequate. But Julius seemed to feel otherwise. He smiled like a teacher getting ready to school their pupil.

"Do you want to know something I learned as a child?"

Not if it included why she needed to attend something miserable, but nodded anyway.

"The value of something is not intrinsic. Its value is

what you make others believe it's worth."

"So, what you're saying is that my paintings are worthless."

"On the contrary. They are priceless. Art always is."

She grinned. No one's ever said that to her before. Even Max made her feel like what she did was nothing more than a hobby, that it would never earn anything.

"What?" Julius shrugged, "It is."

"If it's priceless, then, how do I sell it?"

A devilish smirk played on his lips. "By having an ally, that's how."

Intrigued, she leaned toward him. Julius seemed to like that, as his smirk grew into an appreciative smile. His long fingers drummed on the next painting as he examined it with the same reverence as he did the others. "If someone else shows interest in your work, then others will clamor to get to it. And if there is a story behind it, the value doubles."

This much Erica already knew. The trouble was getting the first set of buyers in the first place. Then his insinuation dawned on her. Oh... "You're offering to be my ally."

"Precisely."

"What do you get out of it?"

"The businessman in me tells me I should take a commission for every piece I help you sell. The man trying to get to your creamy thighs says I should do it in good faith."

An unexpected spark of desire thumped through her at his words.

"Wow, that was... very honest."

"We're being absolutely honest here, aren't we?"

She cleared her throat. "Of course, we are. I just wasn't expecting—I mean..."

Her mouth went dry again. The green of his concerned eyes seemed to darken slightly, drawing her in. The air between them threatened to ignite, and for a millisecond, she thought he might kiss her.

"Erica, do my advances make you uncomfortable? Because I won't stop until you tell me to."

She could think of a thousand things she was right then. Uncomfortable was the furthest thing from her mind. Scared was more like it. Her immediate attraction to him set her pulse throbbing in her ear. She never had this

"Are you telling me to stop?"

"Absolute truth?" Her words were small and thin.

It was Julius's turn to nod.

"N-no. And that terrifies me."

His eyes softened for a moment as he subtly moved toward the next stack of paintings leaning against the wall beside the first. "I'm apologize if my advances come off the wrong way... I can be a bit forward."

"It's not you that I'm afraid of," Erica interjected quickly, cursing the distance he put between them.

"I see. You are already spoken for." It wasn't a question. He cast an accusatory glance at the phone in her pocket. For a split-second she'd wondered if he'd overheard the argument she'd had before he'd announced himself at the door. She quickly dismissed the thought.

Her apartment-turned-studio was built ridiculously well. There was no way her voice had travelled through that much concrete.

Erica cleared the lump from her throat. "No, not anymore."

"I'm sorry."

"I'm not."

Again, his gaze fell on her pocket with a look that told her he wanted to ask about it. She prayed he didn't. Unfortunately, fate wasn't in her corner.

"What happened?"

Erica wasn't ready to talk about Max or their on-again off-again, mostly on the rocks relationship that had been teetering on the brink long before their botched anniversary dinner. If she hadn't been the one to call him, they probably never would have spoken again. Instead of blurting all of this aloud, Erica settled on, "It's complicated."

Julius made a sound of disapproval.

"That is the truth! It's complicated. Besides, it's your turn for a secret. Tell me about the girl who broke your heart. Then maybe, I'll tell you all about the guy who broke mine."

"All I want to know is his address so I can kill him."

Erica laughed. "Aggressive much, vampire?"

"What can I say, vampires are known to be territorial."

"You're stalling again." She threw his challenge back at him.

"Guilty." Julius sighed before he faced her fully. "Her name was Cinda."

"Go on."

"You only asked for a name," A sudden sly smile teased her. "And a name is all you'll get. Your turn. Tell me about Mr. Complicated."

"Unfair!" She poked her bottom lip out with a playful frown before turning serious. "It seems like we're both unwilling to talk about our exes."

"Fair enough. I don't want to think of you bedding anyone else anyway."

"Besides you?"

Julius's sure fingers fumbled over the last painting in the stack. He laid a steady gaze on her, direct and pointed. "Are you offering?"

Her retort knotted in her throat. The scent of him pulled her further in. It wasn't until that moment that she realized she was inches away from him. She must have unconsciously drifted toward him. He hadn't moved an inch from looking at her stack of paintings, but there she was, right on top of him. If she so much as exhaled, her lips would brush against his shoulder.

God, you need to calm down girl, she reprimanded herself, squeezing her knees together, trying desperately to quell the budding desire ignited by the thought of kissing every inch of him. "If it's worth my while."

"Believe me, love, if I got you in my bed, you'd never want to leave."

"That sure of yourself?" she asked instead of the 'yes, please' she was thinking.

"We all have our talents," Julius said with a confident shrug. From his demeanor and tone, there was no doubt in her mind that his talents were extensive. He pulled one of her paintings out of the stack and set it against the wall behind him. He hadn't remarked on any of the details, but from the way his entire body seemed to glow, this one was his favorite. He pulled out another.

"What are you doing?" she asked when he grabbed a third.

"Taking the best ones for myself," he said with a grin. "Two weeks from now, they'll all be sold. I don't want to miss out on my chance to secure an original."

"I wish I had your confidence."

"Don't worry love, you will. First, we tackle Saturday. After that, the art will sell itself."

"You're really going to help me?" Erica asked and Julius nodded. "To pay you back for the car or... in good faith?"

"That depends," he smirked. "Are you saying I have a chance?"

"I'm not saying you don't."

"I'll take that." He walked over to the sofa again and sat, staring at her half-covered canvas with curiosity. She usually hated when someone tried to look at her art before it was finished. It was... well, personal. Having someone see the bare color-blocked canvas was like displaying her soul. A deep vulnerability usually squeezed its way to the surface when someone got too close. But with Julius, his presence seemed to calm her. He didn't give off an air of judgement. Only one of curiosity.

"What's that going to be?" he asked of the portrait sitting on her easel.

It was of him. After she met him, he was all her muse would let her see in her artistic eye. The many blank canvases around the room were testament to her art block. After sitting on her stool for hours, she'd decided to just give in to her muse and let his image flow across the canvas. Thankfully, she'd only gotten to the dark hues of Stick's nightclub. Color splotches formed the background of the piece, but she layered nothing on top of it yet. She could tell him it was anything, really. Otherwise he'd think she was a lunatic, painting his likeness like a madwoman after only seeing him twice. He'd probably think she was obsessed with him.

"Absolute truth," he warned, like he could see the lie forming in her mind.

"Okay fine," she swallowed nervously. "It's of you."

"You're painting me?" The awe in his tone made her giddy inside. No one, not even Max, looked at her that way. The way a child looked on Christmas morning after getting the exact toy they'd asked for. His admiration floored her. He looked at the painting again.

"How long before its finished?"

"Depends on the paint." She shrugged, trying to hide a blush creeping up on her cheeks. "Best guess, a week or so if I can get the lighting right."

"I'm in town for a couple of weeks. I'd love to see it once it's completed. Now, let's cover our game plan for Saturday night."

And they did. Dinner was served promptly at 7. He'd pick her up at 6, they'd go to the preceding cocktail hour, glad hand with the rich and powerful, and by the time the dessert course made its way around, invite her high rollers to the show once they were fat, drunk, and merry. Julius's words, not hers. The plan was sound, even if it made her jittery.

"Now that dinner is squared away. Time for rapid fire truth," Julius announced.

"What's that?"

"I'll ask you a set of questions that you must answer, no thinking it over. Just whatever comes off the top of your head."

"Turnabout is fair play. We'll take turns."

"I'm going to love you in my bed." He grinned with a shake of his head.

She rolled her eyes playfully. "Alright Casanova, let's not get ahead of ourselves. Are we playing or what?"

"We'll start off easy. Then, the questions will get tougher. Favorite color?"

"Seafoam green. Lately, it's been more emerald green."

"Well, you can't go around answering questions like that and not expect me to have a follow up."

"Rapid fire, remember?" she teased with a laugh.

"We should amend the rules. Answers require an explanation."

"Fine."

"Why the change?"

"You."

Julius paused again, a burning look in his eyes like he wanted her to explain. But she was already asking a question of her own. "Favorite holiday?"

"New Year's. New beginnings for new things. Ever

have a pet?"

"A chow chow named Dave. You?"

"A Yorkie named Pudding, until my father found it and made me put him down."

She gasped at the horror.

Julius shrugged it off as if it were no big deal. "I had a rough upbringing."

"I thought you said you came from a powerful family?"

"I do. We never wanted for anything, but that didn't mean we had everything. Love and gentleness were often lacking in my father's house. Our mother did dote on us when he wasn't looking."

"Us? You have siblings?"

"I do. Six."

"There are seven of you?"

"That's right. You mentioned you were an only child."

She nodded, unable to fathom that many kids around as a child. "What was it like?"

"Chaos. What's your idea of the best date?"

"Looking for ideas?"

"Maybe."

"Is it too cliché to say a paint night or go on a midnight paint run? You?"

"It's not. And, I'm not particular about the date as long as it ends with a pleasurable evening in bed."

Erica laughed. "You're a dirtbag."

"Excuse me, but I'm an honest dirtbag, thank you very much."

Julius laughed alongside her. He had to be the easiest person she'd ever talked to. When he laughed and poked fun at her, it felt as if they'd been the best of friends their entire life. There was a genuine person underneath all that bravado.

He was also interesting, that was for sure. Even more so after he finished telling her about his travels through Europe and how he practically had a bar brawl in each country he stopped in along the way. According to him, fist fights seemed to find him, he didn't seek them out.

He yawned right after she did. "It's getting late."

She glanced at the clock on her microwave and her eyebrows nearly touched her hairline. "Wow, I hadn't realized it was three in the morning."

"I should get going."

"I get that vampires are creatures of the night and all, but you don't want to walk around in this neighborhood alone until sunrise."

"Are you saying I can spend the night with you?"

"On the couch."

"Good, we get to sleep together after all." His hopeful gaze was punctuated by him taking off his shoes and peeling off his suit jacket.

She eyed him when he went for his belt. "With our clothes on."

"I will tell you, Erica," he went on chipperly, "this has been the most enjoyable date I've had in years."

"This was not a date," She said with a laugh.

Julius shrugged. "It's ending with a pleasurable night in bed, so it qualifies."

"Even fully clothed?"

"We have to start somewhere. First on the couch, next

in a bed. First clothed, next... unclothed," He wiggled his brows like Groucho Marx.

"We have very different ideas of what a date is," she replied, trying to quell the fluttering in her chest, picturing the man in front of her without his clothes on.

He shrugged as if to say 'semantics,' then patted the broken leather of her couch. "Are you getting in?"

She definitely couldn't trust herself to lie down so close to him right now. Even sleepy, the man was walking sex on a stick. If he so much as breathed on her, she'd probably jump his bones.

Get yourself together. She was only there for flirting, she reminded herself. Flirting didn't mean bedfellows, even though that's all she could think about.

"I will in a minute, I just want to finish the next color block so it can dry overnight."

"Then you'll crawl into bed with me?" He asked hopefully.

"Don't get any ideas. If you try anything, I will fight you in my sleep."

"Hmm, I love a fighter."

"You are relentless." She chuckled, handed him a throw blanket, and dashed to her easel before she could get caught up in the intoxication of being so close to him. "Alright, Casanova, get some sleep."

He didn't right away. From the corner of her eye, she could see Julius's keen gaze studying her as she mixed her paints and began putting them on the canvas. Having him watch her didn't make her feel uncomfortable, not the way it usually did when someone saw her work in the raw. His presence was almost like being enveloped in a warm hug.

He didn't say anything, only watched. She wasn't sure how long. As soon as she finished putting down the first layer that would be his face, she turned toward him to get the exact mischievous glint he seemed to wear so often, however, he was laid out on her couch, his light snores filling the room.

She stayed up for as long as her sleepy eyes would allow, then did as promised and crawled onto the couch beside him.

Immediately, his arms were around her, hugging her close, and she didn't mind. In fact, it felt... nice.

She breathed in the comfort and let herself relax. If every day could end like this, relaxing next to someone who was easy to talk to, she could revel in it for the rest of her life. Karma, on the other hand, had other plans.

8

ERICA

ERICA WAS JARRED AWAKE. Bleary-eyed, she tried to figure out what to shut up first. Her alarm, her phone, and a ringtone she didn't recognize all competed for her attention, but the most pressing was the pounding on her door. She tried to move, but a solid body resisted.

Oh.

Her head popped up for a fraction of a second. Julius, in his rumpled button-down shirt with the top few buttons undone, was still fast asleep. And laying very much between her legs.

Knock. Knock. Knock.

Who the heck was at her door? Besides the man laying between her knees, she never invited anyone to her studio. Her only visitors had been...

Frick.

Mr. Hinkley, her ornery, nothing-is-right-in-the-world neighbor, or heaven forbid, her landlord. It was entirely too early in the morning for their crap, and her thoughts turned sour as she grabbed for the phone between her and the sofa to turn off the ringer.

"Open up." The voice was muffled.

Yeah, well, she would if she could figure a way out of her current entanglement without waking said entangler. As gently as she could, she extracted her leg from behind him and eased her way to her feet before heading to the door. Light snores escaped him as his head leaned in an awkward angle against the sofa, but he didn't wake.

Another knock.

"Erica! Please."

She stopped dead. That was not Mr. Hinkley. That wasn't even her landlord.

It was Max.

And Julius was still there. And she was... she looked down at her boy shorts and rumpled t-shirt. God, why did she have the habit of undressing herself while she slept? If Max saw them like this, he'd think the worst.

Crap.

No, double crap.

"Please, I need to talk to you."

Instead of opening the door like the insistent knock demanded, she forged toward a pair of stretch jeans that had ended up in a ball, tucked underneath the very much still sleeping body of Julius.

"Wake up," she pushed his solid body.

"Erica, I know you're in there." The voice was muffled,

but now that she'd identified it, there was no mistaking it.

"Come on Mr. Craul, wake up please."

As much as she tried to keep her voice down, the businessman currently sleeping on her couch didn't move right away.

"Julius," she begged, pushing against the hard planes of his body. It hadn't escaped her that nothing but muscle greeted the palm of her hands. Completely solid. When that didn't work, she tried for a nearby window. A spray of light cascaded across his face and into his eyes. Instantly, his hands flew up to shield them.

"You have to get up."

A sleepy groan answered her, but he moved just enough so she could grab her jeans and put them on in a rush.

"You have to hide," she said, buttoning her pants while trying to coax the large man from her sofa and into the bathroom.

"What's wrong?" In an instant, Julius sat straight up and looked around her apartment.

Knock. Knock. Knock.

"Who's that?" He asked, watching the door curiously, looking ready to answer it himself.

Not on her watch.

"That's why you have to hide in the bathroom," she plucked his suit jacket from across the couch back and stuffed it into his hands. Julius stalled, then his curiosity turned to disbelief.

"The bathroom?"

She needed him to hurry it along.

"It's either that or the closet, but you might pass out from the paint fumes in there." When Julius's feet didn't move quickly enough, she explained, "That is my Mr. Complicated. And you can't be here."

Thankfully, he moved in the direction she led him.

"Don't come out until I come back."

Julius looked ready to protest, but nodded his consent instead and allowed her to close him inside the bathroom. Before Max could knock again, she rushed to the front door and opened it.

"You answered," Max's worn face brightened with relief as she cracked the door just a little.

She gasped at the sight of him. Dressed in old, stained sweatpants and the oldest T-shirt he owned, Max looked awful. He looked like he hadn't slept well in days. The fierce attention to detail he usually showed had turned lackluster and limp. His clothes, usually pressed to perfection, were crinkled and creased. His cheeks looked more angular than normal. Hollow, like he hadn't eaten. Despite it, the boyish handsome face she'd fallen in love with was still there. Her heart ached for him.

"What are you doing here?"

"I didn't mean what I said yesterday," he said in a rush. "You're everything to me."

A lump formed at the base of her throat. Guilt squelched at her gut.

"Eri, I'm sorry. I don't want to take a break from you. I'm just stressed and not thinking clearly..."

No words came to her as she watched in stunned silence as her ex-fiancé unraveled in front of her.

Ordinarily, she'd invite him inside. With Julius hiding in her bathroom, it was completely out of the question.

"Are you going to say something?" he asked timidly.

A loud clattering came from inside her studio.

"What was that?" His head shot up.

"Nothing," she quickly replied, pushing herself forward into the doorframe. "I'm just getting ready for my show, probably some paints or something fell over."

Max's brown eyes flickered to her face then behind her, trying to get a view of the apartment.

"Are you with someone?"

This time an accusatory stare swept her frame. Her cheeks burned for a moment before she stared into a face she hadn't seen in over a week.

"Shouldn't I be asking *you* that? Where have you been?"

"You were upset after our anniversary," Max drummed against her doorframe, "I wanted to give you space."

"And those girls going up to your office, who were they?" Erica's eyebrow raised in suspicion, despite the dread overcoming her. Tears started to well in her eyes at the thought of Max actually cheating on her.

"You came to my office?" He sputtered, before turning serious. "That was Cav's doing..."

"She called you by name."

"A lot of people know who I am Erica, it doesn't mean anything."

Her face scrunched in disbelief and Max's hand jutted out to stop her from going back inside.

"Wait. Let me explain. We were having a business

meeting, and Cav invited them as the entertainment for our investors. He didn't let me in on his plan until they arrived. My investors were there, what was I supposed to do?"

"Make them leave."

"I couldn't do that, so I left instead."

"Then why'd you stay away?"

"You were mad at me, so I figured you wouldn't want me around. So, I stayed at Aiden's. But I swear to you, nothing happened between me and those girls."

The earnestness in his voice made her falter.

More clattering came from her bathroom. She cleared her throat loudly to mask the sound. "Come on, let's go for a coffee."

"You don't drink coffee." Max's head bobbled over hers as he tried to see what was in the background.

"But you do, and you look like you need one." She pushed against Max, forcing him out of the doorway. "It's just Mr. Hinkley."

"In your apartment?" He glanced behind her.

"He's banging on the ceiling because we're talking in the doorway." It was plausible. He'd done it before.

Max considered it.

"Coffee?" She distracted him as he stared in disbelief.

"Yeah, if that means you'll talk to me again. I mean, after calling your mom..."

"You called my mother?" She stopped walking and wheeled around, pulling out her phone to the barrage of text messages she'd received overnight. Each one from her mother, telling her not to screw things up with Max. After the first three, she exited the conversation before the urge to throw her phone down the hallway overwhelmed her.

"You weren't answering your phone."

"I spoke to you yesterday, Max, and you said you wanted to take a break."

"I called you back to apologize, but you didn't answer."

"So, you called my mother?" she asked again, furious. "You know how it is between me and her. We don't get along."

"Well, I tried your friend first, but she's angry…"

Like he didn't know why.

"So, you thought a phone call to my mother would do the trick?"

"I was desperate! You weren't answering, so I asked her to reach out to you for me."

This time, it really was Mr. Hinkley who banged on the floor below them.

"Come on, before I get reported. I don't want my landlord to cancel my lease."

Silence followed them the half a block it took to get them to a little coffee shop on the corner of her street. Coffee Cozy had what many hailed as the best coffee on this side of town. She didn't drink the stuff, but their fruit teas weren't half bad. They hopped into line behind a half dozen other people.

"So, your mom said you'd be at your father's dinner."

So, he didn't just plead his case. They had enough time to chat about her father's birthday dinner. She tossed him a scathing look. He backed away with a sheepish look.

"I won't call her again. I promise."

The line shifted forward.

"So... Are you going? If you need someone to go with..."

She hesitated. She couldn't tell him she was going with someone else, so she choked out a lie instead, "I'm not going."

"Oh. It would be a good opportunity though."

The line moved and Erica encouraged Max forward.

"Not for me," Erica needed to quell the budding hopefulness in his voice. Of course he'd want to go to the power grab. With his new commercial real estate venture, his quest to be in the right circles almost matched her father's. However, with Julius going, she had to do everything in her power to keep him away.

"You know how it is. My parents are social climbing, and the others can smell it like blood in the water. I'd be surprised if anyone showed up."

"I guess you're right." He sounded disappointed.

A breath of silence passed between them.

"So, you were telling me where you've been."

"I had a lot on my mind."

The line shifted again.

"That's what fiancées are for, Max. They're there to talk to you about the lot that's on your mind. And, conveniently for you, you had one until yesterday when you broke it off with me."

"Don't say that," he muttered. "I don't want to think of us not together."

"Well, it's true isn't it?" She turned to the barista when it was her turn and told him her drink order. Blueberry

Acai hot tea. Plain. She wasn't in the mood for anything fancier than that.

"I'll pay for it," he said to the barista before ordering his own drink.

Her phone vibrated in her pocket. Please don't let it be her mother. She could not handle another text from her mother.

Julius: I've been stuck in the bathroom forever. Can I come out now?

Frick. Her sheepish laugh blew the steam from her hot tea as the barista handed her a mug of hot water with a tea bag in it. Quickly she looked over to Max, who was still ordering the most elaborate coffee she'd ever heard of. A splash of double foam in the coffee, the rest in a cup. Only the new Max would do something like that. Old Max had his coffee black, no sugar. At least he was distracted. She turned back to Julius's text message.

Erica: OMG. I hadn't realized you were still there. You can go now. I'm going to be a while.

Julius: Where? I want to show Mr. Complicated what a real man looks like.

Erica: Alright keyboard gangster, let's not get ahead of ourselves.

Julius: Tell him you found someone else.

Erica: You are relentless.

Julius: Seriously, I really hope he screws up. Again.

When she didn't answer right away, another message

came after it.

Julius: Too much?
Erica: A tad.
Julius: We're still going on that date. I don't care if he does try to weasel his way back in.
Date? She smiled, teasing him. **I thought this was a business venture.**
Julius: Creamy thighs remember?
Erica: You're still a dirtbag.
Julius: Remember, I'm an honest dirtbag.
Erica: Haha.

"Who are you talking to?"

Max finally made his way over, double fisting his coffee and double foam cup, craning his neck to see why she was trying to suppress a smile.

She quickly switched messaging screens to the heavily one-sided text message string from her mom.

"My mother," she replied.

"Yeah, sorry about that." He nodded, guiding her to a secluded table near the back.

She sent one single message to the fifteen she'd sent: **Calm down, I'm with him now**.

At least now she wasn't a liar. She was talking to her mother. Sort of.

"How's your tea?" he asked.

"Can we skip this? My tea is great. Your coffee is good. Now, let's get back to why you've been MIA this week."

"Yeah," he breathed into his coffee. Erica waited

expectantly. His tone hushed, he looked around. "I don't even know where to start."

"Just out with it, Max." Whenever he was going to tell her something he knew she wouldn't like, he stalled.

"Things aren't good with the family. My father's in deep with the wrong people."

Erica was stunned into silence. "What kind of trouble?"

"He owes a lot of money to someone who's willing to hurt as many people as it takes to get it back. So, over the past few weeks Cav and I have been trying to scrounge up as much cash as we could. I haven't been around because if I don't come up with the money, they'll hurt my father. Maybe even kill him."

"Kill him? What do you mean, kill him? Have you called the police?"

"Keep your voice down," he hushed her. Then lowered his voice to conspiratorial levels. "Splinters is not the kind of person you call the police on. That'll only make things worse."

"Why didn't you say something?"

"I tried to, but how do you tell someone something like that? Besides, it's going to be over soon. Cav and I are going to secure this deal, pay our father's debt, and it'll be out of our lives for good."

The phone between them buzzed. He sighed. "That's Cav now. We have to get to our meeting, and I'm already late. I need to get changed."

"You can't drop that bombshell then leave. Are you safe? Is he?"

"We're fine," he assured her. "I'm sorry. This deal is so close. Once the contract is signed, I promise, I'll tell you everything," he pleaded, but stood up from the table. "Just tell me you'll reconsider us. You don't have to answer right now. Maybe at your art show. I can still come right?"

She sat in shock. She was more concerned about his dad than anything else.

"Can you promise me you'll think about it? For us?"

"Y-yeah, of course," she said automatically.

"Thank you! I don't deserve you," Max landed a kiss on her cheek and rushed from the coffee shop.

Erica sat, blowing into her tea, wondering what the heck she was going to do next. And, as if the universe was giving her a colossal middle finger, her phone buzzed again.

Julius.

I locked up on my way out. See you at six on Saturday.

One thing at a time. She took a sip of her tea. First, she'd get through her father's birthday dinner with Julius. Then, figure out what to do about Max. And hopefully, make it out in one piece.

9

ERICA

ERICA'S PULSE THUMPED IN HER EAR as Julius turned the corner two miles from her parent's house. Julius looked over.

"Hey, you're going to do great," he said, his hand found hers on the armrest and gave it a gentle squeeze.

Yeah, tell that to her roiling guts.

The car slid to a stop in front of her parent's oversized home—what her mother affectionately called their new passion project—but passion was the last thing that came to mind. Her nerves intensified when she took in the monstrosity in front of her.

A car attendant who looked barely old enough to drive walked up to their car with a giddy look. He opened the doors of the two-door rental Julius drove them in. She opened her mouth to apologize about the car again, but stopped. He made her promise not to bring it up anymore, since she was paying her debt to him.

"Take a deep breath," Julius murmured once he'd walked around the car to join her. He placed a reassuring hand at the small of her back and handed the attendant the key. "You'll do fine."

Yeah, if only it didn't feel like walking into a room full of vultures, she thought wearily as they moved up the stone walkway and into her parent's new home.

It had certainly changed since the last time she'd been in it. She was sure they'd bleed themselves broke before finishing. Apparently, she was wrong. They walked into a grand entrance and were escorted into an even nicer dining room. A woodworker must have spent months getting every curved detail that adorned the ceiling perfectly right.

This was not the standard issue dining room of her childhood. Just a few years ago, her family functions always revolved around a six-person dining table that barely fit the room. This, by comparison, was the picture of elegance.

To top it off, everyone was dressed to match the richly decorated walls. She, on the other hand, was dressed like a little grey mouse in a plain black dress. She didn't belong here.

As soon as she entered the room at Julius's side, her mother and father turned toward her. She braced herself for the onslaught of their judgmental stares. Neither of them ever approved of her and weren't afraid to show it.

Her feet hesitated, but Julius's reassuring hand remained steady at her back, encouraging her forward. Finding it calming, she inhaled and stepped into the room as much confidence as she could drum up.

"Erica," her mother called as soon as she spotted her. "I'm delighted you found the time to join us." Her mother's tone was polite but mocking. She may have seemed cheerful, but there was a nastiness underneath.

"You know I wouldn't miss dad's party for anything," the saccharine smile she returned was just as fake as the hug her mother pulled her into.

Her mother's cheeks moved into a frown beside her face as she hissed, "What in God's name are you wearing?"

"It's a dress." She tried to pull away, but her mother's hold tightened.

"It's *off the rack*."

"There's nothing wrong with it."

"It's a disgrace."

Heat rushed up Erica's throat.

"Don't keep her all to yourself," her father said beside them, probably sensing the tension. Finally, her mother let go but didn't let her get too far. This time, her eyes were scathing.

"If you'd come home, you wouldn't have to dress in rags."

"This is not a rag, and I'm fine where I am."

A few heads turned in their direction. Noses turned upward as they pretended not to show interest in the family squabble.

"Erica, you weren't raised in a sewer, keep your voice

down. Please be nice tonight. It's your father's birthday. Oh, and who's this?" She turned to face Julius as if she hadn't noticed the gorgeous man walk into the room on her arm.

"Mother, this is Julius Craul. He's my..." she trailed off, at a loss for words.

"Investor."

"Friend," they both said at the same time.

Julius took her mother's hand with a shake and gave her a charming smile.

"Investor?" Her mother's eyebrows raised, looking like she was debating whether to be impressed or suspicious.

"A friend who happens to be an investor," she corrected unnecessarily. Her nerves made her want to apologize, but she didn't.

"Well any friend of Erica's is a friend to us. Welcome."

Julius returned her smile with one of his own.

Her father perked up beside them, his interest peaked at the prospect of dollar signs. "What do you invest in?"

"Trade routes, mostly," Julius replied. "Although we are diversifying our ventures to entertainment and real estate."

"You're not meddling with that bar she's got herself tangled with, are you?" her father asked.

"I am a sucker for prime business," Julius replied with a charming laugh.

"I hear that." Her father joined in, but the laughter didn't meet his eyes. He was not enthused.

"You have a happy birthday, Mr. Wallace."

"Thank you, son. I hope you have a good time tonight."

Just as they were moving away, her mother muttered lowly. "Can you believe she brought someone else to your party? Does she know how that's going to make her look?"

Julius chuckled once they were out of earshot. "I'm guessing they liked Mr. Complicated?"

"My parents are... set in their ways."

"Reminds me of home. Do you remember the game plan?"

"Wait until people are drunk, then sell my work while they are impressionable and try not to embarrass myself."

"Precisely," Julius nodded, pointing at a couple across the room. "We'll start with them. They look pretty far gone."

She clutched at Julius's suit coat before he could stalk over to Delores Scotts and her husband Reginald. "Let's start someplace easier."

"What's wrong with them?"

"Those two are the most powerful people in the room. They're practically royalty."

"Royals?"

"No, not like real royalty. But they are probably just as powerful. We should warm up first before approaching them."

"Gotcha." He nodded in understanding and motioned to another couple sipping cocktails close to the Scotts. "What about them? They're not royalty, are they?"

"No, they're regular civilians. We can start with them."

The nerves in her gut rumbled as they walked over.

"Ah, Erica," Mrs. Novak greeted her.

"Hello, Mrs. Novak," she smiled politely in return.

"How are you enjoying the party?"

"As long as they keep the drinks flowing," Mr. Novak cut in, but grunted slightly when his wife elbowed him and amended, "Spectacularly."

Mrs. Novak shifted. "How are you? Your mother said you were on sabbatical?"

If she called quitting her receptionist job at her father's firm in favor of following her own path, then sure, sabbatical worked fine.

"I wanted to strike out on my own," she said instead.

"A pioneer," she said enthusiastically. "Do tell."

"I wouldn't call it pioneering," Erica began, but Julius stepped in and gave her elbow a gentle squeeze.

"Oh, I would," Julius smiled knowingly before turning back to the Novaks. "Artists are always modest, aren't they? If I were fielding so many offers, I'd boast a little harder."

"Offers?" She was intrigued, a perfectly died eyebrow lifted.

"Erica, here, is an exceptional painter. It's a wonder her father hasn't put her pieces on display." Julius looked around the room with a cavalier look that masked one of contempt. Immediately, the couple looked around with the same look.

"I wonder why he hasn't either," Mrs. Novak said in agreement.

Wow, he was good. The way the Novaks' eyes glanced toward the walls in disapproval was shocking.

"Wait, that's right. He's generously decided to donate them to the auction." He must have seen Erica trying to hide a look of befuddlement, because he continued, "For the showcase."

"Showcase?" They asked nearly in unison.

"The Friday after next, Erica is debuting her latest collection. It's already being said she's the modern Rembrandt."

"Really?" Mrs. Novak's eyes bulged.

"Yes," Julius said. "It's being touted as the event that cannot be missed."

"Erica, please send me the details. Your mother has my information."

"So, I can count on your attendance?" She asked, completely shocked that the Novaks seemed genuinely interested.

"We wouldn't miss it." Mrs. Novak smiled, then turned to her husband. "You know, dear, we should invite the Alondales. They were talking about securing a few pieces for the new addition they're putting on their house."

"That is right..."

"If you'll excuse us, we're going to get a drink," Julius said.

"The tonic is exceptional," Mr. Novak recommended as they parted.

Walking away, Erica was floating on a cloud. Just like that, she'd secured two guests. Maybe even four. She bounced on her toes and readied to thank Julius, until Mrs. Novak opened her mouth.

"That entire family is tragic. On sabbatical to *paint.*" She snorted quietly. "Martha will absolutely love that train wreck of a show. *Auction,* really?"

"It's probably because they can't sell it." The Novaks shared a hearty laugh at that.

Erica's back stiffened, her fingers curled into fists.

"Just breathe. They're not worth the fight. Don't give them the time of day," Julius said, guiding her away.

"How do you do this?" The elation she'd felt devolved into rage.

"I've been practicing my entire life." He gave her a wink. "Besides, they're idiots. Art is auctioned all the time. I hope she doesn't say that to *Martha*. She'll make a fool out of herself."

Erica stifled a laugh.

"Your work is exceptional. And because of it, there will be many who will root for your defeat. But you will rise anyway."

"If you say so."

"I know it. Now, who's next?"

"You're ready for more? Already?"

Julius nodded in understanding. "We should get that drink first, then."

"Erica," her mother called from behind her before she had the chance to head to the bar.

"Yes, mother?" She fought for every ounce of patience she could muster.

"Come with me. You didn't greet Delores."

Her eyes flickered to the queen of the city. "Right now?"

"Yes, dear. We can't appear to be rude."

She took a patient breath, with half a mind to tell her mother what the Novak's really thought of them, then turned to Julius.

"Alone, dear." Her mother eyed Julius with a hint of a frown crinkling the corners of her lips.

"I'll go grab us that drink," he said, unperturbed by her mother's thorns.

"That was rude," she muttered to her mother as she scurried her away.

"You're involved, sweetheart. You can't be introduced with him."

Thankfully, Julius was out of earshot. Before she had the chance to tell her mother her engagement had been broken off, she was already taking strides across the room, claws digging into her arm as she led her over to Delores Scotts, one of the richest socialites in the city. Her arm was blue from lack of blood by they stood in front of Mrs. Scotts. Her mother was super eager to impress her.

"Delores!" Her mother perked up when Delores, wearing a long purple velvet gown, pulled another glass of champagne from a tray and turned to her.

"Rachel," Delores brightened for half a second at the mention of her name.

"I see you've brought your daughter with you," Her mother said. "Annie, I didn't see you come in. You're all grownup now."

"Yes, she's just arrived. You know eighteen-year-olds," Mrs. Scotts answered for her daughter.

"Eighteen? You look so young. You clearly inherited your mother's good genes."

Her mother was trying too hard, but Erica stood silently, counting the seconds until she was back at

Julius's side.

"Rachel, you're a doll," Mrs. Scotts replied again. Wow, was the girl not allowed to talk?

"Delores, how are your other children?"

"They are very well. Annie, here, is currently fielding offers from the Berlin Philharmonic and the London Symphony Orchestra."

The woman had six kids, but Mrs. Scotts patted Annie like she was the Stanley Cup and they'd just won the championships.

"Did you hear that, Erica? The London Symphony Orchestra. What a talent."

The way she clutched at the side of her dress and leaned into the pair, Erica could smell her mother's jealousy from a mile away. She forced herself to smile and agree, fighting an eye roll at how disingenuous her mother was being. Annie could have been the first woman on Mars, and her mother couldn't have cared less.

Across the room, Julius seemed to be having all the fun, glad handing with the high rollers. He looked at ease. Comfortable. How he found comfort in the shark tank, she'd never understand.

"T-thank you, M-Mrs. Wallace." Annie finally spoke up, her voice soft and meek. The waifish girl seemed perpetually afraid. Not that anyone could blame her. Being in the shadow of Mrs. Scotts would have been difficult for anyone.

"And what are you up to dear?" Mrs. Scotts turned her attention to her. Immediately, she felt like she was put in a fish tank.

"You know how children are." Her mother spoke before she could, her voice light and cavalier. "Unfortunately, mine decided to start her rebellious phase late in life."

"I wouldn't call it rebellious," she ground her teeth so hard she was sure the enamel was going to turn to powder in her mouth.

"Oh?" Delores asked curiously, but she could have sworn there was nothing but gleeful judgement in the way Mrs. Scotts tapped her glass of wine with a long blood-red fingernail. "You're a painter, are you not?"

"She's on a one-year sabbatical from her father's firm," her mother clarified quickly.

"Oh," Mrs. Scott's eyes brightened, eager to talk about herself. "My eldest took a gap year to travel Europe. It's all the rage with kids today. What are you up to while you're away?"

"Painting," She said with an ironic smile.

Her mother bristled.

"So, you *are* a painter. Where are you exhibited? I'd love to see it."

"I'm not, currently." Erica took a deep breath, trying to stave off the sense of worthlessness that usually accompanied having to admit her failures in front of this crowd. Just as she was getting ready to say that she only sold to private vendors, Delores's face upturned in obvious disapproval.

"I see. And your boyfriend, what does he do?" Delores's gaze dashed across the room in search for Julius.

"You mean, her fiancé." A very familiar voice came up

behind her, and two equally familiar and very much not supposed to be there arms enclosed her into a hug. Oh God, this could not be happening.

What the hell was he doing there?

"Max," her voice cracked as she turned around to the ripe scent of alcohol on his breath. "What are you doing here?"

Alarmed, her gaze darted over to where Julius was shaking hands, but he was no longer where she'd last spotted him.

"Your mother invited me, remember? I thought you weren't coming."

"You can't be here," she said firmly.

"Of course, he can, dear," her mother interjected. "It's well within his rights as your fiancé."

"Fiancé?" Julius's deep voice rumbled behind her a moment later. When they turned, his eyes widened in shock. "Max?"

"Mr. Craul? What are you doing here?"

Somebody shoot me, please.

"I'm Erica's escort."

"Instead of her fiancé?" Mrs. Scotts clarified, glancing at her mother with a look that said *'so, this is what you allow in your house.'* The room seemed to be shrinking around her. The air became thick.

"Ex," Erica corrected as quietly as she could, hoping this whole thing would fizzle into nothing.

"We're working it out," Max said quickly as he swayed on his toes. His inebriation didn't stop him from staring Julius down.

Julius squared his shoulders. Mrs. Scotts, Erica, and her mother watched them like a game of tennis as the ball was volleyed from one side to the other. Erica stood frozen between them, unable to move. Or think. Or do much of anything other than wish for a bottomless pit to open under her shoes.

"He's your Mr. Complicated?" Julius turned to her. The betrayal that set into Julius's voice made her cheeks flush in embarrassment. Well, it was out now.

"Yes."

"*He* knows about us?" Max moved between them. "How do you know him?"

"He's an investor," she said, feeling herself shrink to the size of an ant.

"This, I know. But that doesn't explain why he's here with *you*."

"He's also a patron of the arts."

Max snorted. "Is that what he told you? I'm sure the fact that you're pretty makes him a patron of the arts."

"Do you think so little of Erica's talent that you'd think anyone after her work must only be interested in her?" The offense in Julius's tone was unmistakable.

Max rolled his eyes. "I know what my fiancée's good for."

Julius's jaw clenched as he eyed her ex-fiancé. They stood the same height and were equally matched in build. Equally ready to pounce on each other.

Her mother cut in with a smile. "Perhaps, you'd like a drink."

The last thing Max needed was another drink. Mrs.

Scotts excused herself and scurried over to her husband. There was no mistaking the gossip she was spreading as they both stared their way with raised brows and conspiratorial looks.

"I think he's had—"

"Yes, I would. Come, Erica," Max said.

"Erica's not a dog who barks on command," Julius replied.

"Erica can speak for herself." She eyed both men sharply. The small group turned toward her, and the room was suddenly out of air. "Julius is here to help me tonight. That's all. So, no thank you to the drink."

Even though she desperately needed one. Or two.

Max was not happy about that. "Fine. We'll talk about this later."

No sooner had he left them, he was at the makeshift bar in the corner of the room, ordering a double shot. She wondered when they'd stop serving him. He clearly arrived intoxicated.

"Young man, I need to speak with my daughter." Her mother frowned at Julius, not hiding her disapproval. The pads of her fingertips dug into Erica's arm as she led them away from the dissipating group.

"That hurts," she protested. Her mother continued to pull her to a lonely corner, away from prying ears.

"Look at the trouble you've caused."

"What?"

"You're embarrassing us. If you didn't come here with that... that *man*."

"Julius is helping me get my showcase set up."

"Showcase? Erica, when are you going to give up your little hobby already?"

"What I do is much more than a *hobby*."

"I told your father not to let you wave around paint brushes and pretend that it's worth something. It has gotten out of hand. We've indulged you too long."

"It's talent," she said through gritted teeth. "Isn't that what you said about Annie? Her talent is for music, mine is for paint. Is it too hard for you to say that about me?"

"There's a difference between you and her, sweetheart. She's wanted. You're not."

The hurt that thrashed inside of her brought angry tears to her eyes.

"Let's all calm down." Her father intervened when their quiet corner bubbled over. He tossed her a look of disapproval. "Erica, what are you doing? My two best ladies can't be over here fighting."

"Why are you looking at me? I didn't start it."

"Erica, apologize to your mother," her father demanded. How could he not defend her? Her mother who was wrong. Not her. She'd never given much to the term 'seeing red' until that moment. Enough was enough.

"No. *She's* the one who should apologize."

"Erica! Stop this right now," Her father's voice dropped into a low hiss, the warning in it unmistakable.

"Or what? You're going to send me to my room? I'm so freaking tired of this. Why do you hate me so much? My entire life, I did everything right, and still you peck and peck. Is it too much to ask that you believe in the one dream I've ever had?"

"It's not acceptable to have a daughter who revels in being a starving artist," her father said. "To be in the right circles, we have to have the right presentation." No matter which words he used, they all sounded the same to her.

You're not good enough.

She'd been hearing different variations of it ever since her father's business took off. Blood rushed to her head, making it harder for her to think.

"What you're doing is unacceptable," her mother said. "What would the Scotts say? Or the Novaks? Don't you understand, we are in a room of influen—"

"For goodness sakes!" The dam burst. The entire room fell silent. Erica's voice echoed off of the walls. "For once in your life, could you stop trying to impress these people?"

"Erica, that's enough," her mother spat through clenched teeth, eyes darting around, cheeks enflamed with embarrassment.

"Why? Because you're afraid of what your fake friends might say about me? Oh wait, you don't care as long as you don't look bad. News flash. They. Don't. Even. Like. You."

"Erica, you're embarrassing us." Her mother chuckled nervously and looked around pointedly, encouraging her to stop with a painful grip on her wrist. There were many ears listening to their conversation.

"Rachel, don't entertain her," her father said the turned to her. "You are acting like a spoiled brat. If you're going to be disruptive, you can leave." He pointed to the door.

"Fine. I don't want to be here with all of these fake people, anyway."

She clutched her purse and made her way toward the exit. This was the reason she hated visiting her parents. No matter what, she ended up the bad guy. The outcast. Tears brimmed through the anger. As if feeling her distress, Julius appeared at her side. His warm, reassuring hand was at the small of her back.

"It's alright," He said softly. His presence brought her some relief. Julius leaned in to speak quietly. "Don't let them get to you."

"Get your filthy hands off of her," Max snatched Julius's wrist and pulled his hand away.

Julius's entire body stilled as he looked at Max's hand with disgust. "Excuse me?"

"You heard me." Max pushed between them. Barely able to hold himself upright, he made a show of sizing him up. "Get your hands off of my girl."

"Max, please," Erica said. She just wanted to get out of there as fast as she could.

"I brought her here, I will take her home."

"I'll take her home," Max slurred.

"Max, you're drunk. You can't take anyone home." She tried to inch her way to the exit. The heated gazes from the room, the disapproval from her parents, and her own humiliation was starting to set in. The cloud she floated on when she spoke her mind disappeared.

He ignored her, eyes on Julius. "She's mine."

"If she were yours," Julius said calmly, "then she wouldn't be here with me."

With a gentle hand, Julius reached for her shoulder. Again, Max ripped it away. This time, the force of the momentum turned them both around. The tension between the two men broke.

"Touch her again, and I'll kill you."

"I'm not your enemy." Julius stepped toward her, but was quickly shoved backward. Just as Julius nudged her out of the way, Max swung, his large fist hurtling at Julius's face. In a graceful move, Julius stepped back, avoiding the blow. Max staggered forward with a grunt. A deep scowl etched lines in his brow, and he growled in frustration.

"Max, stop," she pleaded, watching him wind up like an angry bull. "That's enough."

Max charged Julius, knocking them both into the table and onto the ground. Max, on top, swung again. This time, his fist connected with Julius's face. As painful as it looked, it didn't seem to faze him. Max hit him again.

"Do something, Rich!" Her mother cried out.

By now, the crowd had created a loose circle, everyone too entranced to look anywhere else besides at the brawl in her parents' dining room.

Max went for another blow, but Julius kicked him off. Max staggered into the marble tabletop with a crack. Grunting, and disoriented, he fumbled to rise. When he finally came up for air, someone shrieked.

"Oh my god, his eyes."

Max and the woman made eye contact before he swiveled away from her, rubbing his eyes. Blood seemed to gush from one of them, staining his fingers.

"Are you okay?" she asked, but fear pushed her away from him instead of toward him.

Her father stepped in. "It's time for you all to leave before I call the police."

To her surprise, Max didn't disagree. Clutching his face, he rushed into the foyer and staggered out of the front door without a backwards glance.

"Make sure he doesn't drive," her father called to the man at the front door who radioed the valet outside.

Erica looked around in horror. No one moved as they watched. The full realization of what had happened hit her, and shame flooded her.

"Let's go." Julius's steady voice was beside her. "I'm sorry Mr. and Mrs. Wallace."

Neither one of her parents responded to his apology.

Disheveled, Julius seemed okay for the most part, just as apologetic as she was. A slight trail of blood ran down from the corner of his mouth.

"You're bleeding."

"It's fine. Let's get out of here."

She nodded and followed him back to the car waiting for them at curbside. Too much in shock to do anything besides get into the passenger seat, she stared back at her parents' house for perhaps the final time.

One thing was completely certain: her life had gone to hell.

10

JULIUS

JULIUS THREW OPEN THE DOOR to his brother's room as soon as he arrived at their hotel suite.

"Tell me you didn't know."

Evan didn't have the decency to looked shocked when he stormed in, nostrils flaring, fangs down. Instead, his lanky brother sat unperturbed, calmly reading through a stack of papers under the glow of his desk lamp. His impassive face made Julius want to punch him.

"Hello? I'm talking to you."

Evan finally looked up from the paper stack. "You have blood on your face."

"Really? I hadn't noticed." Julius was past the point of sarcasm and heading straight into fury.

"You could be a bit more discreet if you're going to feed in public."

"I was attacked by a wolf tonight."

Evan perked up, concern bleached his features. From the look of concentration on his face, Evan was trying to piece together the blips of memories that flooded his mind. "Max attacked you?"

Us. Thinking of Erica, shaken and quiet in his passenger seat the entire ride home... The vampire inside of him still wanted to rip Max's arms from his body. The wolf should have known better. Putting a human between two giants was dangerous. She could have gotten hurt. He thought of Erica's forlorn silence as he drove her back to her apartment. By the all gods, he wished he could take away memories like his brother could. He'd erase this entire night from her memory and start over.

"Did you know she was engaged to him?"

Evan didn't say anything right away. "You assured me that she was a catch and release."

"When were you planning to tell me?"

Evan shrugged. "I didn't think it was relevant. It never seemed to bother you before."

"Well, it does now. I don't want to be with someone who's already with someone else."

"Isn't that what you do? Find the already attached so they don't leech onto you?"

"I don't do that anymore."

"Since when?"

"Since..." *Erica.* Her name wrenched from his throat. Was he really admitting that she was different? That this— whatever they had—was slowly changing him? He'd barely known her a week, and it bothered him to think of her with someone else. Julius pictured her beside the wolf, and his fangs sharpened. She was taken. No, *engaged.*

"I need blood," Julius said, not bothering to put his fangs away.

"The synth blood is in the storage safe under the bar."

"I need something stronger." His vampire agreed. If he was going to war with a shifter, he'd need human blood to become stronger.

"Don't you have another way to decompress that doesn't include inciting a bloodbath? I rather like these clothes."

"Not to be an inconvenience to your dry cleaner, but there are only two ways I relieve stress. And fucking Erica's brains out is out of the question at the moment."

That would only happen if she ever spoke to him again. Which she might not. Seeing as there was a wolf standing in his way. His vampire didn't like that idea one bit.

"I'm sure you have hobbies outside of sex," Evan said. "What about drinking? You love to drink."

"Do I look like I want to have a drink right now?"

"You look like shit, so it's statistically likely."

"If this is your attempt at calming me down, you're failing."

"I should call Dani. She'd know what to do."

"Don't. I don't need our little sister in my business."

"She knows we're in town. There's no escaping her. Eventually, she'll find us."

True enough. Julius wondered why she hadn't made it her business to be in theirs since they arrived in town.

"Exams," Evan replied to his thoughts.

"Well then, it looks like our dear sister needs to focus on school. And don't distract me. I'm still upset with you."

"Then I probably shouldn't tell you the upside in all of this."

Julius absolutely hated when Evan did this. Tell him just enough to keep him on the edge. It was clear from the way Evan slowly poured an ice-filled highball glass with dark liquor, his brother was waiting for the anticipation to build.

"Are you really going to make me ask?"

Evan shrugged and filled another glass with ice, one cube at a time. Painstakingly slow.

"Fine, what's the upside? And it better be good."

"They're not doing well."

"Explain."

"Ooh, you channel the King very well."

"Talk already," Julius pressed impatiently.

"Alright, alright. Apparently, the night we met. You know, when she destroyed your prized possession? She thought it was Max's car."

"And...?"

"She thought he was cheating on her, but this wasn't the first time she'd thought something like that. So, to teach him a lesson, she took a bat to his car. Only, it turned out to be yours."

"And... what happened after?"

"You were there. They ran."

"Seriously, Evan. Did he cheat on her or not?"

"My telepathic abilities only stretch so far."

"But, they're not together," Julius clarified. His mood

started to brighten again.

"I wouldn't think so, considering she seemed pretty fed up. And she's agreed to see you more than once. For only the gods know why."

Julius snorted. "I'm not nearly that bad."

"You're worse. Feel better?"

"Marginally."

"Excellent. Now, tomorrow we apologize to the wolf."

"What?" Julius sputtered. "I didn't do anything wrong. He picked a fight with me."

"We have to move on this deal. The building Max is sitting on is prime. We can double our money plus interest within six months."

"That quickly?"

"Yes, the mayor approved a rehabilitation program. They're flooding that area with cash. The funds are due to be released within the next few months. We can sit on it for that long, then refinance and take out our cash."

"You got all of this from reading *that*?" Julius motioned to the stack of papers on his desk.

"I'm a mind reader," Evan said. "I only needed to get close enough to the people involved. We'll just have to check in on the investment periodically."

The thought of staying for six months had its appeal. At least he'd be able to stay with Erica. Maybe even camp out on her couch and watch her paint from time to time. That was quickly becoming his favorite pastime in the human realm. His vampire wouldn't leave her so soon, anyway. Now that he was pretty sure her relationship with Max was over. But it burned his ass to think he'd have to apologize to the shifter in order to make this deal happen.

"Suck it up buttercup, we're making this deal."

Text between Dani, Julius and Evan

Dani: Morning nerds!

Dani: HELLO!

Julius: It's four in the morning.

Dani: Not for me it isn't. Did you two dickheads think you could avoid me forever?

Julius: Dickhead? What's fuck is a dickhead?

Dani: Evan, can you please stop teaching Julius how to curse. He's doing it wrong.

Evan: I'm not teaching him anything. He's probably learning it from that girl.

Julius: Leave her out of this.

Dani: Uh oh. What girl?

Evan: The girl who wrecked his car.

Dani: Wrecked his... You mean, he's met someone?

Julius: No.

Evan: Yes.

Dani: And he's seen her more than once?

Julius: No.

Evan: Yes.

Dani: Before or after he's slept with her.

Evan: Both.

Julius: I did not sleep with her. Well, I did, but not in the manner you're implying.

Dani: I see.

Dani: Why do you always get serious about the crazy ones?

Julius: She's not crazy.

Evan: She and her friend took a bat to the car you had custom made for this trip.

Dani: WTF? Custom made? WE'RE SUPPOSED TO BE LAYING LOW, JULIUS!

Evan: Told you.

Dani: Julius?

Evan: He's sulking.

Julius: I am not sulking.

Evan: He's sulking more now than when she ruined his car.

Dani: And you've been seeing this girl... regularly?

Julius: SHE IS NOT CRAZY!

Dani: Whoa, calm down there. Looks like I need to meet her.

Julius: No.

Dani: Too late. I'm already boarding a flight, be there in six hours. And please for the love of the all gods, bring me a blood bag. Not that synth shit Damian has been making us drink.

Evan: Danica...

Dani: Don't use my full name, jackass. Besides, I'm a vampire, I have a thing for blood. Sue me.

Julius: When you get here, please don't embarrass me. I just met her.

Dani: As your sister, it's pretty much my job. □

Julius: I can't even go to a different realm without my

family getting into my business.

Evan: He can't wait to see you btw. He's doesn't understand why you wanted to go to school in the alter realm. It's too far.

Julius: Stop reading my mind Evan.

Evan: Fuck off.

Dani: Take notes Julius, that's how you're supposed to swear. See you suckers soon.

11

JULIUS

THE HIGH-RISE ON 114TH AND Broadway was in desperate need of repair. Even through the rough, Julius could see its potential. Apparently, the shifter acquired it just before the mayor passed legislation to gentrify the neighborhood. Evan was right, the entire area was transforming. Many of the buildings had been sold off, vacated, and roped off as construction equipment sat outside, ready for demolition.

"Your abilities never cease to amaze me," He praised his brother as they waited for Max and his business partner to arrive, but Evan was too busy fretting to accept it.

"Now, don't screw this up. You know what needs to be done."

"Try not to attack him."

"And apologize," Evan tossed him a wry, don't-fuck-this-up glance, then checked his phone for the fourth time since they'd arrived. His brother was nervous.

"They'll be here," he reassured him. "They need us just as much as we need them."

"I apologize for assuming they might bail on us since you two are feuding over the same girl."

A block away, a car moved through the early morning streets.

"See?"

Evan looked toward the sound. The car hadn't turned the corner yet, but once it did, relief eased Evan's tense shoulders.

The shine of the black car bounced in the early morning sun from several blocks away. He had to admit, it would have been easy for Erica to mistake the two—except for the classless pinstripe detail that laid against the hood. Behind the glass, two figures were in deep conversation. With the streets empty and clear of noise, it was easy to hear what the two shifters were discussing as the car drove toward them.

"For the love of God, don't let your dick get in the way of this," Cav said. It seemed they both were being scolded by their brothers for their behavior. "I had to beg Evan to meet up again."

"You think I want to do a deal with a fanger?" Max replied.

"Seeing as you have Splinters up your ass, pun intended, you should be willing to spread her legs if it gets you this deal."

"I can't whore out my future wife to a fanger. He's not even one of our own kind."

Cav laughed, clearly caught off guard. "You've considered it?"

"Anything is better than getting a bullet in the head. Besides, Erica wouldn't go for it." Max shook his head.

"You asked?" His brother sputtered.

"Do I look insane to you? Of course, I didn't ask. She's already pissed at me for our anniversary."

"Maybe it was because you were fucking other girls on your anniversary..."

"You know how my wolf is. He has certain needs. Erica wouldn't have gone for a threesome." Max leaned into the backseat to grab a file folder. "Which reminds me, if she ever asks, you brought them and I left to sleep over at Aiden's house. She saw them coming up to the office that night."

"Jesus, you're a savage. I'm surprised she's still talking to you. How the hell did you get out of that one?"

"I told her Splinters will kill our father if we don't get this money."

"You told her about Splinters?"

"I had to do something. She cornered me with that whole, 'I saw two half-naked girls going up to your office' thing. And I sure as hell wasn't going to tell her I owe Splinters a personal debt for gambling away his yacht after sleeping with his mistress. Erica would never forgive me."

"I'm starting to feel bad for the poor girl. She's kind of a sweetheart."

"Don't go soft on me. She looks pretty on my arm

when we sign deals like these." Max pulled out several papers from the folder in his lap. "Plus, she can cook, and she's not bad in the sack either. She's an artist, how could she not be. That also doesn't hurt."

The car stopped just behind where they'd parked, but he dared not look up. If he did, he'd be liable to kill Max. He stared at his feet, on the precipice of letting his vampire out. His breathing quickened and his fists clenched, preparing to launch at Max. Erica was not a plaything.

"Julius," Evan's voice was purposefully calm beside him.

"You expect me to apologize to that?" Julius's fighting fangs began to expand and draw down. A hatred he'd never known curled up his back and tightened in his muscles as his vampire surfaced. Blackness pooled in his eyes.

Yes, he's a piece of shit, Evan said into his mind. *But you can't go beast mode in the middle of the street.*

Yes, he could. His transformation was already starting. It felt good, having his vampire break through the surface. In the eighty years since he'd reached maturity, he'd never let his vampire out. Not truly. The beast inside of him was always to be kept at bay. The darkest part of every vampire was too vicious—too carnal—to let out without restraint. After many years of practice keeping him contained, Julius had finally found a reason to let his vampire run rampant.

Then he felt it again. A mouth numbing tingle traveled up his spine to the base of his skull. It was Evan.

"You have to do this," Evan said. "On your honor as Prince of the realm. Our people need you."

When Evan put it that way, his vampire softened. The spindles of his rage broke apart. His kingdom depended on this deal. They wouldn't accept that he'd let the head between his legs decide what was best for his kingdom. His vampire cared more for his people than he did for ripping Max's throat out. Begrudgingly, he retreated and Evan lifted his hold.

"Keep perspective," Evan advised. "Think of the starvation that's sure to come if we don't get this money. Remember the last time rampant famine blew through the realm? Millions of young innocents died."

"Understood," he said through clenched teeth. He'd put his petty differences aside and think of the plight of his kingdom. They needed money to buy blood, and that's what he'd deliver on.

"If he mentions her, do nothing," Evan said, a pleading note in his voice. "I can help remind you."

The tingle at the base of his skull fortified Evan's claim. Julius nodded his consent, resigned, knowing he wouldn't be able to keep himself from ruining everything if he had to speak first.

I'll do all the talking.

When the two shifters exited the car, Evan stepped forward to greet them. He did little more than eye the scumbag in front of him. It was a wonder they'd do business with someone with such questionable morals.

We'll do whatever it takes for our kingdom. Even negotiate with the devil himself, Evan said.

That was precisely what they were about to do.

"Thank you for meeting us." Cav shook Evan's hand.

"Thank you for coming."

"Let's go inside. It's a bit chilly out."

Julius remained silent, barely looking at either brother while they were ushered inside. Just as Cav handed them the blueprints for the new space, Max turned to Julius.

"About last night," Max began, his stare cold and calculating. "I was surprised to see you there."

He stared at him through slits, his expression equally frigid.

Just try your best, Evan encouraged.

"I can let it go if you can," he said. The words were tight on the way out. It was as close to an apology as he could get. An awkward silence stretched through the expanse of the first floor.

Cav nudged his brother hard. Max cleared his throat. "No hard feelings."

"That's settled, then." Evan said, then turned the subject to other things. "Where was the pool going to go again?"

"Right this way." Cav pulled Max in front of him.

It seemed both of their brothers were keen to keep as much distance between them as possible. For most of the second visit, they did. As Cav showed them the pool and layout of the state-of-the-art fitness center, Max was cordial. By the time they reached the rooftop, Max was more animated.

"This will be one of the dual penthouse suites. One on either side."

"How do you ensure privacy?" he asked, wanting to throw Max off the high-rise. It would do him no good; a shifter could survive a fall from this height if he shifted in midair. The regenerative properties from their shift would heal most breaks. It would be painful as all hell though. That alone would make it worth it. But he shoved his fists into his slacks instead. If Max was willing to play nice, so was he.

"There will be a dividing wall in the center. It will be designed to muffle most sounds. We thought of a glass enclosure as a possibility as well depending if we can secure a frosted option with the right thickness."

"What about security?" Evan asked. "Currently, the design looks pretty open."

"Let me show you," Cav said, pointing down at the proposal in his hands. "I think we left the security plans on the pool level."

"We have a bit of time before we have to go to the airport. My sister is flying in this morning," Evan explained. "So, we can go down to look at them."

Do you think you can handle being alone with the wolf for five minutes?

I've been fine so far.

Be nice. Was all Evan said as he boarded the service elevator with Cav.

Once they were alone, Max turned toward him abruptly. "I take it she hasn't told you yet."

The wolf was baiting him. He steeled himself. From the smirk on Max's face, he must have known he had no idea what he was talking about. But curiosity bested him.

"Don't worry," Max continued. "She will."

"What does she need to inform me of?"

"We're working things out."

Julius's jaw clenched as he stared into Max's dark, mocking eyes. It made him want to beat the blithering smile off of his face. He could rip the wolf's throat out right now, and no one would know it. Cav was already descending the service elevator with Evan, discussing terms. Max was a lone wolf. Unprotected. A familiar numbness ran up the back of his neck and settled there like novocaine.

Evan.

I'm not going to kill him.

I can't take that chance. Just tell him you'll leave her alone.

No. If Erica came to him, he would never turn her away. But then realized, she hadn't come to him. Did the scumbag in front of her get to her too? She hadn't spoken to him since the party. Probably because he slammed her ex into her parent's dining room table. He deserved it, of course, but perhaps Erica didn't see it that way.

"If you two are working things out, then you won't have a problem with me," he said, proving to both of them a lesson of his restraint.

"Then we are aligned, Mr. Craul?" Max asked, the undercurrent of challenge clear. He wanted Julius to back off of Erica. Like that would ever happen. In fact, he knew just how he was going to win her back. He'd show her that she didn't need a manipulative scumbag in her life. Of course, he wasn't going to let Max know this.

"If everything remains in order, you'll have no issues on my end." Julius said, his voice level despite the churning of the beast inside of him. His vampire itched to come to the surface.

"I know how to keep order in my own house," Max said. We'll see about that.

"Then, you have your answer," he said instead.

"Excellent, we're agreed."

The wolf put his hand out. He eyed it with disgust.

Take it. Evan said harshly.

Begrudgingly, he took hold of it with a firm grasp of his own. Hard, unyielding. Inwardly, his vampire paced and hurried him to let go. He'd rather die from a poison-laced dagger than touch skin with the enemy.

He's not our enemy.

He is now.

12

ERICA

"SO, LET ME GET THIS STRAIGHT. You're seeing the guy whose car we completely wrecked? Are you insane?" Marie's voice screeched over the line as Erica cradled her cell phone with one hand and mixed paints with the other.

Thankfully, at Open Studio, her professor didn't care if she was on the phone or not. Neither did her classmates—or rather, classmate. This late in the evening, just one other soul had braved the chilly weather to come to class. Across the room, he had his headphones on full blast. So, he was definitely not disturbed by her phone call.

"It's not the worst thing I've ever done," she replied.

"This is *you* we're talking about. Of course it is."

"That's not fair. What about when I dated Tommy Richards in high school?"

The entire school was shocked when they'd started

dating. She was the class sweetheart and Richards was the very definition of a bad boy. The kind who skipped class and smoked pot in Smoker's Row behind the boy's baseball field. Really, he only had a hard appearance, on the inside he was soft as a teddy bear. Behind his grunge hair and leather jacket, there was a heart of gold underneath.

"Tommy Richards was a pothead slacker. He's a baby deer compared to this. Not that I'm complaining. I've been waiting for someone better to scoop you up for ages. Please tell me he's hot at least," Marie sighed hopefully.

"You didn't notice?" Shock bled into her words.

"I was running for my life! I wasn't thinking about whether the guy was hot or not."

"OMG, he's gorgeous." She all but swooned, then described every bit of the sexy man who made it impossible to think of anything else. "And his eyes! It's so freaking cliché, but they're dreamy."

Marie whistled over the phone. "Does he have a brother?"

"He does, but he's not your type. Well, he's got plenty of brothers, I think. He's one of seven."

"Ask him! If he does, and if any of them have half the genes you've described, we're going to figure out how to spread the wealth immediately."

"Down girl." She laughed. "Besides, we haven't spoken since the party—"

"What party?"

"My father's birthday dinner."

"You mean to tell me he's met your parents? So, soon?

He's one brave soul."

"It's not like that. He came to help with my showcase."

"I like him already. How did it go?"

"It was a disaster!" She cried, then filled her friend in on the mess that was her father's birthday party. "And well... we haven't spoken since."

"Wait, what do you mean you haven't spoken since? Why not?"

"He hasn't called."

"So? You have his number, don't you?"

"I do."

"We're living in the 21st century! Interest is a two-way street. If you want him to know you're still into him, call him."

"What do I say? Hey, I know we haven't spoken since you broke my parents' dining room when you decked my ex, but..."

"Man, I wish I was there to see that." Marie's voice rose with glee.

"It was so embarrassing! Plus, Max and I still haven't had a chance to talk..."

"What's there to talk about? His loss."

"You're very quick to dismiss Max. He's got a lot going on right now," she said earnestly. She didn't go into detail about his father or the debt they were trying to pay back, but he was going through a rough time right now.

Marie remained silent on the line, despite her usual vocal thoughts about her ex. They never got along since the day they met to the point where they hardly hung out if Max was around. It was surprising she was so reserved.

It was short lived. Marie sighed heavily.

"We've been best friends since we were in the third grade. Believe me when I tell you, I know exactly when someone is not worth your time. And I'd be a shitty friend if I didn't say that. He doesn't treat you right."

"Like how?" she found herself becoming defensive.

"For starters, he got into a fight at your parent's house, left you with another man to take you home and didn't even call to ask if made it home safe."

"I didn't call him either," she argued.

"Okay, then what about him ghosting you on your anniversary."

"He had a reason for that," she said defensively.

"He always does," Marie reminded her. "Listen, all I'm saying is you should take some time to think things over while you're on a break. I get it, I know you've been with him for a few years, so it'll be hard to just turn the switch off, but..." There was a contemplative pause. "You know what you need? A Max detox. Don't see him, don't talk to him... Don't even think about him for a week. Let your brain settle. You'll be able to think much more clearly."

"What do I do in the meantime?" Erica asked, holding in a chuckle. Now that her relationship was over, her best friend seemed on a personal mission to keep it that way.

"The best way to get your mind off him is to put it to use on someone else. It seems Hotness Overload fits the bill. Aren't you dating him anyway?"

"We're not dating."

"If he is brave enough to meet your parents, you're dating."

"He's only in town for a couple of weeks."

"No one says you have to have forever with the guy. Get in there, do the horizontal tango and get out. At the very least, he'll be one hell of a distraction."

"Isn't that the truth." Even thinking of him now gave her the tingles.

"Give the guy a chance. If it doesn't work out, there's plenty of tall and sexy in this city."

Her phone beeped twice in her ear. When she looked at the display, she could have sworn her best friend was in cahoots with the universe. Julius's name sprawled across the screen. A flash of excitement burst through her, making her hands shake.

"OMG, that's him." She tried to temper her excitement.

"Hotness Overload? Or... that other one," Marie said in disdain.

She laughed at her friend's brashness. "Julius. What do I do?"

"Answer it! Remember, no Max for a week. Not one single thought."

Her phone beeped again.

"I'm going before it disconnects."

"Don't forget to ask Julius about his hot brothers."

"Sure thing." She chuckled before switching over to the other line and putting her paint brush down. "Hello."

"So, I've figured out how I'm going to make it up to you."

Well, that was unexpected. Her temporary confusion slightly dimmed her budding excitement.

"Make what up to me?"

"For getting into a bar brawl at your parents' house. When I told you they seemed to find me, I didn't think I was going to get into one in your presence."

She bit her lip and tried to play it cool. "What makes you think I'd be willing to forgive you?"

"I can be persuasive." Julius played along, likely catching onto the excitement in her voice.

"And how would that be?" She couldn't help the grin that appeared.

"I can show you later tonight."

"You know, I'm beginning to think you really are a vampire. I don't think I've ever seen you walk around in the daylight."

"Sure you have. We slept together, remember?"

An involuntary snort charged out. "You make it sound like it was more than it was."

"It's all in perspective. So, I'm thinking we meet up at eight o'clock. Unless you're otherwise engaged."

Funny choice of words.

"I'm not engaged."

"Would your fiancé agree?"

Ah, he wanted to know about Max. Of course, he did. Any sane man would. The conversation with her friend echoed in her head. *Don't give Max another thought for a week*. Let her brain settle. Little did her friend know, it was already settled. The more she thought of Max, the less she felt romantic feelings for him. And worse, every time she pictured his face, Julius's mischievous smirk seemed to push any thoughts of him out of the way.

"Lucky for you, I don't have one. My situation with Max is complicated, but we're not together. Not anymore."

"I should say I'm sorry, but I'm not."

She stifled a laugh. No, she guessed he wouldn't be.

"What if I've been inconsolable?"

"Can we meet up in an hour?" he asked. "I can console your heartbreak."

"I'm not sure there's anything to console, but I'll be there."

As soon as she hung up the phone, she raced to put her paints away, eager to be with Julius again.

"Are you done for the night?" Her professor barely looked up from his phone, too distracted by the video on it to pay her much attention.

"Yes, I've had enough for one day."

"Stay warm out there."

"Will do."

Keeping warm was an understatement. By the time she'd gotten off the bus and walked two blocks to the address Julius provided, icicles were threatening to form on her nose.

To her surprise, Julius was waiting outside, half an hour early. More surprising, she almost didn't recognize him without his signature suit. Frick, she'd grown to love him in a suit. The way it fit tight to his body and exuded power gave her chills. But to look at the man in basic black pants and a knit sweater made her wonder how she'd ever thought a suit made him look powerful. It exuded from his pores no matter what he wore.

"You're not wearing a suit," she blurted out and

immediately wondered why in the heck she didn't have something more profound to say.

He gave her a lopsided grin.

"If I'd known you preferred me in one, I would have worn it." Julius's voice dipped, and the way he watched her made a small blush crawl up her cheeks. She'd never been so grateful for cold weather. With the biting chill, her cheeks were already red so her blush was indistinguishable.

"There's no need," she cleared her throat.

To distract herself from the lure of the man in front of her, she cleared her throat and looked around the art district. Many of the shops were closed for the night. What was even more jarring were the two extremely large canvases resting against the door of the sports car behind him.

"How did you get those here?" she asked. Judging by the size of his car, there was no way those massive canvases fit inside. They stood higher than the car itself.

"We all have our secrets." He wiggled his eyebrows as he turned the key in the lock of the studio adjacent to them. "You said you've always wanted to do a paint night. So, here we are."

She smiled. "This is a date."

"It was the only thing I could think of to ease the hurt of our other outing."

"Does this mean you're expecting a pleasurable evening in bed?" She intended it as a joke, but as soon as the words were out of her mouth, she felt a growing heat inside of her.

"There are no beds in here, but I'm sure we can make do." He tossed her a playful wink.

Laughing, they hauled the oversized canvases into what looked like an artist's warehouse. A small gallery was in the front, but in the back was a loft she could fit her entire studio into, plus some.

"Wow, how'd you come by this?"

"A friend owed me a favor." He shrugged and turned on the lights. Erica's eyes bugged out of her head when she slid her coat off at stared at the back.

"This place is amazing," she took in its soaring ceilings and brick pillars that seemed to go on forever. Even the concrete floors looked just the perfect shade of chic grey. The small gallery in the front did not do the space justice. They were even more gorgeous in person.

"Are you sure we can paint here? It doesn't look like anyone works here."

The surfaces were pristine and shined to glossy perfection.

"We're welcome to use anything in the warehouse," he reassured her. "The owner hosts paint nights here a few times a month."

The owner must have an exceptional cleaning staff. Or very neat and tidy painters. She looked around again. Not a spec was on the floor. Julius seemed impervious to its glory as he fidgeted with several bottles of acrylic paint.

"I wasn't sure what paint to get. The clerk at the store assured me that these were best for my value. Whatever that means."

"All paint is good paint," she reassured him. The

acrylics in his hand would serve their needs for the night. "Let's set up."

She immediately got to work, bouncing around the studio, getting two stools in case they wanted to sit, grabbing a few spare towels, and filling two tall glasses with water from the sink in the back before placing them by the canvases on top of the stools. A spare tarp laid neatly folded on top of a ten-foot table slab at the far end of the studio. She grabbed it, and they stretched it out underneath the canvases he'd leaned against the wall. It surprised her how easy it felt for her to be in someone else's studio with such familiarity.

"We're set up," he said with pride, looking at their handiwork.

"Where are the brushes?" she asked as she thumbed the primary colored bottles of paint.

"I'm sure there's some around here."

"To use another painter's brushes is tantamount to treason. And it's wicked bad luck." It wasn't, but some artists hated for others to use their stuff. Good paintbrushes weren't the easiest thing to come by or the least expensive.

"I did not realize this."

"That's alright," she quickly amended when his beautiful features frowned in disappointment. "We can use our fingers. I've always wanted to try the hand painting technique. We just need palettes."

She bit her lip and lapped the studio, searching several drawers until she found two unused palettes.

"Are you sure we can use these?" she asked, holding

them up.

"We can use anything in here," he said, rolling up his sleeves.

Erica squeezed several globs of the primary colors onto each of their palettes and handed one to him. They turned to the stretch of empty canvas in front of them.

"Where do we start?" he asked after a minute.

"Follow your muse."

"What if I don't have one?"

"Everyone's got one. Yours might not be cooperating?"

"No, I don't believe it is." He shook his head. "What does one do when that happens?"

"This." She dipped a finger into a glob of red paint and flicked it toward his canvas. Splatters rippled across it.

"Hey! That was my canvas."

She laughed. "Oops."

"I see what this is. Art sabotage!"

"Or inspiration," she feigned innocence, but Julius was already dipping his hand onto the palette and smearing the paints across his palm. Huge globs coated his fingers. Julius poised for his strike.

"Don't you dare!" Her warning came too late. Julius was already flicking the paint at her. A glob of it hit her arm. "You dirty, rotten..."

Julius moved out of squirting distance when she squeezed a pool of paint onto her palette. Following his lead, she drenched her hands, then ran after him with palms open.

"Stop, I need to construct my masterpiece!" He laughed, holding his hands up in surrender. She went for his canvas instead. In retaliation, he went at hers. His large hands did tons more damage than her dainty fingers ever could. But as the slashes of paint came together, they didn't look bad.

"We paint well together. It actually looks pretty."

Julius followed her gaze, his expression turned serious. "It does, doesn't it?"

"We should do a duet."

"Seriously? You'd paint with me?" He asked like a fan whose celebrity idol called them on stage to sing alongside them.

"Of course. It would be my honor."

Julius's reverent look was steadfast. He grinned. "The pleasure is all mine."

This time, they turned back to the canvas and painted side by side. To her surprise, Julius met it with a confidence that only those with extensive hours sitting in front of one would possess. His hands were sure and calm as the paint glided from his fingers and onto the canvas effortlessly.

"You didn't tell me you could paint," Erica said in awe, watching him swirl blue and red together to make a stunning shade of purple. "Why didn't you say anything?"

Julius shrugged. "It's nothing compared to what you can do."

"Yes, it is. This is really good. It looks like a galaxy."

His smile stole her breath for a moment.

"I think my muse has finally appeared. I see why you've always wanted to try this. Feeling the paint under your fingertips, it's otherworldly. It's fluid and graceful, but also primal and instinctual."

He turned back to the canvas, vigorously dipping his fingers into the paint and spreading it in large strokes. Even under Julius's paint-stained clothing, she could see every ripple of his muscles work. It was as if he were making love to the painting in front of them. Watching him was... erotic. The more she watched, the more turned on she became. She wondered if he felt the same when he watched her in her studio.

He paused to look at her. "You've stopped."

"I'm just taking in our creation." She wet her lips and stood back and wiped her hands on her towel. He backed away from the painting as well. She tossed him the remaining paper towels. He wiped his hands, then stood behind her.

She was greeted by every single muscle of his stomach as they considered the painting in front of them. Static charged the air between them and all she could sense was Julius. Her heart jumped when his warm breath blew on the spot on her neck that made her toes curl.

"What do you think?" Julius's lips grazed her neck as he spoke, his voice husky and thick.

"I love this. It's beautiful." Her words were breathy and short. She tried to focus on their work, desperately trying to keep hold of her breathing. It was becoming more erratic as Julius subtly traced her curves with his large hands. "And you? What do you think?"

"It's rousing." He kissed the side of her neck softly, no longer looking at the painting in front of them. She moaned when his hardness swelled against her back. Then again when another kiss pressed against her shoulder.

Julius was not a cautious man. He was demanding and unyielding. Not once did she stand a chance when he pressed his lips to hers. Not against the fire that erupted from Julius and into her, burning straight through her veins.

She let his demanding tongue in without hesitation, eager for him to quell the fire that only he could extinguish.

Her fingers clawed at the hem of his shirt, whimpering when it didn't come up right away. Julius broke apart for only a moment and pulled it over his head.

Fuck. His exercise regimen served him well. He was a god.

Her palms raked against the hard planes of him, reveling in the feel of his cut abs against her palms. When her hands touched his skin, she lost all thought.

In a flash, his body was back against hers. She grabbed the soft tufts of his hair and pulled his lips to hers again. She needed more. Julius's sure fingers danced at the hem of her pants, gliding into her jeans and under the lace of her panties. She widened her legs for him and moved to undo the button. Her lips never parted from his.

"You're going to be the death of me," he groaned as his fingers dipped lower, finding her wetness.

Suddenly, the door slammed open.

She broke away from Julius. He didn't let her get far, stepping behind her and pulling her against him. She let him, but a flush of embarrassment spread across her cheeks as a gust of cold wind swept past them and she stared into a very angry, very feminine face.

"What the hell is going on here?"

13

JULIUS

JULIUS HAD NEVER BEEN SO CLOSE to ripping someone's heart out. A deep scowl settled on his face as he watched his former subject brazenly enter the room. Verna, a powerful mage, had a low current of purple electricity emitting from her fingertips. A glance at Erica assured him she couldn't see it. Even still, a low growl that only he and the mage could hear rose deep from his chest in warning. Flustered, Verna bowed deeply at the waist and doused the magic from her hands.

"V, what are you doing?" Julius asked, silently encouraging her to break protocol. He didn't need her bowing to him in front of Erica. The mage shot up and looked around. Her gaze found the human at his side. Understanding dawned on her face, and she spoke again.

"Your highn—"

Julius cleared his throat loudly. There was an

understanding between them. She was never to speak his title aloud when they were in the human realm.

Verna started again. "I'm sorry. I was driving by and saw the lights on and thought... I completely forgot you were using the studio tonight."

"That's quite all right." Julius held his hand up and forced a warm smile.

It was at that precise moment Verna took in his very much naked chest and Erica's disheveled appearance. It didn't take much to put two and two together.

"Wow, I'm *really* interrupting." She took a deep breath and let it out with a huff. "And, I'm going to go now."

Verna pointed at the door and backed away slowly.

"No, you don't have to go," Erica's small voice said.

Yes, she did.

Verna seemed to agree with his train of thought. "Oh, yes I do. Don't mind me, lovebirds, I didn't interrupt. You have a *very* pleasant evening."

"You as well." His smile was tighter than his pants.

"The table slab in the back is more comfortable than it looks." The words flew from Verna's mouth as she opened the door.

"We'll keep that in mind."

He watched his subject scurry out of the front of the shop. All the while, he kept his hands on Erica's slim waist, lightly tracing her outline.

"Did she just say the table slab was comfortable?" Erica laughed, turning back toward the slab where the tarp had been folded, her cheeks tinged a brilliant shade of pink. "Do we want to know how many people have had sex on that thing?"

He chuckled. "I don't think so."

A gust of chilly air blew past them.

"You're not cold?" Erica placed the delicate pads of her fingers on his forearms.

"Is than an offer to keep me warm?" To his delight, her fingers ghosted down his arm. His entire body shivered in pleasure. If he were a cat, he would have purred.

"That feels so good," he murmured.

"You know what else feels good? Your hands on me."

Thanks be to the all gods, the moment was preserved despite their intruder.

"Then, we should pick up where we left off. Where were we?"

"I think we were looking at our painting." Erica whipped around toward their canvases. He closed the distance between them, pressing his hard length into her back.

"I think we were past that." His hand glided into her pants. "I think we were here."

His fingers delicately swiped over her clit.

"Yeah, right there." Erica whimpered, pressing her ass into him.

He groaned. He was painfully hard. "You are trying to kill me, I'm sure of it."

She craned at an angle to look at him. Her hazel eyes were filled with want. Need.

Julius pulled her into a searing kiss, still pressing his fingers into her folds. The pulse of her blood thumped through his fingers. She radiated like a fireball underneath him. He pressed against her clit harder, stroking back and forth, eliciting several moans of approval.

"More, I need more," she gasped.

He needed no other invitation. He pulled her shirt over her head and nearly lost himself. The plump swell of her breasts commanded his complete attention. His vampire rose to the surface, wanting to rake his fangs over every inch of her creamy skin.

"You don't wear a bra." His voice sounded foreign to his own ears.

"Should I?"

"Never." A hunger built inside of him as his attention turned back to her perfect breasts. Julius let his vampire roam and explore. He gave her mouth a short kiss before he left a trail of them down her neck.

She moaned in surprise when he sucked a nipple in his mouth and bit down, then moved to the other one and did the same. "Frick. Don't stop. Please."

"On the tarp," he ordered. "And I'll give you everything."

She breathed deeply and lowered herself down.

The spray of her hair across the tan fabric was immensely satisfying. If he didn't have a desperate need to lick her to pieces, he would sit and admire her.

He joined her on the tarp and stretched out over her. "You're gorgeous."

She gave him a coy smile that struck him to his core and wiggled underneath him.

"Tell me what you want."

"Y-you. I want you to kiss me." Her voice was strained.

She pointed to the crotch of her jeans. "Here."

He loved when she talked to him like that, ordered him. Erica seemed awkwardly shy, even hesitant sometimes. Now, she was sure. The confident woman was budding and there was no stopping it. He didn't want to.

She whimpered when he lowered the zipper of her pants and slid them down her toned legs. For the all gods, her wetness was alluring. Hypnotic.

"Open for me."

She followed his order without hesitation.

It took everything in him not to bite a trail up her legs before devouring her wet center. He settled for delicate kisses. He reveled in the taste of her skin. When her hands tangled in his hair, he knew exactly what she wanted. He could never deny Erica anything.

He licked up her slit and nipped at her clit through the fabric of her panties. Erica moaned.

"You're torturing me."

His beauty was becoming impatient, hips dancing back and forth as she tried to wiggle out of the panties he looped between his thumbs.

"Take them off," she whined. He kissed the sensitive flesh of her upper thighs, then back on her most sensitive spot.

"You taste amazing," he murmured. "Tell me you're mine."

There was no debate.

"I'm yours," Erica panted. Her hips bucked toward him. "All yours. Now, take them off."

He rewarded her by pulling off her panties and putting

his nose to her mound.

"Say it again."

"I'm yours, Julius. Please."

The sound of her begging nearly stole his control. Not that he had much to begin with. He dove into her wetness. She gushed around him. By the gods, he'd never tasted anything so pure. So. Fucking. Good.

Her back arched, and a spray of wetness met his tongue. Her nectar was sweet and exotic. The more he licked and sucked, the more she rewarded him with more of it. Her moans ignited the beast inside of him. He became hell bent on devouring her.

Her fingers twisted in his hair and she pulled him tighter against her. Her body began to shake, soft tremors at first. But the harder he sucked, the stronger they became. Her breathing went erratic, her moans louder, egging his vampire on. He slipped a finger into her folds and Erica bucked up.

His fangs drew down. There was no stopping his vampire now. He'd lost his mind.

"Julius." Her moans built to a fever pitch. Her entire body tightened. "I'm coming."

His fangs sank into her just as she threw her head back and exploded in his mouth. He should have taken them out, but his vampire was in control now. He sucked deeply, pulling her wetness and her blood into his mouth. This was heaven. He sucked again, savoring her essence on his tongue. She exploded again.

"What are you doing to me," she panted as her body tightened and went over the edge.

Alarm wrenched his fangs back and forced him to look at her face. One arm was draped across her eyes as her nails from the other dug into his shoulder. Her body still convulsing under him. His venom was kicking in, causing her a delightful pleasure that would linger for a while.

"I need you inside of me," she pleaded. Eager to oblige, he freed his erection and rubbed it against her. She was so wet. "Please Julius, I'm yours."

He could hear her say that for an eternity and never tire of it.

Erica's wet heat enveloped him like a glove, soft and tight. His head lolled back. In all his life, he'd never felt anything so glorious. He could feel her from the top of his head to the soles of his feet. His eyes rolled to the back of his head when her fingernails dug into his lower back and she bucked again. Ready. Waiting.

"Tell me, you're mine," he breathed.

In an instant, he and his vampire were in sync. He pulled from her. The exquisite pleasure was so acute, it was almost painful. Almost. He pushed back in.

"Fuck!" Erica moaned, her legs wrapping around his waist and pulling him in as far as she could take him. He drew from her again. Then plunged deeper.

"Julius." His name from her lips had never sounded so sweet. Breathy and light, and he wanted more.

He needed her. Hungered for her. He slammed into her again, harder than he thought a human of this realm could take. She was so wet, he slid into her with ease. She cried out in pleasure, clutching the tarp in her hands. "Fuck, I'm yours."

His hips moved on their own accord, not that he was complaining. His vampire had a blinding need to oblige her, to give her everything he had. His thrusts became quicker. Harder. And each time he slammed into her, Erica's moans grew louder and more erratic.

She was close. He could feel her pulsing around him. It made him ride her harder. Faster.

"Erica," he growled, starting to unravel. His fingers were at her clit again, furiously rubbing with barely any precision, drunk on her cries of pleasure.

With one final cry, his name ripped from her mouth as she clenched around him. Her convulsions sent him over the edge right behind her.

Erica refused to let him leave her until he started to go soft. All the while, short shivers rocketed up and down her body. Every time he adjusted, she moaned again and shivered. So, did he.

With them intertwined like this, all was right in the world, like he no longer had to be the vampire prince who needed to set a time limit to his relationships to protect himself. His vampire identified her as his long before he could.

She was amazing. How could he have ever thought for one moment that Erica would be temporary? Nothing about the woman underneath him was temporary. That was a lie he'd told himself and he'd never say it again. He wanted forever with her. An eternity, no matter how long it took for him to convince her of the same.

"What are we doing tomorrow?" He breathed against her ear as he wrapped them in the rough tarp. She didn't seem to mind. Instead, she cuddled closer to him.

"More of this," she said softly, placing a kiss on his shoulder. "Then, I need to get a few things together for my showcase."

"That sounds like the best plan in the world."

Her breaths began to slow, and her eyes were already closed as she drifted off to sleep. For a moment, he watched her bliss turn into peace. He placed a soft kiss on her forehead.

"I'm yours too, Erica."

And he was. Without a doubt, he knew he'd lay down his life for hers. With the shifter still sniffing around her, he might have to do just that.

14

ERICA

M ORNING SUN SPRINKLED ACROSS Erica's face as she went to turn over in her warm bed. Only, a hard as hell surface was underneath her and not the pillow top mattress she was accustomed to. Her eyes snapped open. It didn't take her long to adjust to her surroundings. They'd never left the studio last night. Instead, she lay wrapped in a tarp, the sun beaming on her face, laying against a very warm, very welcomed body.

"Good morning," Julius mumbled against her ear.

"Morn—" she sounded like she'd eaten a shoe. She cleared her throat and tried again. "Morning."

"I'm glad you slept well." He snuggled into her hair. It was probably a ball of yarn, tangled at the top of her head.

"Why do you say that?"

"You snored for most of the night."

"I *did not* snore."

"It's adorable." Julius chuckled, wiggling his eyebrows, a cheeky grin on his face. "It also tells me I did my job well."

Yeah, he did. She laughed and adjusted herself to lay facing him. He was devastating. Even his hair, which seemed disheveled to perfection, lay perfectly on top of his head. Did he ever have a bad day? Julius's lips stretched into a sleepy smile as he let his head rest against the meat of his bicep and stared into her eyes.

"I could get used to waking up like this," he said, though he seemed surprised by the words.

"Don't do it often?"

"No." He shook his head and played with the ends of her hair. "It's part of the rules. If they are temporary, then they don't get to stay the night as if they are permanent."

As she watched the businessman in front of her, she knew he probably never woke up to anyone beside him. Probably taking to skirting off in the middle of the night.

"So, are you saying I'm not temporary?"

"I hope not."

She tried to hold in a smile as shifted again, trying to find a more comfortable spot on the floor. She didn't want to move. Not yet. She wanted to lay there with Julius and just talk. He was so open to her; she could see as much on his face. This was the exact expression her muse was looking for.

Every time she tried to recreate his likeness on her canvas, it dissolved. It wasn't right. She had a litter of crumpled sketches scattered across her studio to prove it. The look he was giving her now was everything her muse needed. She could lay on the floor all day and just study him. Her lower back, though, had other plans. The table slab may have been comfortable, which she still sincerely doubted, but the floor was not.

"I'm going to be sore today," Erica said. "This floor is killing my back."

She sat up and, thankfully, Julius followed her. When the tarp fell, he gasped. She looked down to her naked breasts and covered them with her arms.

"Never hide away from me." Julius grabbed her elbows and coaxed them down. The sternness in his voice made Erica shiver. Made her want to say 'yes, sir.'

"Good morning," he said again.

"You said that already."

"I want to say it every morning."

"If we have more nights like last night, then you may be saying it often."

"Challenge accepted."

"Of course, you'd rise to that."

"Can you tell?" Julius glanced down at where the tarp draped over his lap.

"You're insatiable," she giggled.

He leaned in to kiss her, but she tucked her chin, ducking out of kissing range. His lips landed on her nose. Hurt flashed in his determined eyes.

"I have dragon breath," she explained.

"You don't have dragon breath. Let me smell."

"I am not going to blow my foul morning breath into your face. Thanks anyway."

He shrugged one shoulder. "Then, if you won't let me

have your lips, there's another set I can kiss."

A shot of desire rushed straight through her. She would very much love a repeat performance of last night. Julius was... How could she even describe it? Carnal. Animalistic, but tender and deep.

Instead of kissing her lips, he landed one at the corner of her mouth. Then her cheek. Then her jawline. A hot fever took over her body when his kisses burned their way down her neck.

She moaned when he sucked on a particularly sensitive spot on her collarbone. Now, this is the best way to wake up, she thought as he traveled lower.

"Oh my," someone said from behind her.

"What are they doing in there?" another voice asked.

"I know it's been a while for you, Trudy, but you should know it when you see it."

What sounded like people jamming their noses on glass settled behind her. She glanced over her shoulder.

"Oh God!" She jolted off of Julius and shot halfway across the floor and out of their line of sight. If she'd thought the concrete was pristine the night before, it'd hid the dirt well. Every particle on it raked across her bare butt as she slid out of sight of the archway with an open view to the street.

"What's wrong?" Julius shot up. He was greeted by the same sight. "Oh... Oh!"

Three older women, bundled in thick parkas and wool hats, peered through the glass, pointing at them and giggling their heads off. Mortification iced her veins. They'd slept with each other in that exact spot last night.

Had anyone else seen the show?

"Hey!" She waved her arms, trying to get Julius's attention as he looked at the window with mild amusement. "Pass me my clothes."

He didn't seem to like that idea much, but slid last night's heap over to her anyway. She yanked her clothes across her body so fast, a few of the seams ripped in the process. She made quick work of putting on her pants and trying to flatten out her hair. Bedhead always plagued her unruly waves.

Now, to get Julius sorted. Her gaze skirted around the floor, looking for Julius's clothing. It seemed they both spotted his pants and shirt at the same time, flung into the little shop portion of his friend's studio, back through the open archway.

"I'll get it," she offered, even though her cheeks were still enflamed from embarrassment.

"No, I'm right here."

To her surprise, Julius stood, somehow managing to keep the tarp secure around his waist, and went into the front room to retrieve his clothes.

Hoots and hollers erupted at the window. Did he look embarrassed? Not a chance. He let out a playful, lopsided grin as he sauntered into the front room, giving the women a smile only a habitual flirt could pull off.

"Alright, show's over ladies." He chuckled and waved them off.

"Aww, give an old woman something," one of them begged. "It's been many years since I've seen a strapping stud."

Erica snorted. *Did she just call him a stud?*

"Sorry ma'am, but my girlfriend wouldn't like that too much."

"Hmph, you're no fun," another one said.

"I see there's nothing here," the third butted in. "Let's go girls."

"He was gorgeous, wasn't he?" The ladies snickered, but their voices sounded further away.

"Are they gone?" She said between laughs.

"Yes, they're gone."

Erica was still laughing her head off by the time Julius returned with his clothes and peered at her with an impish look.

"Girlfriend, huh?" She asked as soon as he was out of sight of the street. She watched in disappointment as he covered his glorious body.

"I could have said wife, but I didn't want to freak you out too terribly."

Her heart squeezed in a way

"You handled them well, that's for sure."

"They're harmless."

"Some of them carry knives, you know."

Julius barked out his own laughter. "You're adorable. Now, that you've insisted I dress, what are we up to today?"

"I have to run to the store. There's so much I need to get."

"Ooh, I'd love to join."

"You might find it boring."

"I doubt that," Julius picked up the tarp and began to

fold it.

"We should probably tell your friend to wash that."

He merely shrugged. Once they were cleaned up, she straightened the paint and stared at the canvases leaning against the walls.

"I'll have someone pick those up later," he said when she moved to shimmy one of them out of place. She settled it back into place and turned around.

"This studio is gorgeous." She sighed.

It was even more beautiful in the daylight. The soaring ceilings and light flooding the archway brightened up the space in the back tremendously well. The front shop was a perfect match to the back warehouse.

"Do you like it?" He tucked her shoulder under his chin and wrapped her into a hug.

"I do," she said. "It's very easy to work in."

"What about to show in? What if you could use this for your showcase?"

"Really? I'd love to have it here!" She whipped around and squealed. That was a much better plan than hosting it in her art class's open studio. "Your friend won't mind?"

"Not at all, actually."

"I could only dream of a space like this." Erica twirled around and looked at the studio again, already formulating in her mind how she'd use it to showcase her art. Her smaller paintings would look great in the small gallery, the larger ones would be amazing under the lights on the side wall. It would be amazing to show

"What if you could own something like this?"

"I would in a heartbeat." She played along, liking the

fantasy of many nights painting alongside Julius in a warehouse like this one.

"What if... I said it was yours?"

"I'd sign the papers right now."

"I'm glad you said that." He gave her arm a gentle squeeze before going into the front of the shop, behind a small counter off to the side, then pulled out a packet of papers. "I still have to look over the paperwork, but it's yours if you want it."

The fantasy burst and Erica's eyes nearly thrust from her skull. "I'm sorry, what?"

He looked taken aback. Apparently, her response was not what he expected. He looked no closer to laughing like it was a joke than she was.

"*You didn't?*" she repeated, this time more dubious than before.

"What if—"

"Seriously, Julius. Did you buy this shop?"

"Sort of..."

She grilled him, waiting for a real answer.

"Well..."

She waited.

"Alright, yes. I put a deposit on it yesterday. I had a little cash laying around—"

"This is not a *little cash*, Julius. The taxes alone will eat you alive. Eat *me* alive. I can't own something like this. I can't afford this. Not for real. Can you get your money back?"

"You don't like it?" He looked like she'd slapped him in the face.

"I do like it. I really do."

"But you don't want it?" Julius's face hardened.

Erica placed her hands on either cheek and brought him down for a kiss, dragon breath be damned. He let her and instantly softened. "Julius." She tried to calm the hysteria that was forming at the base of her throat. "This is sweet. It really is. You're completely thoughtful and ridiculously generous."

"But—"

"But if we're going to do this—" She motioned between the two of them. "—it can't be based on gifts. I've made that mistake once already. And you know what I learned?"

"What?"

"I'm a simple girl. I just want you." She pulled him in for another kiss. "Can we do that? Simple?"

"Yes," he stole another kiss before putting the paperwork away. "Except..."

Oh no, what else did he do?

"Except?"

"It's nothing really. Just a small thing. You'll see when you get back to your studio."

"How small?"

"Relatively."

She braced herself.

15

ERICA

NERVOUS BUTTERFLIES THRASHED in her gut the entire drive to her studio. When they rounded the corner, her shoulders slumped in relief. Her building looked the same as it did on any other day. With so many cars parked out front, she took comfort that he probably hadn't brought the place and made everyone vacate. So, at least he hadn't purchased it too.

She didn't think. Either way, her heart thudded as they walked up the stairs to her studio, her palms sweaty.

"It isn't bad," he promised over her shoulder when she put her key in the lock. "It was part of my 'I'm sorry' present, but we never made it back to your studio last night."

What was she expecting? Something crazy like a baby elephant painted pink with yellow polka dots standing next to her sofa. When she opened the door, she most definitely didn't have an elephant in her doorway.

Instead, several dozen vases filled with handmade long-stemmed paper roses adorned her entire apartment. A sea of blues, reds, and pinks adorned nearly every inch of the walkway space.

The feat was nothing to sneeze at. In true Julius fashion, there was a ton of them. One would have sufficed, but Julius didn't play small. Each of them was gorgeous and unique. It must have taken hours to make these by hand. She gasped in awe.

"You made these?" She was gleeful now, almost giddy.

"I tried. My sister did most of it, though."

"I think I see yours," she said, pointing at a vase with flowers that looked more like golf balls than flower petals with a teasing chuckle.

"Hey, I tried."

"And I love it all the same. These are beautiful."

"So, this is your kind of romance?"

"Yes." Erica kissed his shoulder before picking a couple of vases up off the floor and placing them on her counter. "Did you get scented paper? Nice touch. Thank your sister for me."

"It was my idea," he protested.

She pulled Julius into a hug. "These are beautiful. It must have taken forever to haul all of these up. How did you get these in here anyway?"

"I sort of paid your landlord a small sum to arrange these."

"A small sum?" Like he had a little cash to put down on an art studio in one of the trendiest districts in downtown.

"Oh, I have to get that." Julius rummaged in his coat pocket.

"Get what?"

"My phone."

On cue, the ringtone became louder.

"You heard that?"

"It buzzes first." He squinted at the screen, then gave her an apologetic frown. "Sorry, it's my brother, I have to take this... Evan."

From the sound of it, Evan was not happy. She couldn't hear what he said—the words were too quick—but from the sheer volume, he was pissed.

"I can explain." Julius's voice was level. "Another opportunity arose."

More yelling followed.

Curiosity piqued her interest, but Erica made herself busy instead of staring at Julius's mouth like she wanted to. She tried to pick up as many of the vases as close to the phone as she possibly could. Too bad, she still couldn't hear Julius's brother. She wondered what he did.

"I understand. I know what I'm doing."

Julius seemed calm, although the raging voice on the other end was livid.

"I'm more than happy to discuss the particulars." After one last yell, the phone went silent. He turned back to her with a guiltily amused expression. "Well, he's a bit miffed this morning. I have to go talk him off the ledge."

"Being called to the principal's office?"

"Something like that," he said with a wink. "Can I

make it up to you and take you out for lunch?"

"I'm going to be out all day. Dinner?"

"Delightful." He leaned over and gave her a small chaste kiss on the cheek. One just wasn't enough. She found herself wanting more, but he pulled away too soon. "Tonight then."

After a quick shower, and a great deal of cooling off, she turned herself to her tasks. The date to her art showcase was approaching rapidly, and she needed to be ready.

Getting extra pallet knives, easel stands, and decorations for her upcoming show provided her with just enough of a distraction to not be drooling over the night she'd had with Julius. Although, blips of it seemed to flash into her mind at the wrong times. Why her lady bits wanted to act up while she was searching for fake flowers at her local craft store was beyond her. No, not beyond her. Everything seemed to remind her of Julius. The paper flowers Julius had crafted for her was the most thoughtful thing anyone had ever done for her. He deserved an award for such good behavior.

By the time she exited the last shop, she was completely famished. Skipping breakfast and lunch was a mistake. The sky was already darkening, and she was sure most restaurants would be ridiculously busy if they didn't call ahead. She dialed Julius. He picked up on the first ring.

"Did you get detention?" she asked.

"We've come to an understanding."

"Meaning, he reamed you out, didn't he?"

"My ass still hurts."

"Well, I can rub your sore bottom if you wanted to come over for a while before dinner." The growling in her stomach was forgotten as the delicious man on the phone distracted her.

"I'd like that. There are other parts of me that are sore as well. Will you be rubbing those too?"

"Other parts?"

"Yes, my pants have been ill-fitting all day. A little tight in the crotch area. Can't fathom the reason why. However, it has made me incredibly sore there too. Will you rub it out for me?"

She snorted. "You are shameless."

Julius joined in with her laughter. "Are you home?"

"At the studio. Well, almost."

"Good, I'm on that side of town. Do you need a ride?"

"No, I'm on the bus now, just a few stops away." She thought of getting off at the next stop just so she could ride alongside Julius. It was much too cold for that sort of insanity.

"I'll be waiting for you by the time you get there, I think," Julius said. "I'm almost there now."

"If I'm not there, just bribe my landlord again. I'm sure he'll let you right in."

Julius chuckled. "I'll see what I can do."

The bus route took the longest it ever had. It seemed like the driver intentionally stopped at several places where no one got off the bus just to piss her off. To her dismay, he waited at several of the busier stops longer than necessary. There was no one hauling ass from three blocks down, yet he waited like they were. Heck, she'd taken this route long enough to know that those people were usually left in the dust.

To go seven blocks took them nearly fifteen minutes. Thankfully her studio was just off the corner. Her gaze swept the block, looking for Julius's car, but she didn't see it parked outside. Hopefully, he didn't have to park too far away. This time of night, with most people home for the evening, parking was at a premium.

Hauling several bags upstairs was the least amount of fun she'd had all day. By the time she reached the fifth floor, she was exhausted. To her surprise, her door was already unlocked.

That rat bastard. She smiled without a hint of ire. He really did bribe her landlord again.

"Julius," she called as she opened her apartment door and walked in. "When I said to bribe my landlord, I didn't really mean—"

One of the vases rattled before toppling over in the studio. It fell but didn't break. "Yeah, I meant to put those up. Why are you in the dark?"

Erica flicked on the light. "Jul—"

His name died on her lips when she saw a strange man leaning against her counter. Thin and dressed in a plain leather jacket, she didn't recognize him. She should have run. She should have screamed. Something other than asking, "Who the hell are you?"

"I need you to deliver a message for me." His voice was raspy like he'd spent his entire life smoking Marlboros and drinking whiskey.

Yeah, no. She stepped backward to find the hard body of a man pushing her forward.

"What are you doing?"

"This has to be some kind of mistake." She panicked, struggling against him. Her bags dropped to the floor at her feet, and she dug her heels in. Dread soaked through to her bones as her feet were forcibly moved toward the man in her kitchen. "Please. Just leave now and it's forgotten, I swear."

"We're in the right place, sweetheart." The gaunt man gave her a nasty sneer.

Stunned into incoherence, her thoughts froze into a brick.

"Tell Max I know where you live."

Max? What the heck did he have to do with this? Then her mind flitted back to their conversation at the coffee shop. Splinters. The man in front of her with a thick scar running down the side of his face was here for her. He'd stop at nothing to get back what was owed. Erica struggled harder against the body behind her, but his viselike grip wouldn't let her go.

Oh God, this can't be happening. She needed to call for help. At this hour, Mr. Hinkley would be pissed if she started making a racket. She needed to count on that.

She screamed, but a thick hand that smelled like a dirty car engine wrapped around her mouth and made it nearly impossible to breathe. His rough calluses squeezed painfully at her cheek bones. Bile etched the lining of her throat.

The gaunt man straightened from the counter and

walked toward her. She struggled against the man behind her, tears leaking from her eyes. She'd seen enough movies to know what was next. He was going to make an example out of her.

That singular thought gave her all the fight she needed. She pushed against what felt like a giant boulder.

"Hold her, Binks."

Fight like hell, run like hell. It was the code every woman should be taught in her lifetime when faced with an attacker. That's all she could think of when a skinny, overly tanned hand patted the top of her head like she was some sort of family pet. The man's dark beady eyes, blacker than coal, were cold and indifferent.

"You're such a pretty thing. It would be awful to have to—"

She kicked out as hard as she could.

Caught by surprise, the gaunt man in front of her doubled over for a moment before the eeriest laugh came from him. She'd never heard a sound so foul before.

"She's a fighter, Binks. Look at that." His eyes found hers. "I'm going to love tearing you apart."

She tried to kick him again, but Binks slammed her against the wall, knocking her into one of her stacks of paintings awkwardly. A hole gouged out of one of them as her foot went right through it.

Suddenly, he let go. She didn't realize she was free until she heard glass shattering across the room as the man was thrown into several vases.

Julius was in her doorway one moment, then pulling the man off of her the next, like he'd sprouted from the ground.

When Binks tried to get up, Julius launched himself at him, throwing him off balance and offering blow after blow to his face. This was not the brawl in her parents' house. There, Julius was on the defense. Now, he was full of rage.

Julius broke his nose. Binks let out a howl, a painful yelp akin to a dog being kicked as he clutched his face.

The bones in Binks's face started to crack and break. Her eyes were playing tricks on her. They had to be. His nose broadened, the bridge extending. His face started to change. Julius's hands were back on the man's face, this time pressing hard against it as if trying to put it back into place.

Adrenaline and fear rooted her legs in cement, making her part of the furniture. Sickness roiled her gut.

Reaching out with a thick arm, Binks grabbed a glass vase and smashed it against the side of Julius's head.

A shard of glass the size of her palm cut into Julius's face, settling deep into his cheek. To her horror, he staggered backward. He must have been in shock as he pulled it out. Blood stained the glass as he let it drop to the floor, never taking his eyes off of Binks. When he turned, the mark on his face slowly closed, exposing new skin. If she hadn't seen the glass shard in his face, she wouldn't have believed he'd been cut save for the blood dripping to his shirt.

"Binks, let's go." Splinters looked wearily at the scene in front of them. Binks didn't follow the command right away. Splinters didn't wait for him. Instead, he moved to the door and out, leaving his comrade to fend for himself. Maybe he could sense a losing battle when he saw one. Or knew that something much worse was coming.

A vicious growl answered the thought. One that was equal parts rage and deranged. Julius's eyes darkened, then flooded with black, like tar being poured in the road, but deeper, shinier like glass. His teeth elongated into points. His canines first, then a second set that seemed to protrude from just behind the first set.

The intruder didn't have any more fight left in him as he scurried from her apartment after Splinters. For a moment, Julius locked eyes with her. He was completely feral. Unhinged.

Then, he followed them out the door and at least down the hall, but she couldn't hear much past that.

The silence in her studio was deafening. Yet, there was no peace. Not a single ounce of relief that the men were gone.

She couldn't focus on that. She could only focus on the man she'd slept with the night before. All this time, she thought it was a joke. That he was playing around. But no. The monster in front of her was real. Very real.

The light eclipsed her doorway. Julius was back, eyes alert. And thankfully, back to normal. Her heartrate spiked in fear at the sight of him.

"I can track them, but I need to make sure you're alright." The sound was throaty and came out like a hiss. His fangs were still down, pearly whites in sharp spires.

"You're a—"

"Erica..."

"You're a—"

"You're safe now." Julius's voice sounded like his own again.

"You're a—" The words were stuck on repeat.

"Erica, I'm not going to hurt you." His canines receded.

"Don't come near me," she trembled and grabbed two paint brushes. When he took another step, she hopped up onto her couch as if Julius were a freaking mouse scurrying across the floor. "Get. Out."

"I can explain."

"Get out!"

"You shouldn't be alone right now."

"Help me." At first the words were breathless, but then they became louder. She yelled again, praying like hell Mr. Hinkley heard it and called the police.

"All right," Julius said in a rush and backed away. "I'm going."

Erica's gaze followed him to the door, and as soon as he was out of it, her feet let her move again. She threw all of her body weight against the door and locked herself behind it.

Her throat was coming out of her mouth. She still felt open and exposed. She rushed to the bathroom and locked herself in there too.

He really was a... a.... Goodness, even thinking the word made her want to join the ranks at the asylum. But there was no doubting what she saw. A flash of his fangs, the way his eyes morphed into a black abyss. He was a demon.

No.

Julius Craul was a monster.

16

JULIUS

JULIUS PACED.

When that did him no good, he went to the bar and grabbed another blood bag. He ripped open the main port and put it to his lips. Blood sloshed into his mouth; its thickness was euphoric. He could feel himself getting stronger with each gulp. Thank the all gods, his sister was in town. He would not suffer synth blood again. It made him vulnerable. Weak.

He'd nearly failed to subdue the wolf in Erica's apartment when he began to shift. If his vampire hadn't been so close to the surface—hadn't come out—Erica would have gotten hurt. Now, she was terrified of him because of what he was.

"There is a way we can solve that particular problem." Evan's soft voice was at odds with his usual spry tenor.

"How? Travel back in time and prevent this from

happening?" he smeared the sarcasm on thick. "I come from a line of very talented brothers, but as far as I am aware, none of you can do that."

"You also have talented sisters, you know." Dani entered the common room in a thick linen bathrobe, scrunching her wet dark hair in a towel. "What are we solving?"

The two of them went quiet.

"Did I miss something?" Dani looked between the both of them. "What aren't you saying?"

Julius locked eyes with Evan before turning to his sister. "Erica saw me."

"Yes, you were with her last night." Dani shrugged, but then her eyes widened. "Oh! You mean she saw *you*. How much of you are we talking?"

"Everything."

"Holy macaroni. I thought Evan was kidding when he said you were going to screw this up for us."

"Not helping," Evan said.

Dani carried on anyway. "When did this happen?"

"Last night," Evan answered.

"And you've been holding on to this all day? No wonder everyone's been in a pissy mood. How exactly did you let your vampire out for her to see it?"

"She was attacked. I lost control."

"What do you mean attacked? Is she okay?" Dani asked in concern. "Do we need to kick someone's ass?"

His face tightened into a wry smile. His sister hadn't even met Erica, yet she was already protective of her. He couldn't have asked for better siblings.

"Shaken, but she's fine."

"Well, where is she now?"

"At home. Asher is guarding her apartment."

"I'm confused." Dani tapped a pointed fingernail on the bar top. "Erica was attacked, you're here, and Asher—my scary vampire palace guard—is at her door? Who thought that was a good idea?"

"He's been ordered to be a bit more discreet than that," Evan said. "He's keeping his distance, blending in."

Dani's face pinched in disbelief. "This is Asher we're talking about. Have you seen him? Tall, thick like a train, no table manners? I can't even have him on campus without turning heads. Asher is the definition of a sore thumb."

Evan cleared his throat and stared pointedly in Julius's direction.

Dani quickly backtracked. "I mean... He is, but she will be safe."

"I know she will. I'll make sure of it." The ache inside of him amplified at the thought of failing her again.

"I see. That explains the blood." Her golden eyes flickered down to the bar top, littered with a few empty blood bags. "You might want to go easy on those. You've been on rations for the better part of a year."

"Dani, leave him," Evan warned.

"In just a minute. I want to make sure I understand this." Dani sat on the sofa beside Evan and gave him an unreadable look. "Our dear brother here has lost control, exposed vampires to humankind and our plan is to sit in the hotel suite while Asher guards her door?"

"Do you have a better solution?" he asked in annoyance, slamming a hand on the bar in frustration.

Dani paused, as if choosing her words carefully. "All I'm asking is, how do we keep her from exposing us further?"

"What are you insinuating Danica?" His face turned cold, his body hard.

"I didn't say we were going to do anything. All I asked was how we were planning on getting her to conveniently forget we exist? If she tells anyone or if someone were to find out what she knew—"

"No one will." His voice was harder than stone. He shot to his feet and headed to the window. Even this late in the night, lit windows were sprinkled throughout the city.

"How can you say that for certain?"

He cut her a vicious look that dared her to bring harm to Erica. They both knew a secret was only silenced one way. With death. That was what their father taught them. There was no way they were going down that path. He'd rip the entire alter realm apart if any harm came to her.

"I know of an alternative," Evan interjected.

Curiosity made him turn to face his brother.

"I can remove her memories."

"Out of the question."

"Evan, you can't do that," Dani said softly.

"You know how dangerous it is." He had to agree with his sister's concern.

"It hurts you. Remember the last time? You almost didn't survive it."

And if he remembered correctly, the person whose memories he swiped barely survived it too. He was not going to let his brother near Erica. Not when removing her memories could put them both at risk.

"What are our other options?" Evan asked.

"Even if we did take her memories—" Julius eyed them both. "—which we won't, and even if it worked, she'll have someone after her, only she won't know why."

If his sister's personal guard hadn't been there, Julius would have never been able to pry himself away from her door. Not while the shifters were still out there. Retreating didn't mean they'd given up. Only regrouped.

"We don't know that for certain," Evan said.

Dani looked between them again. "What don't we know?"

"He thinks the shifters will be back."

"I have no reason to doubt they won't." Even thinking of them still prowling the streets made him itch with anger.

"We're going to find them." Evan reassured him.

"I should have tracked them when I had the chance."

By the time he'd gone back for them, they'd changed forms. Their scent wasn't strong enough to track in an open street. Not like a human. He could detect a human heartbeat from a mile away if absolutely necessary. Shifters were a different breed entirely, virtually undetectable to him unless they were close.

"What did the shifters want?" Dani asked.

He looked up to his sister. "I could barely think of anything besides killing once I realized she was in danger." Julius tried to level the anger boiling in his gut. It was unsuccessful. Instead, he checked his watch and squeezed at another blood bag. Asher should be calling in a report soon, as he did every hour.

At exactly the one-hour mark, the phone in his pocket buzzed, then rang.

"Your highness," Asher said.

"How is she?"

"We're on the move."

"Where?"

"I don't know. Someone picked her up ten minutes ago. Human female, long black hair, piercings. Likely a friend. However, I'm not the only one keeping her company."

The words felt like a cold wind chilling his bones to ice.

"Explain."

"Two shifters are in a car in front of me. What are my orders?" Asher asked.

"Make sure she's safe." His throat tightened. "Call me when they reach their destination."

"No need, they're stopping now. Doesn't look like much. Brick building, red door."

Savu. He stood abruptly.

"Are they going inside?"

"Looks like. Their company too. I'm headed in."

"Don't take your eyes off of her for a second. Understood?"

"Yes, your highness."

He disconnected the call and looked into the stricken face of his brother and the determined one of his sister.

"Let's go," Evan said.

"I'm coming too." Dani nodded, then scurried off to her room to get dressed. He eyed the closed door. He wasn't going to wait for his sister to get dolled up. But, by the time he was at the elevator, she'd already pulled on a dress and had her hair pulled into a tight bun at the top of her head.

"That was quick," Evan said.

"Vampire, remember?" She opened the door to their hotel suite. "Now, let's go kick some ass.

———————

AS PER HIS GROWING EXPECTATION, Savu was busy, even for a weeknight. The bar at the front of the house was packed end to end. He knew Erica was at one of the bars, somewhere. The challenge lay in getting from the entrance through the ocean of warm bodies screaming for him to take a sip. His vampire inhaled deeply, reveling in the scent. He swallowed the dryness that formed in his throat. His thirst was awakening.

Evan's thoughts invaded his own. *Keep it together for one minute. We'll grab Erica, then we'll leave.* He didn't miss the worried glance, nor the mind-numbing tingle that started to curve up his spine.

"I don't think he can do this," Evan said to their sister.

"Sure, he can. You've got this." Dani was at his side, pretending to bounce to the music, dancing as they searched the crowd, looking for the two shifters. "I can get more blood if you need it."

He couldn't go on a blood binge, no matter how badly he craved it. If he was going to be around Erica, he needed to keep it under control. He'd had enough to revive his strength. Overfeeding would be to his detriment.

"Where's Asher?" Julius scanned the room, focusing his attention on something else.

"How could you miss him? I told you he stuck out."

"North wall." Evan nodded in the guard's direction. Asher did look out of place amongst the humans dancing around him, not that he wasn't comfortable. His mate was human, but the former vampire warrior wasn't used to trying to blend in amongst them. "I'm going to go talk to him. Get a read on the shifters."

He pushed the thoughts of his thirst away and focused on scenting Erica. She wasn't in the crowd.

"At least try to blend in." Dani nudged him and pulled two drinks from a tray girl who was circling the crowd and handed one to him. He wasn't in the mood to drink liquor. He didn't need anything else clouding his senses.

He kept his vampire focused on tracking Erica. Finding her scent was difficult at first, but he set his vampire to the task. Her perfume was weak under the much stronger scent of blood. As faint as it was, it was there. He held onto it.

"Now, what does she look like?" Dani asked from beside him.

"Gorgeous. Wavy blonde hair that goes down to her waist. Tiny, compared to me. Maybe about your height. Hazel eyes and a smile to kill for. She'll likely be working behind the waist-high benches."

"I know what a bar is. I think I see her." His sister pointed at the far end of the club. Erica wasn't stationed at the main bar, but an annex one to the side.

"Mr. Craul... I didn't expect to see you tonight." The dragon intercepted them before he could go further. Stick offered his hand and a questioning look.

"An unexpected situation brought us here." Julius's face drew into a tight smile.

The bar owner seemed to sense the alarm in his voice. Apparently, the dragon lore had gotten some things right. Dragons were said to have keen senses. Even better than a vampire's.

"Is there trouble?"

"Some things are best said behind closed doors."

Stick nodded and motioned for him to follow. He didn't.

"I'll explain. You get Erica." Dani said.

Like he had any other intention. He moved toward the bar while Dani introduced herself to the club owner.

Behind the bar, Erica's movements were fluid. Naturally graceful. She smelled just as intoxicating as she had the first night they met. After having so much blood, his senses were becoming more heightened. Every neuron fired and pulsed as he drew closer to her. The feeling was otherworldly, like they were vibrating on the same frequency and she was subconsciously pulling him to her.

She was serving a group and didn't see him. Erica placed several shot glasses in a row and poured a strange mixture in them before splashing alcohol at the top. Then she lit it on fire.

The small crowd around her bar wooed. Each of the guys, all human, grabbed a shot glass for themselves, blew out the flames, and gulped them down. The scent of shifters wasn't close to her. He briefly glanced over his shoulder. They must have been keeping their distance.

They are. Evan's voice slithered between his thoughts. *One's by the door. The other is near the emergency exit.*

Julius looked and spotted them immediately. Dressed in plain black, they looked normal amongst the crowd, if a bit understated. Julius memorized their faces.

What do they want?

Not sure yet. Remember the plan. Convince Erica to leave with us. When they follow, Asher and I will track them.

Got it.

"Erica," He grabbed her hand before it left the bar. A zing of pleasure shot through him. Her pulse spiked and surprise recoiled it back to her chest when she saw him.

"Oh shit," she gasped, fumbling with a large bottle in her hand. Then dread rearranged her features into terror. For a moment, it looked as if she was going to hurtle the bottle at his face and run.

"I need you to listen to me. You're in danger."

"Yeah, I know." Her gaze swept his frame before scanning the crowded club. He tried to brush off the hurt.

"Not from me."

You need to hurry, Evan said quickly. *You've been spotted, and their alpha has given them the order to take her if you showed. We have to go.*

He looked up. The shifter near the door moved from

the wall. From across the room, the other nodded and they made their way through the crowd toward him.

Asher and I will intercept. Focus on Erica. Take her if you have to.

Take her? Ice surged through his bones. If Evan wanted to steal Erica away, his brother must have seen what nasty plans they had in store for her. He turned back to Erica.

"There's a man by the door coming toward us. Bald head. You see him?" He leaned in closer to her. She looked over his shoulder, eyes searching through the crowd until they paused near the entrance, just next to where security was checking people in and out. She nodded, eyes never looking away from the heavyset man. "He's been following you."

Her head volleyed from the man coming toward them and back to him.

"Following me? Why? W-what do they want?" Erica backed up into a case of bottles, looking for a way out.

"You. We have to leave right now."

17

ERICA

ERICA WATCHED THROUGH the darkness as a man, thick like a Sequoya, weaved through the thicket of patrons. Her heart lodged in her throat.

"What do I do?" She hadn't realized she'd said the words aloud until Julius responded.

"Come with me."

She looked into his emerald eyes. A larger part of her than she cared to admit found comfort in them. She shouldn't have. Not after finding out what he was. But now that Julius's reassuring presence was in front of her, things felt different. Easy. Normal.

She nodded and placed the bottle of liquor in her hand down in its cradle. In a daze, she pressed the comms in her ear.

"Stick." Her voice was shaky.

"Erica, are you okay?" Her boss sad worriedly.

"I'm fine there's just..."

Julius appeared next to her like he'd mastered teleportation. One moment, he was on the opposite side of the bar, the next he was standing right next to her. Standing much too close for her sanity. She wasn't sure if she should be deathly afraid or completely aroused. Despite what her body was telling her, her brain chose the former.

"You have to do this on the way out." Julius grabbed her forearm and pulled her from the platform and down into the crowd. Pleasure erupted from his fingertips and across her skin. Small zings at first. But it became stronger the longer he held on. Just like it had felt when he'd licked almost every inch of her.

"Hey, stop that." Her words were at odds with her feet's compliance. Her feet, the stinking traitors that they were, would probably follow for as long as the pleasure coursed through her. She yanked her arm away from him. Despite feeling a sense of desperate loss, she let Julius take a stride away from her. What the heck was happening? She looked down at her forearm then back to Julius. Was he doing that?

"Erica, you have the night," her boss said over the comms in her ear, jolting her back to the present. "Your friends explained everything."

Her friends? They were not her friends. As soon as she opened her mouth to tell Stick that, the heavyset man was bulldozed by someone equally as large and slammed into the side wall.

"This way." Julius navigated away from them. It didn't

take long for a fight to start. Several bouncers were already running toward it, poised to break it up.

As with any disruption, curious heads turned toward the men throwing fists. Bodies caught in a stasis watched the fight. Except one. The second man, just as intimidating as the one behind her, cut toward them.

Julius murmured something against her ear that she couldn't make out. He didn't touch her this time, but the vibrations from his voice sent shockwaves of pleasure shooting down her neck. The music down in the pit was loud. Much too loud to keep focus. Even though she tried to drown it out, she couldn't hear anything but the pulse quickening at Julius's featherlight touch.

"An exit," he repeated. This time, the sound clarity was marginally better.

Before she could reply, Julius tugged her toward the entrance. They weren't going to make it out. Not with the line that had formed. A wave of screams erupted in the middle of the pit.

"Oh my God," a girl screeched from behind her. Someone bumped into them.

"Don't look back." Julius weaved through a crowd too distracted to notice they'd cut ahead in line.

Then chaos erupted. Several screams rang out. Julius tugged her out the door just as the club burst. He hastily led her down the stairs. Groups of people stampeded behind them and onto the sidewalk.

"Come, we can't stop." Julius didn't look down at her, only kept his attention focused ahead of them. His fingers twisted with hers. Waves of pleasure made her shiver. She suppressed a moan and followed his large strides to the road.

"Jules," a voice called out from the street. A girl with black hair and golden eyes pulled up to the curb alongside them. She didn't look old enough to drive. "Get in."

Julius ushered her into the backseat, then got in behind her.

"Where's Evan?" the girl asked.

"Inside. He hasn't come out," Julius replied.

The girl pulled away from the curb and honked at several people loitering in the street, looking ready to run them over if they didn't move.

"Aren't we going to wait for him?" She asked, pointing back at Stick's nightclub.

"He can take care of himself," the girl in the front said, then slammed on her brakes and laid on the horn. Several partiers yelled for her to watch where she was going. She gave them the finger and shouted, "Move, or I'll move you."

The nose of the car bucked forward in warning. The sea parted to let them through. She gunned it. Erica flinched, thinking she was definitely going to run over a few people with how close they were. The girl wasn't worried.

To her surprise, they made it past the collection of patrons that waddled into the street without taking anyone out. As soon as they drove through the crowd, the girl flipped her hair over her shoulder and looked in the rearview mirror at her.

"I feel like I know you already. I'm Danica. But you can

call me Dani."

"Um... I'm Erica."

Dani looked between her and Julius. "You mean, you haven't told her about me?"

The screech in Dani's voice made Erica jump in her seat.

"Oh, come on Jules. You promised."

"Hardly the time." Julius was preoccupied with his phone.

"I'm his sister, and it looks like dufus here didn't say anything even though he promised to soften you up to me."

"You're the one who helped him with the flowers."

Dani beamed with pride and nodded.

"At least he didn't take all the credit, like he usually does." She gave her brother a pointed look. "Julius has been falling all over himself for you. You must be special."

"Dani, focus on the road."

Immediately, the animated girl in the front seat stopped talking, lips squeezing into a pucker.

"Erica, I need you to be honest with me. Who were those men?" Julius asked from beside her. Even his voice washed her with pleasure. She hadn't realized she was leaning up against him until he adjusted himself. Immediately, she flung herself to the opposite side of the backseat and strapped in. She needed to keep herself together. There were two men after her, and she was completely entranced by the vampire beside her. She focused on his question.

"I never seen them before." Panic rose in her throat.

Dani groaned from the front of the car. "He's gotten ahead of himself. The two men in the club were shifters."

"Dani, you could be a bit more discreet," Julius said, chiding his sister. "You're going to scare her."

"What discretion? She already knows what you are. No point in cutting corners now."

"A-are you one too?" She cringed at the thought of being in a car, trapped between two vampires.

Dani was silent when they came to a stoplight, then sighed. "I see there's a lot my brother has to tell you. We're not going to hurt you."

"So, I've heard. Why does everyone keep telling me that?"

"Your heart is racing." Julius's voice was soft. Comforting. But he didn't look at her, only stared at his phone. "It's an earmark of fear."

She clutched at her chest as if putting her hand on it would placate her heart and make it slow down. "Is it—distracting?"

"No, why would it be?" Dani turned the corner and entered an underground parking garage. "Now, the shifters in the nightclub."

"I don't know who they are. I've never seen them in my life."

"What about the ones in your studio?" Julius asked.

The air left Erica for a moment, and her heart thumped erratically in her chest at the memory. Her brain told her not to think of it. To forget it ever happened. It was too scary to relive.

"He said something about Max." Her voice pinched

inside of her throat.

"Who's Max?" Dani asked looking at them again.

"Her ex."

"What's he doing in bed with shifters? That's nasty business."

"His father owes Splinters money."

"I'm sorry, did you just say Splinters?" Dani asked. "THE Splinters? For the all gods, Splinters is after you? What the hell did you get yourself into?" The questions were directed toward her, but she had no answers.

"Who's Splinters?" she and Julius asked in unison.

Dani's golden eyes flickered over to Julius, who'd hardened into stone. "Haven't you been paying attention, Jules? He's a trader."

"Then what does he want with Erica? She's not supernatural. I'm sure once he's made aware of that fact, he'll leave her alone."

Dani hesitated. "You don't understand, Jules. Splinters is ruthless. Anyone in the body trade has to be, but Splinters is his own kind of sadistic. If someone owes him, he'll find a way to get it back. No matter the cost."

"If Max owes him money, we'll arrange a payoff," Julius said but his sister didn't look convinced. "Things will be fine. Come, let's get up to the suite. We can discuss this further up there."

"No dice. I have to go back for Evan," she stopped at an abrupt halt at the entrance. Julius nodded at his sister as they got out.

"Find him safe."

"Will do." Dani shot off in the car, tires screaming as

she took several turns more wildly than necessary as she went back for her brother.

"Will he be okay? We could have waited..."

"My brother knows how to defend himself." His voice was like gravel. Rough. "Our first priority is you."

"Me? Why me?"

Julius's expression was unreadable as he ushered her into the hotel lobby. She looked around at the gold-plated elevator doors and marble floors. It definitely wasn't the kind of digs she would've expected a clan of vampires to hole up in. "Is this where you're staying?"

"It is. I got stuck in this dump since my coffin is in the shop." Julius shrugged.

She tried to hold in a laugh. He'd make a joke out of everything. "Yeah, what a dump. Much too clean for my tastes. Give me cramped quarters and claustrophobia any day."

A long, awkward silence passed between them as they waited for the elevator to open.

"For as long as I can remember," Julius said, "I have always known the right thing to say. But now, I find I am at a loss."

"You can start with the truth."

The elevator doors opened and they boarded. She felt the tug of the elevator pulling them upward. An even stronger one pulled her toward Julius.

"Nothing I have said to you has been a lie."

No, it wasn't. He'd told her that he was a vampire. She'd just refused to believe it.

"How could I believe you? You're... well, *normal.*"

"Most of us are."

"Y-you walk around in the sunlight, for crying out loud!"

"We are light sensitive, but we do well at all times of day once our eyes adjust. In most ways we are the same as humans."

"Except the..." She swallowed a lump that formed in her throat, the last bit squeezed out in a whisper. "...blood thing."

"No creature of size can survive without it. We have a genetic defect that makes it impossible for us to produce it on our own. So, we must ingest it."

"From humans?" Her voice squeaked.

"Human blood is preferable. Although my kingdom has been looking for alternate forms. There's one alternative that shows promise. We call it synth blood. My siblings and I have transitioned to it for nearly a year. It doesn't make us as strong as human blood does. But it will suffice. If we can produce enough, it'll keep my people from starving. But, it's really expensive to produce. That's why we're here, in your world."

"My world?"

"I should probably start over. Hi, I am Julius Craul, third son to the great king, mid-prince of Elder. I hail from the vampire realm."

"Vampire realm... There are realms too."

"Yes, there are several known realms. Many have yet to be explored. But there are three that we've studied extensively. This one, which we call the alter realm or human realm. My realm, which is the vampire realm."

"The third?"

"Primarily inhabited by shifters."

"I can't believe I'm having this conversation right now." she studied the ceiling of the elevator, trying to wrap her mind around what he was saying.

"It is a lot to take in."

"And you're a prince? That explains the buckets of money and how you handled my parents and their pretentious friends so well."

"Thank you... I think."

The elevator glided to a stop. When it opened, the entire city came into view. Her jaw dropped.

Yeah, he was a prince all right. Only royalty could afford something like this. If she thought her parents' home was a monstrosity of elegance, it paled in comparison to the penthouse suite she currently stood in. She wondered if the toilet was gold too.

"This is your suite? This is way better than a coffin." She looked around in awe. There were more doors in it than any hotel she'd ever stayed in. With its own kitchen, dining room, and living area, no expense was spared in its luxury.

Julius leaned behind the bar across the room. Keeping his distance as she made her way to the couch. An anger she couldn't explain burned across her skin that he was so far away. Close but out of reach. She needed to feel him touch her again.

"We do well."

"You know, only rich people say that. But it does explain how you were able to buy an art studio with just a little cash laying around."

"Cash laying... By the gods." Julius's outburst was sudden. "This is my fault."

"Come again?"

"The money I used to purchase your studio was earmarked for Max. If I'd just laid down my pride and given him the money, you'd be safe. Splinters wouldn't be after you." Julius looked utterly ashamed of himself. An apologetic sorrow steeped his face. "I am very sorry."

She took a step toward him, the call of him making her want to comfort him. "Sorry for what? Not knowing that my ex's father was in bed with the wrong people?"

"That's the problem. I did know. I knew he owed a debt to someone, but I was so angry that he was toying with you. So, when the opportunity to screw him over arose, I didn't think twice. But now it's blown back on you. And that is my fault."

She'd drifted across the room, leaning against the other side of their en-suite bar, his warmth reeling her in. She placed her palms on the cool bar top next to his, wanting desperately to stroke his hand to give him comfort. The draw to touch him was nearly impossible to resist.

"It's still not your fault," she said. "You didn't get entangled with Splinters in the first place. Don't blame yourself for something someone else did."

He was silent for a moment. "Why are you such a saint?"

"I'd hardly call myself a saint. Saints don't usually have the kind of thoughts I'm having right now."

"Hmm." His voice dipped low. Seductive. "And what kind of thoughts are those, Erica?"

Once the words were out of his mouth, the pull between them intensified. Much more intense now that her nerves had settled.

"Not the kind you should have when there are people after you."

"You don't have to worry. You're safe here with me."

"I know. I feel it." Her hand found his, stretched out on the bar. When she touched him, sharp, shooting pleasure surged through her. Closing her eyes, she groaned and leaned into it.

"Wait." He pulled his hand just out of reach. "Before we continue, there's something I should tell you."

"What's that?" She breathed in the scent of him. Clean. Safe.

"This feeling you're having right now, it's because of my venom."

"Your venom? Like a poison?" She did a mental check. Completely drawn to him, check. Pain, nada.

"Yes, but it is my pleasure venom that's running inside of your veins. It's what's been drawing you to me, trying to forge a bond."

"How did you get your venom inside of—" She didn't have to finish. He'd bitten her when he went down on her. Funny, she hadn't even felt him break the skin. Only a slight pressure, then a lot of pleasure. Her thighs squeezed together at the thought, trying to stay her budding arousal.

"The closer we are to each other, the stronger it is." His breathing was slow, controlled. Unlike hers, which was becoming more ragged.

"You want me too?" She licked her lips.

"So much it hurts. Just being with you drives me insane, but nothing has to happen if you don't want it to. Tomorrow, the venom will be out of your system, and we can talk."

"I don't want to talk. I just want you." She pushed aside any lingering serious thoughts and launched into just feeling.

"I was hoping you'd say that." His large hands wrapped around her shoulders. Another shiver of pleasure erupted from them. Like a slow drug, even the pressure from his hands made her want him more.

His fangs elongated. She gasped. A swirl of excitement blipped through her. She wasn't afraid. This close to him, her mind and body could only focus on the pleasure he brought her.

"I apologize." Julius's large hand covered his mouth. "It's hard to keep them contained when we're like this."

"If I can't hide from you, you don't get to hide from me either." She grabbed his wrists and tugged his hand until his fangs came into view.

Julius's eyes darkened slightly as he watched her intently. He was nervous. Afraid that she might shame him.

"Your fangs," she murmured. A vicious need burned through her. "Do they hurt when they come down?"

"No."

"Will they hurt me?"

He shook his head in the negative.

"C-can I touch them?"

"You wish to touch my fangs?" His eyes widened.

"Is that wrong?" she asked, then wished she hadn't said anything. Of course it was wrong. That much was evident by the stunned look on his face.

"Fang touching is very intimate. Usually only done between mates."

"Oh." Her eyes drifted to her feet as if she found her black stilettos more interesting than the onslaught of Julius's scrutiny. She didn't. But facing Julius's hesitant gaze was more daunting. "Of course, that would be inappropriate."

"No, it wouldn't. I would be delighted."

"You would?" Was he saying what she thought he was? That she was his mate? His sexy chuckle pushed the budding questions away and made her insides warm.

"Of course I would." Julius whipped around the bar and escorted her to a large plush sofa and sat. Erica shimmied next to him. He grinned. "Full disclosure. It will be a very pleasurable experience. For both of us because of the pleasure venom. Can you handle that, Erica?"

She nodded and reached up to his fangs. There was no hesitation when she put her finger to one and stroked the length of it. Erica wasn't prepared for the nirvana that erupted through her fingertips and shot straight to her core. Her body jumped.

"Don't stop." He grabbed ahold of her wrist like he thought she was going to rip away. She couldn't even if she tried. The pleasure racing through her veins wouldn't allow it.

He brought her legs around his waist. Through their clothes she could feel his hardness against her, straining for relief.

"Wow," she said. "This feels..."

"Amazing," Julius finished with a moan. Yes, but it was more than that. It was orgasmic.

Julius's large hands dug into her hips and he ground her against him with abandon as she stroked his fangs. She moved in time with him. Her lips pressed against his neck, then nipped at his jaw, aching to feel more of the sweet wash of pleasure that ran through her every place they touched.

"Don't stop, Erica." His voice was guttural and raw. She didn't. She pressed down on him harder. His breathing went uneven. His head flew back into the seat cushions. His entire body tightened. "By the all gods."

Seeing Julius come apart under her touch was the most mesmerizing thing she'd ever seen. His irises contracted and widened as spurts of pleasure made him tremor. He ripped her hand from his mouth and pressed his lips against hers. Hard. Consuming. She reciprocated. At that moment, she decided she didn't care if he was a vampire or that the supernatural even existed. All she wanted was him. Unfortunately, her phone rang inside of her pocket. She ignored it and kissed him again. She didn't want to pull away from his lips.

"You should get that," he breathed through another kiss.

If she must. She shifted, but Julius didn't let her get far. He hooked his hands on her waist and kept her straddling him. She pulled the nuisance from her pocket.

It'd better be good, or she was going to find whomever it was and throw them out of a window. When she looked at the screen, it took her a moment to fully comprehend what she was seeing.

A name she hadn't expected flashed across her screen. Her eyes connected with Julius's for a moment then flickered back down to her phone.

Max.

18

ERICA

THE GLOW OF THE PHONE'S blacklight pierced her eyes as she stared at Max's name on the screen. She chewed on her bottom lip, caught between being hopelessly awkward and feeling terribly guilty for being with someone else while her ex may have been in distress. Erica answered the call and put the phone to her ear.

"Max, is everything okay?"

He didn't say anything at first.

"Max?"

There was a faint noise in the background. She strained to hear it. It sounded like labored breathing. Worry wrenched at her chest.

"Max? Are you alright?"

She listened in a daze, immediately jumping to the worst conclusions. Until the sound became louder.

Oh.

Max most definitely was not hurt. In fact, he was the furthest thing from it. He was... he was *with someone.*

Mortification slackened her jaw as the sound of bodies colliding with one another, punctuated with moans, met her ear.

She should hang up. That was the sensible thing to do. But she could do nothing but rake a hand through her hair in astonishment as she listened. Her emotions jumbled into a stew. She was unsure of what to feel. It wasn't like she and Max were still together. Heck, she was even with someone else herself. But to hear the reality of it was... *awful.*

"Yes, Max!" The girl, whoever she was, squealed.

Julius placed a hand on the wrist that held her phone. "Hang up."

She couldn't. It was as if her hands were permanently stuck to her ear as the woman screamed her release in the background.

She was going to throw up.

"Jesus," the girl cried out. "Even after six months, we still go at it like crazy."

Wait. Did she just say six months?

"I told you. I'm an animal," Max replied with a laugh.

Six months? She wrenched herself off of Julius in one go and stormed over to the window. Despite the view, she couldn't see it. Everything was whitewashed and blending together. It felt as if her heart was going to turn itself inside out before it exploded. How could he? How dare he?

To think, he'd made her feel crazy! Now look at where

she was. Standing there with a phone jamming into the side of her face, listening to her ex-fiancé confirm that he'd been cheating on her for months. What was worse, she couldn't even hang up the phone like she ought to. She needed him to know that she knew. That what they had was completely over.

"Max!" She screamed. Her breaths drove into deep, angry huffs. Of course, he didn't respond. He didn't even know she was on the line. But that didn't quell the anger of his betrayal. "That bastard! I'm going to kill him."

She didn't notice that Julius rose from the sofa and took several large strides toward her until he cupped his hands around her arms. She could feel the pleasure of his touch, but it seemed duller now. Not even his pleasure venom could wrench her out of the onslaught of emotions that gushed through her.

"Erica," Julius finally broke through, placing a delicate hand on her shoulder. His head cocked to one side as he tried to get her attention. "Hey. Let me take that."

He motioned for the phone. She hesitated, watching him with wide eyes. He could hear it too, she realized.

"I'll take it."

His words were the grease that unhinged her elbow as she shakily lowered the phone into his hand. Julius ended the call. At a loss for what to say, she turned back to the window and stared out at the city. She couldn't face him, even though in the reflection of the window she could see a shadow of his expression. He looked hurt for her.

If he thought she was a saint, he was the epitome of His Holiness himself.

"Are you okay?... Do you want to talk about it?"

She couldn't respond. How could she even begin to explain it when she couldn't even reconcile it for herself. She was angry at someone who she didn't harbor romantic feelings for. Hadn't she confessed as much to herself? She and Max barely hung on. Their on-again-off-again relationship had been... what? A convenience.

On paper, Max was everything she thought she should have. He was ambitious. A go-getter. Charming and terribly handsome. With Max at her side, it was the first time since her father's business started booming that she'd thought she wouldn't be seen as a disappointment. When she saw the shine in her father's eyes when she brought him home to the dinner table, it confirmed it. Then, when he charmed her mother into submission, the deal was sealed.

Ever since then, she'd been holding onto him so tightly, she hadn't realized she'd been living for someone else. But after spending time with the businessman behind her, things had changed. She'd found confidence in herself again. She knew she could stand on her own two feet with or without her parent's approval.

Julius wrapped her in a strong embrace. Every bit of him providing her with just the right amount of comfort.

"We can kill him if you want to."

She snorted. "Believe me I want to. I have people after me because of him, and he has the nerve to—"

In a sudden motion, Julius jolted upright, then turned around in a blur.

"What?" She looked at Julius's alarmed face.

"Get behind me." He pulled her behind him and faced the elevator. The same alertness he'd had when they'd raced away from the men at the nightclub was back. It only took a moment for her ears to catch up. As the elevator rose to their floor, she could hear the noise growing louder. It sounded like someone was giving it a good throttle. She clutched at Julius's shirt and tried to peak behind him, dreading what was inside.

The elevator doors opened and the commotion inside spilled out. It didn't take long for either of them to assess the situation. Something was wrong. Very wrong.

"What happened?" Julius immediately rushed to the elevator.

"Your highness, Master Evan has met a poisoned blade." A vampire of severe girth and more muscles than she'd ever seen up close looked to Julius in desperation.

"Let me see, Asher." Julius sidestepped him to reach his brother. "Bring him in."

Julius glanced at Dani, who looked just as distraught. Between the two of them, Dani and Asher strung Evan between them, shifting their weight to drag him inside of their suite. As they moved, Evan let out a howl of pain—a strange screeching that settled somewhere between a dog's howl and a bat's sonic screech—and bucked against them.

"Be careful with him."

When his body came into view, she gasped. A long knife jutted from his gut. Dark red-black blood, much too dark for it to be the right color, stained his clothing. Julius lifted Evan's shirt to assess the wound, then jumped back.

A dark black resin spread from the knife and up onto his torso like tar spread through his veins.

She gasped. "Oh my God. He needs help."

Evan contorted in pain when they set him down in the middle of the floor. His fangs had elongated, his eyes pooled to black.

"He needs blood." Julius raced to the bar and swung a large black box from under the counter onto the granite slab.

"What are you doing?" Erica looked between them. "We have to take him to the hospital."

Asher wasted no time on pretense. "You've seen what he is. He cannot be fixed there."

"Where's the blood?" Julius asked, digging through the box. The room filled with silence. "Dani, where's the rest of the blood?"

"You're asking me? You're the one who went on a binge," she said, unwilling to take the blame.

Julius swore and threw the box down with a heavy thud. Several black packages scattered at their feet.

"Evan." Dani shook her brother when he'd gone too still. "Look at me."

Evan lulled in and out of consciousness.

"What about the synth blood?" Dani asked.

"On flesh wounds, sure, but this is poison. It won't be strong enough." Julius shook his head.

"Do you know this for certain?"

"No, but—"

"We have to try something!" Dani's voice cracked with desperation.

Julius plucked a package from the floor and was at his brother's side in an instant, murmuring something only they could hear. He ripped open the side of the bag and put the corner to Evan's lips. "Come on brother, drink."

With some coaxing, Evan's pale ashen lips suckled the bag. It didn't take. The blood came back up in a cough.

"He may be too far gone to save," Asher said with a shake of his head.

"No, he isn't. We have to encourage his body to heal." Julius grabbed the hilt of the knife and yanked it out of his brother's stomach. Erica flinched. Evan's pain-filled growls gnashed his elongated teeth together as his body convulsed.

"Hold him down."

Asher and Dani moved to either side of Evan and bound his limbs to the floor so he couldn't move. He fought against them, teeth gnawing, trying to get to his stomach.

"We have to press his wound."

"Jules, he's poisoned," Dani whispered. "You can't."

Then, he turned to her. Their eyes met. His were pleading, his voice was strained. "Help me, please."

Numbly, her feet moved toward him on instinct.

Dropping the blade on the floor, Julius pulled off his shirt, balled it up, and tucked it between her hands.

"Apply as much pressure as you can."

She nodded. The warmth of Julius's body was drastically different than Evan's, who was cold and waning. At first, she shrank away, but Julius's steady hand pulled her forward and pressed the shirt to Evan's stomach. Shaking, she pressed the shirt down.

"What kind of poison is this?" Julius asked, the question directed toward Asher. Asher looked at the weapon on the floor.

"I've only ever seen wounds like this with Shifter blood," he said.

Alarm dotted Julius's emerald eyes as he looked at the wound on his brother's stomach. The confident businessman had vanished. In his place, lay someone shattered. He glanced worriedly down at his brother.

"Press harder," Asher's voice was gruff. "You're not going to hurt him any more than he already is."

She tried to press the balled-up shirt into Evan's abdomen, but it felt like jamming a key into a hole that it didn't fit into. Gritting her teeth, she pressed down as hard as she could.

"How do we fix him?" She asked.

Several vampires looked at her at the same time.

"If we give him time, he may heal on his own."

"Not without a mage healing drought. Your highness, forgive me, his best chance is human blood." Asher's words were flat.

Then, she was at an advantage. "I-I can help him."

Each vampire in the room wore a different expression. While Asher's strong brow quirked in disbelief and Dani looked relieved, Julius was torn.

"Will it work?" She asked when they shared a look between them but didn't say anything.

"It will, but it is a lot to ask." Julius shook his head. "He'll need a lot. It won't be pleasant."

"I'm not going to let him die." Erica looked down at Evan. "If it'll work, you can take my blood. As much as you need."

"Thank you!" Dani looked like she wanted to give her a hug.

Evan's eyes rolled upward and he let out a gurgle.

"He's losing time," Asher brought their attention back. She looked down at Evan again. There was no way she could press his wound and feed him blood at the same time. The others sensed this as well.

"Here. I'll take it." Dani grabbed a hold of the shirt in Erica's hand.

"Dani, don't!" Julius warned.

But she was already pressing the shirt into Evan's stomach. "I have to help."

She flinched as his poisoned blood met her fingertips. It sounded like the butt of a lit cigarette was being put out against her skin. The skin around her fingertips and knuckles began to blacken. The poison was burning her.

She gritted her teeth and pressed the ball of blood-soaked fabric further into Evan despite her obvious pain.

Julius nodded, then moved to her. "Blood drinking is a bit different than—"

Asher cleared his throat. "Your highness."

"Right." Julius nodded and turned to her. They didn't have time for the mechanics.

He took her hand and held it to his mouth. His fangs drew down and pressed into her flesh. She felt the pressure before blood pooled in her palm. He pressed it gently to Evan's lips.

"Drink brother."

Evan didn't.

"Come on Evan. Drink."

Her blood trickled over his lips, and it took a moment for him to respond. He latched on, eagerly suckling the side of her hand. Softly at first, but as he gathered his strength, the sucking grew deeper.

"He's drinking." She was relieved. When she looked at Julius, he was watching her intently as Evan sucked at her hand so hard it was painful.

She winced, bit down on the inside of her cheek, and made herself calm down. She was going to be fine. Sensing her discomfort, Julius's warm hand stroked her shoulders. It fueled her forward. He leaned in and murmured softly against her ear. Thanking her for saving his brother. For being so brave. So, she had to be, even if it felt like her hand was drying into a raisin. Erica closed her eyes and let the vampire under her take deep gulps of her blood. Blood rushed to her head. She swayed forward.

"It's working," Dani said.

Peeking under her eyelashes, she stared at Evan's stomach. Dani had removed the balled-up shirt. The dark viscous substance retreated back toward the wound. The black veins started to fade, leaving pink streaks across his skin until the wound closed up. The tightness in the room eased when Evan let go and relaxed back onto the floor.

"Is he okay?" she asked, trying to keep the room from spinning. "Does he need more?"

She surveyed the bites on her hand. Two small round circles puckered under her pinky; the wound closed. She

SABRINA C ROSE

held it back up to Julius for him to bite her again. "Here."

"He has had his fill. His body heals," Asher looked at the wound on Evan's stomach.

"Are you alright?" Julius asked her in concern when she flopped back onto her butt.

"I'm fine." Exhausted, but she'll live after a nap. She pointed at Evan, who lay unnaturally still. "Is he? He's not waking up."

"He will," Dani said, folding the soiled shirt in her hands.

"Dani, your hands." Julius reached for his sister. The tips of her fingers had completely blackened like she'd dredged them in soot.

"I'm fine," she tucked them away inside of her fists. "It hardly hurts."

"Good," Evan's scratchy voice said from underneath them. "Now get off my arm. It's hurting."

"Well no one told you to put your arm right there," Dani retorted, but hopped away. There was only relief in her voice.

"You're okay?" Erica asked, looking at the pale brother.

"Yes." He nodded a fraction before his blue eyes found Julius. His voice was weak, but its intent stern. "He won't stop."

"Evan, you need to rest," Julius placated.

"No," he said, shaking his head weakly. "You have to understand. He won't stop until he has her."

When Evan glanced at her, she knew exactly what he meant. Splinters was coming for her.

"Why me? Why not—" She stopped short of saying Max's name.

"An eye for an eye."

She didn't understand. What did that mean?

She didn't do anything to Splinters. Apparently, Julius knew something she didn't because he rose to his feet and the exhaustion in his face turned into one of determination.

"Then we'll set up a meet."

"No, you're not understanding. They want her. Bad."

19

JULIUS

ERICA'S DELICATE HAND FOUND HIS at his side. He intertwined his fingers with hers. His vampire crooned. Her skin was velvety soft and the only thing keeping him from scouring the city in search of her ex and killing him.

"I don't understand." Her voice was shaky. Scared. "Why? What if they come tonight?"

He looked to Asher and Dani. Asher stood straighter. "I assure you, your highness, we were not followed."

He turned back to Erica. "We will handle this at first light."

"I still don't understand why this is happening."

"There's a lot you don't know about your ex," he said with a heavy sigh and avoided her gaze. Her curious stare turned into one of scrutiny.

"Besides the fact that he's a cheating, lying jerk?"

Bitterness coated her tone.

"There's more to that." He glanced at Erica but wished he hadn't. Her wide eyes stole his breath. She was innocent in all of this. She deserved the truth. Instead, what came out was, "You have to trust me."

From the determined look on her face, he knew she was never going to swallow that whole. If anything, he'd learned Erica was full of surprises.

"Trust is earned with the truth," she said. "There are people after me. I need to know why."

An unfamiliar feeling settled inside of him—one he hadn't felt in a long time. He almost couldn't identify it at first. It made his vampire want to make more of those paper flowers, although he was no good at making them. He wanted to buy more buildings he couldn't return, even though he promised Erica he could. But not as a gesture of his affection. He wanted to do it because he was sorry because he felt guilty. She had always had every right to know about her ex, and he'd withheld it from her. He had no right to do that. There was only one way to ease it. The truth.

He nodded after a while. "Yes, you should."

He looked over at his siblings. Evan laid on his side and Dani hovered over him. Even though they were doing their best to try to make it seem like Julius and Erica had privacy, they were failing miserably. The pair looked like two statues erected in the middle of their suite. They could have at least made a show of talking to each other. Or moving.

"Maybe we should talk in private." He motioned to his

bedroom. Erica nodded and went first. He followed, closing the door behind him.

"Perhaps you should sit." He motioned to his bed—a bed he very much wanted Erica in. His fangs elongated when she sat on the edge of it. He was already devising ways to keep her in it. He forced his vampire to behave. Now was not the time.

"So, why is Splinters after me?" Erica asked. Her voice was plain, her eyes inquisitive.

"I shouldn't be the one to tell you this."

"Just say it. What's so bad that I now have a maniac after me?"

He should keep it simple. Tell her that her ex cheated on her with a sadistic trader's mistress, gambled away his boat in the process, and now owed him a debt equal to that which included her. Sure, that was going to go over extremely well.

"Max slept with Splinters's mistress, and now he wants to avenge it."

"I'm sorry, I must have misheard you. Max slept with a maniac's mistress and now said maniac is after me?"

He nodded, knowing it was probably unwise to use too many words right now. With the way her entire body tensed up, he could see the anger start in her toes and travel up to her hair follicles. She turned a bright shade of red, then it darkened the more she thought over what he said.

"I have people after me because he couldn't keep it in his pants?" Erica clutched her hands into a tight ball in her lap. She stared at the floor. Then she went silent.

Much too silent. He started to worry.

"Erica, are you—"

"Just when I begin to think he can't be any more of an asshole!" Her outburst was furious and sudden. He stood watching the woman in front of him come apart in a fit of anger. She began to pace alongside the bed, looking completely in a dazed. The way her veins bulged in her neck was worrisome. Her face was completely shaded in a blistering hue of red. Then her gaze found him. When her eyes travelled up the length of him, it made him shift his weight from one foot to the other. She was frighteningly angry.

"How do you know? Did Max tell you this himself?"

"I overheard him."

More silence. Then she said, "When? How long have you known?"

"Erica..."

"When did you know?"

"Before we painted together. I overheard him when we went to survey a property that we might invest in."

"Why didn't you say anything to me?"

"What was I supposed to say?"

"Anything besides nothing," she shouted.

"It didn't seem to matter." His voice began to raise to match.

"It mattered to me," she cried. Her hands slapped at her own chest. "We had history together. I might have been considering going back to him."

Just the thought of her even thinking of someone else irked him. No, it infuriated him. By the gods, he wanted to claim her and leave his mark where everyone could see it. Mate her for life. So both she and everyone else she'd ever come into contact with would know she was his. He clenched his teeth and bared his fangs. His vampire growled and took control of their conversation. "You were never going to go back to him."

"Max and I were going to get married once upon a time, you don't just throw that away."

"You. Were. Never. Going. Back." He enunciated each word and moved into her space and looked her directly in the eye.

"How do you know?" For all her determination, he saw her succumb to his intensity. By the way she faltered, he knew she'd never once looked back. He softened, only a hair.

"Because you're mine, Erica. You belong to me now." When she opened her mouth, he didn't allow her to speak. "He was *never* going to have you again. I'm here now and there will be no one after me. Understood?"

"That's the thing. You're here *now*. We haven't even hit the three-week limit yet. My life will be in shambles, and you'll be free back in your vampire world with your princely duties, living your best life."

"There's no life for me without you."

"How can you say that so definitively?"

"I won't mince my words because I need you to understand me. You are my mate Erica. For a vampire, that means you are everything to me. There is no best life without you in it."

"Don't you have to go back to the vampire world?" It

was a last-ditch effort to convince herself out of falling for him. Clearly, he wasn't the only one in denial.

"Only long enough that I can leave it permanently."

"You can't do that. You're a prince."

"Elder has many princes. It can live without me. I, on the other hand, cannot live without you."

"I-I," she was clearly searching for the truth.

"Tell me you'll continue to allow me to woo you relentlessly until you can't live without me either... since you're dangerously close already."

That earned a laugh from her, along with a playful shake of her head. He couldn't help but smile because he'd made her smile.

"There you go again, always knowing exactly what to say to make me feel better."

"It's a gift. Some of us have natural charm," he joked with a nonchalant shrug, although his insides cheered. His jubilation was short-lived. The phone inside his suite rang. He looked at the phone for a moment. It was the front desk. What the hell did they want at this time of night? He picked up the phone.

"Yes?"

"I-I'm sorry to disturb you, um, Mr. Craul. You have a visitor. I'm putting her through to your monitor."

He looked up at Erica with a dead weight in his chest. He should have been focused on getting her out to a safe place.

In a flash, he was at the front door checking the monitor near the elevator. When he saw a shocking shade of purple hair, his brows nearly met his hairline.

"Verna?"

"Who is it?" Dani asked from the sofa.

"She's a friend."

"What is she doing here?"

His thoughts exactly. She'd already told him she wouldn't refund him the money for the studio he'd purchased. But there she was, standing in the lobby of his hotel. He reached for the phone beside the monitor and greeted the front desk attendant.

"Let me speak to her. Keep the monitor on."

After a moment of shuffling, Verna answered. "Your highness, I know it's late."

"What do you want?"

She cleared her throat. "I came to talk to you about our contract."

"I think you've made your terms quite clear." He watched the monitor, soaking up the image. Nothing in the mage's movements were out of the ordinary. She tucked one arm under the other for support as she stretched the wire over the front desk to talk.

"I've reconsidered." Her voice was level and calm.

"At this time of night?"

"Yes... I've been losing sleep over this..."

Of all the nights, she chose this one to have a conscience. He asked her to hand the phone back to the woman behind the desk and said, "Send her up."

"Jules, is everything okay? Who's coming up here?"

"A business associate of mine. It should be quick."

He looked around the room. It was devoid of the necessary people. Only Dani sat on the sofa, but now her back was completely straight as she sat turned toward him in concern. It was misplaced.

"Where's Evan?"

"He's washing his wound. Asher's helping. Or trying." Her golden eyes flickered to Evan's closed door. Julius could only imagine the shenanigans his brother was up to.

"At least he's healing."

He looked up when Erica eclipsed his doorway. He smiled when he saw her. By the gods, he was smitten.

"Hey." He walked over to her. "I just have to handle something, and we can settle in for the night. We can deal with everything else once morning comes."

Erica gave him a grateful nod. Small folds creased under her eyes. Her tiredness was showing.

"You can get started without me."

"No, I'll wait." She yawned.

He gave her a half-grin. Whether she realized it or not, she was acting like his mate already. They were in sync. Dani made room for them on the sofa as they waited for Verna to come up. Erica leaned her head against his arm but he moved it so she could settle into his chest. He and his vampire were on a cloud. Her sweet honeysuckle and lilac scent smelled like home to him.

Evan's bedroom door swung open with a swift, sudden motion.

"Who did you let up here?" Evan asked, his voice more alert than it had been since he regained consciousness.

"Verna." His voice hiked, matching the agitation in his brother's. "Why?"

Even though his brother hadn't returned to his normal

color, he was beginning to walk around thanks to the aid of Erica's blood. He clutched at his side and leaned against the door frame and stared at the gold-coated elevators in their suite.

"Don't let her in."

"What?" Julius sprang to his feet, jostling Erica in the process. Several alarmed expressions followed. "Why? What is it?"

"I have my doubts." Evan said aloud, but pushed into his mind, *I can't read her thoughts. I can tell she's coming, but I can't see inside of her mind.*

Instantly, Julius relaxed. "Is that all?"

Why would she be hiding her thoughts?

"It's Verna," he said, then added only to Evan, *She doesn't trust anyone.*

When Asher appeared from inside of the room, Evan pointed to the elevator. "Guard it with your life."

"Yes, your highness." Asher bowed and walked up to the elevator. Julius rolled his eyes. They were completely overreacting. He was going to tell them as much, but when he looked down to the woman on the sofa, he closed his mouth. It wouldn't hurt to use a bit of caution.

When the elevator dinged, the doors opened to only Verna. He relaxed. At least she wasn't hiding henchmen in her coat.

"V!" Julius greeted her from behind Asher.

Asher blocked her way for a moment, then searched her. "She's clean."

"I'd like to think so." Verna made a show of straightening her leather jacket back into place before tentatively looking around. "I didn't mean to disturb the whole house."

"We've had a long night." Julius brought her to the table and encouraged her to sit. "Would you like a drink?"

"No, thanks," she thumbed the back of the chair but made no move to sit down. Then, he saw the crack in her veneer—the flash of something that was well-hidden by the camera in the lobby.

She looked more weather-worn than when she'd busted in on him with Erica in the studio. Usually, magic kept a mage from appearing as aged as she was. Now it seemed her magic had waned. Her skin was ashen and pale, her lips cracked and dried. Even the violet of her eyes had weakened to more of a lavender. She was completely forlorn. Spent. The only thing with any vibrancy was the shocking shade of purple on top of her head. But there was something more.

"Verna?" He looked at the mage. "What's wrong?"

When her eyes darted over to Asher, then Evan, he saw it. Fear. Guilt.

"I'm sorry your highness," Verna mumbled. "It shouldn't have been *you*. I didn't know, I swear. He said she was a shifter's girl..."

"Verna, you're not making any sense."

"You don't understand."

"Then, make me understand. What happened?" Immediately, his insides curled.

Verna's careful gaze skirted across the room again, sweeping into every face, except one.

"Not even selling you my studio was enough. I have to

pay him."

"Pay who, Verna?"

"I'm sorry, your highness." The mage shook her head, sorrow filled her eyes. "I am bound by magic to pay him. And I owe him big. He always gets what he's owed."

That was not the first time he'd heard that expression, and as soon as she said it, he knew exactly who she owed.

"Verna, whatever you owe, we can pay it."

"You don't understand."

Finally, Verna's gaze settled on Erica. Then, it became very clear she was the currency Splinters was expecting. No amount of money would do. He only wanted Erica. This is what Evan saw in the shifters' minds. Their collective consciousness was compelled, solely focused on his mate, to bring her to Splinters.

"I'm sorry, your highness. I swear, I didn't know."

"Verna," he tried to reason, stepping in front of Erica. "I will kill for her. You know that. Whatever you're thinking of doing, don't."

"You don't understand. I *have to*." Her voice was soft. "It's a magic debt. I have to pay it. I have no choice."

"We protect Erica," he said, alerting his siblings. They were already ready. "No matter the cost."

Tears bubbled in the mage's eyes as she put a hand to her mouth like she had no control over her actions.

"I'm sorry your highness." Verna blew an orange powder into his face, then forced more of it around the room. It looked like colored chalk being puffed into the air. It stung. His eyes watered. He blinked several times, trying to clear it away, then staggered backward. It was an irritant. At quick glance, the entire room was affected. Except Erica.

"What is this?" he asked, inhaling some of the powder in the process. That was a mistake. It felt like someone put their mouth to his and sucked all the air out of his lungs. His airways were blocked. He coughed, unable to catch his breath. It forced him to his knees.

Asher sprang up, plugged his nose, and lunged for Verna. The warrior was precise in his movements and swift, but Verna was quicker. A spurt of energy blanketed them, freezing Asher in the air just before he collided with the table. She blew more of the powder into his face. It constricted him just the same.

By then, it felt like Julius had grown a mountain on his shoulders. He looked up at Erica. He had to get to her but was helpless to do anything but watch while his body was forced flat to the floor.

"Wh—" The words wouldn't form around the coughs. He looked to his mate. "Er—"

He tried to tell her to run, but the words wouldn't form. He pointed vehemently at the elevator doors instead. Erica got the hint. Her golden hair bounced against her back as she raced to the elevator.

"I'm sorry." Verna appeared in front of Erica, lay a single finger on her, and Erica stopped like she'd been frozen in ice. No. She had to get away.

"You—" the word barely made it out before he coughed again. This time blood ended up on the floor by his face.

"I'm sorry, your highness. He said if I did this, I'd be free. He's offering me a fresh start. I didn't know it was you. They said they traced her here. It was supposed to be the wolf. *Not you.* I wouldn't have agreed if I knew. I wouldn't betray the crown."

But she was. Julius tried to force the substance from his lungs, but whenever he tried to get air in, it wouldn't come. His chest hurt. It felt like his lungs had been burned to ash.

Please Verna, he pleaded inside of his mind. *Please don't take her. I'll do anything. I'll trade my own life. Just don't leave.*

The mage couldn't hear it, but his brother could.

We'll get her back. Evan said to him. *Verna sides with us.*

She clearly didn't. Not when she was taking Erica away. He cursed and he screamed inside of his mind. He was ripping from the inside. It started in his chest, then gouged his insides when Verna put her hand on Erica's shoulder. He tried to get his body to work. Tried to force it upright, but her magic was too strong. Verna stirred a green electric glow around Erica. It traveled around the base of their feet and swirled up their bodies.

"You'll heal soon. Doc 94 in Bingham Park." Verna said, staring at his immobile body. She bowed deeply. "Hurry."

Then, she vanished.

20

JULIUS

WHEN THE MAGE LEFT, HER MAGIC lifted. Julius sprang to his feet as soon as the heaviness fizzled. Breathing was still hard, but manageable. Rage ripped through him.

"Calm, brother," Evan said in an even tone.

He seethed. "She took her. Splinters has Erica."

"We'll get her back." Dani was already calling for their car to be valeted to the front of the hotel.

"Verna said something about the docs in Bingham park. Where is that?"

"I'll look it up." Dani's nimble fingers dashed around her phone.

"Julius, Verna's not our enemy," Evan said.

His eyes cut to Evan. If his brother thought for one moment Verna wasn't an enemy to the crown, he was vastly mistaken.

"She tried to warn you. She let me into her mind, and I saw it. She's bound by blood magic. She couldn't help it. She tried to warn us. That's why she had the front desk call the room. That's why she told us where she was taking her."

"I don't care." Julius grabbed his coat to search for his keys. His mate was gone and it was Verna's fault. Blood magic or not.

"I've got it," Dani finally said, looking down at her phone. "Doc 94 is a warehouse in Bingham park."

She pulled it up on a digital map and showed it to him. He and Evan shared a look. That was the heart of shifter territory.

That's uptown," Evan said. "Half an hour out."

"How do we get there?"

"The map will guide us."

Good. He zipped to the elevator and mashed the button.

"Wait," Evan called, babying his stomach as he hoisted himself to his feet.

"What the hell do you think you're doing?" Julius asked.

"We're going to get Erica," he replied. "It makes the most sense for me to go. I can read minds."

"You're still hurt."

"I can take care of myself."

"The last time you said that, you ended up with a knife in your stomach."

"To-may-toe, To-ma-to," Evan said with a wave of his hand. Then, reading the question forming on his face, and explained, "It's a human saying—"

"We don't have time for this," He cut him off abruptly and pushed the elevator button again. Where the hell was this thing? "You're not coming. I can't protect her and look after you at the same time."

"I need to help."

"You want to help? Rest. Get better. That is how you help me. Asher will secure more blood for you."

"You need backup."

"What the hell do you think I'm here for?" Dani cut in, putting a hand on her hip and giving Evan a frown. When Dani reached for her own coat, Julius grimaced. She was coming with him, of course. She shouldn't. Her fingers weren't completely healed. But it seemed his busybody sister couldn't help herself. For the all gods, where the hell was the elevator?

"You should stay here too."

"No dice, you heard Evan. You don't know what you're up against. You're not going alone.

"Your hands are not yet healed."

"They're fine." She tucked them into her pockets. "Besides, I should be the one to do the talking. I'm a better negotiator."

Julius remained silent. He had no plans to talk. If his sister wanted to believe that he'd be able to keep his vampire from ripping throats out, she'd be better off staying behind.

"Accept the help." Evan made a face but settled back into the sofa and clutched at his stomach.

You think I want to put my little sister in danger? His

sister had not trained like a warrior the way the rest of them had. Basic self-defense, nothing further. If the stubborn fool on the sofa had been more careful, he'd be in fighting shape already.

You know I can hear you.

"You should," Julius said aloud. "And you should feel very guilty about it."

"Go to hell."

"I'm already in hell. My mate is gone. Asher, guard him with your life."

"Yes, your highness." Asher nodded despite Evan's reluctance.

With that, Julius boarded the elevator and pushed the express button to the garage and took off after Erica. Both of their lives depended on it.

———————

DOC 94 WAS ABANDONED. When they stopped at the address the GPS said was the correct one, Julius thrashed at the steering wheel. Not a soul lurked around it.

"Are you sure we're at the right place?" He looked at Dani, then down to the phone in her hands.

"Yes, this is Doc 94."

"Does it look like anything exists here?" He pointed at the empty building with several broken windows.

"Looks can be deceiving. If I were trying to hide a secret operation, I'd put it here."

He had to believe that, even though everything inside

of him twisted in doubt and refused to relinquish its hold. Erica was there. She needed to be. He shot off to the warehouse.

"Jules, wait!"

He ran inside despite his sister's protests. He couldn't wait one more minute. He had to get to his mate. When he got inside, it looked no less vacant. Large wooden crates and metal shipping containers were stacked on top of one another in an endless labyrinth. If she were here, she could be anywhere. His vampire rose to the surface and sniffed the air. Shifters. Faint, but it was a concentrated sort of faintness.

Focus. He forced his vampire to think of Erica's scent. *Find her.*

To his surprise, she *was* there. But locating her was going to be like pulling a needle from a hay heap. Everything seemed to hold traces of his girl, but none of it was distinctive. He couldn't pinpoint her exact location.

"Your highness! What took you so long?"

Julius's vampire took control when Verna appeared in front of him. His eyes pooled to black. His fangs drew down. He hissed at his subject. So much for her oath to lay down her life for the crown. She'd poisoned him, left him for dead, then took his mate. If she was on their side, the mage had better show her allegiance, fast.

"Where's Erica?"

"I'm sorry, your highness" The mage backed away, a current of purple electricity floating around her fingertips.

"Tell me where Erica is. Evan says you side with us."

The mage looked over her shoulder for a split second.

He rushed her and put his hands around her throat.

"Where is she?" he roared.

"She's in the back by the dock," Verna choked out. "But—"

He squeezed tighter, cutting off her words. "You will never cross the house of Craul again."

"Jules, stop!" Dani gripped his wrist. "Let her speak."

"No." Seething, he tightened his grip. His vampire was thoroughly enjoying the feel of the soft tissue in his grasp. Verna gathered just enough of herself to put her hand on his other wrist. Electricity jolted through his legs, forcing his knees to buckle. By the gods, it was excruciating. As if trying to outdo itself, the pain traveled up his spine and ripped through his skull like someone was driving a nail through his temple. He let go, and she dropped unsteadily to the ground. She started speaking before he could launch another attack.

"He's draining her," Verna said between gasping breaths, pressing her fingers at her neck like she was trying to rip his phantom fingers away.

"Where?"

"In the back..."

He sidestepped her.

"Wait, she has a healing drought. It'll work, but you have to get there in time." Her pale purple eyes flickered between Dani and him. "Which isn't going to be easy. He's well protected."

"How many?"

"A handful that I saw, but they're shifters. They can regenerate. They also carry poison-laced weapons."

"Anything else?"

The mage shook her head. "You're running out of time. I wish I could make this up to you."

In a split second, he knew exactly how. "You can. Get my sister out of here."

Dani backed away from them. "What? No."

She nodded, then bowed. "To the crown."

"Stop, Verna. I command you."

"I outrank you, sister." Julius nodded at Verna.

"Wait," Dani protested. "He can't go alone. Stop. You can't."

The mage latched on to Dani despite her protest, and just like with Erica, a green hue swirled around them before they vanished.

Good.

At least he wouldn't be worried over his sister. He turned back in the direction Verna had pointed and ran at full speed, trying to trace her scent. It became both stronger and weaker as he ran, coming in plumes, then vanishing.

What the hell were they doing to her? Dread urged his vampire to push harder.

Thankfully, he didn't run into anyone on his way to the back of the warehouse. Gusts of late autumn wind swirled around him, and in an instant, he could smell it. Blood.

A lot of it.

He sprinted.

In the middle of an open area, flanked by an opened bay that led to the stench of the river, was Erica, tied to a chair. Her head hung. She wasn't conscious. Her heartbeat was irregular. Although she had a needle taped to the inside of her arm, there was no blood around her. That bastard had harvested it from her. He took a step forward. Everything about the scene in front of him should have screamed caution. But with Erica like this, he didn't hesitate.

He didn't think.

He raced to her.

"Erica," he said softly, cupping her chin and lifting it. "Love, can you hear me?"

She murmured something, but otherwise didn't respond. He looked down at the restraints and began to untie them. His senses were off. It wasn't until he heard several steps behind him that he realized he wasn't alone.

"I told the wolf he had one hour. I didn't realize he'd send a fanger instead." The voice was greasy, slick, and rough. "What is it with her? You all have some sort of threesome or something?"

Julius jerked upright and spun around to find a collection of men in dark blue construction uniforms surrounding him. They parted, allowing a much smaller, gaunt man through. He looked sickly. Frail. Perhaps it was the sagging of his near translucent skin or his weathered, beady eyes. He was the one in Erica's apartment. The man she called Splinters.

"It seems you have stolen something from me." He looked the gaunt man directly in the eye.

"Is that right? What is it you presume I took?" Splinters's smile was vicious and taunting. "I think you're barking up the wrong shifter, son."

Julius's jaw snapped tight for a moment, staying his vampire from lunging. He needed to see if more shifters would emerge from the catacombs of the warehouse.

"I'm here to make a trade."

"A trade?" Splinters looked surprised. "What could a fanger possibly want with a human? If it's her blood, I'm afraid you're a bit too late for that. It's gone, being shipped. Unless you want what little there is left."

Julius forced himself to calm. Splinters was taunting him, testing to see how much leverage he had. He'd betray no more than he needed to.

Julius took control of their conversation. "What I want with her is my business. Are you ready to hear the terms of my deal?" When Splinters didn't speak right away, he added, "It would be in poor form to turn your back on prime business. Especially when it will keep you and your pack eating well for years to come."

When a gurgle of murmurs rippled through the men behind him, a vein in the trader's jaw jumped. They were itching for their next big payday. From the look on the trader's face, he didn't seem pleased by their collective excitement. He turned to his men. Immediately, they went silent. When he turned back around, the trader spit at the floor between them. Julius didn't flinch.

"Fine. What is it?"

"You let us walk out of here, and I let you all live."

Splinters laughed, and the collective joined in.

"You have a lot of nerve coming into my house and threatening me. Especially after all I do for your kind." His voice became raspier, more hostile, but he noticed no more shifters joined them.

"This is why I've never had much patience for traders. You all talk incessantly. Accept the terms or don't."

Splinters looked flabbergasted, shocked that he had the audacity to speak to him in such a way. The gaunt man took a step forward. Julius matched it. He was not afraid of a shifter. Especially not the one in front of him.

"No, I do not accept." Splinters backed off, then raised his arm. With a flick of his hand, he signaled for his men to attack.

Adrenaline suffused his body when the shifters rushed him. Against his tenacity, they would not win.

One of them pushed him backward into another, trying to knock him over. He needed to find the upper hand, some sort of advantage in a six against one fight. He needed to break the chain by the weakest link.

"Sometimes a bounty just falls into your lap," one of them taunted.

"We should save him. Stuff him and post him up," another said.

Julius found an opening. He bulldozed their weakest link, a thin shifter with a mop of what looked like straw on his head. His eyes bulged in surprise when Julius grabbed his neck and twisted.

A sick howl sounded behind him. Each of the shifters bent for a moment, and he wondered if a death in the pack caused them pain.

It didn't. It was their rallying cry.

The other men pulled knives from their clothing and rushed him. He had to keep the poisoned blades away from his skin. He used every tactic he was trained to use. Without his battle armor, he was exposed, a disadvantage they exploited. Before long, several gashes lined his arms and legs, but he'd been quick enough to not let them cut deeper than paper.

This was a street fight, plain and simple. Dirty. Vampire against shifter. Instinct against instinct. Julius knew the outcome; he'd win or die trying. His vampire was completely at the surface as his opponents became a tangle of limbs, punching and kicking and slicing. They were losing steam and breathing hard. They didn't have much fight left. He didn't either. All of the shallow cuts of their blades were starting to take their toll, but every time they closed in, he pushed against one, toppling him off balance and using it to end him. Until one of them made a mistake.

The hilt of a dagger hit his foot with a thud. In a flash, he dove for it, sprang to his feet, and gutted one of his attackers. He met the floor with a thud.

Then, at his feet, he started to shift.

By the gods.

He had to stop the remaining two. There was no way he'd be able to fight against their regenerative properties

He held the blade tight in his hand, thankful his father had the foresight to have all of his sons trained like warriors. He pushed the one whose fur had started to pop out of his back, and slammed the dagger into his heart.

With a short, strangled cry, he fell to the floor and slumped forward.

Julius heard the other shifter too late. As he turned, a

serrated dagger cut into him, this time shredding his gut and twisting deep. His body jerked. With the shifter this close, he pulled him close enough to rip at his throat with his fangs.

His mouth stung like alcohol burning an open wound. To his surprise, he had enough good blood in him for his mouth to scab over and heal. The wound in his gut, however, did not.

The poison spreading inside his body. It felt like hot coals being liquified and thrust through his veins. He had to stop it from spreading. He'd have to risk losing too much blood over having his blood poisoned. Before he could pull the knife from his gut, a sick, sadistic laugh erupted behind him. His body swayed as he turned toward their leader.

"You will die for this, fanger, and I always get what I am owed." Splinters's bravado masked his fear well. The rapid fire beating of the shifter's heart was even loud enough that Julius could hear it. In a sudden motion Splinters didn't see coming, Julius pulled the dagger from his stomach and launched it at him. Accuracy was not his ally that day. It didn't pierce his heart, but his lungs instead.

The thin man looked shocked as he fell to the floor. He clutched at the blade in his chest.

"Go ahead, take it out. You'll bleed out like your mutts here. Or I'll do it for you. Either way you die." Julius's gaze was deadly. "You've stolen from me. And *I* always get what *I am* owed."

"You won't have enough time to save her anyway. The

closest hospital is miles away." He laughed again, but this time it ended in a bloodied cough. "She'll be dead by the time you get there." Splinters's slick voice gurgled as the blood churned in his lungs. "Either way, I still win."

"No." His eyes blackened. "You don't."

He lunged at Splinters, digging his hand into his chest adjacent to the blade. The shifter's body resisted, but Julius didn't stop until he'd broken through his ribcage. Flesh and muscle dug into his fingernails, and the trader's blood burned his hands, charring them black.

"You'll never win." He growled and ripped out his heart.

Splinters's entire body went rigid as a board, stuck in that final moment like he was reaching for his heart but couldn't.

"You should have accepted my deal," he said as the trader's eyes glossed over.

The floor rose beneath his feet. Spent, he staggered backward and dropped to his knees. The poison was still spreading and he was losing too much blood. He was weakening fast. Subconsciously, his fingers found the wound on his stomach. It was worse than Evan's. Evan had had a clean cut. His was ragged, and his insides were shredded. A wave of exhaustion sent his palms to the floor.

No, he needed to get up. His mate needed him. Even if he had to crawl to get to her. She was losing time, and who knew if the healing drought would do her any good at this point. He dragged himself to her.

Julius hauled himself up and released the restraints on

her arms and legs. Her body slumped forward. Catching her should have been easy, but she nearly leveled him. He clutched her and laid her down on the floor beside him. Her heartbeat was faint.

He searched her pockets for the vial Verna promised. At least the mage did not lie. In a small hidden pocket in her dress, he found the small vial. A single serving of clear liquid was inside of it. Uncapping it, he tilted Erica's head back and put it to her lips, praying like hell it took.

She couldn't die. He wouldn't let her.

He waited for her body to make way for the healing drought, but Julius collapsed back in exhaustion, the poison and blood loss having taken its toll. He fought for as long as he could. He had to make sure she lived. He had to stay awake. Darkness crept into the corners of his eyes as he used the last of his strength to cuddle next to his mate. The darkness proved stronger.

"For the all gods, let her live." He let out the single prayer. Then, the blackness overtook him.

21

ERICA

ERICA GAINED JUST ENOUGH consciousness to know she wasn't at home. It was too cold. Howling wind gusted against her, forcing her body to curl into the fetal position. Immediately, she opened her eyes.

Bodies littered the floor. All of them were immobile with blank stares looking past the ceiling at nothingness. Pools of their blood stained the floor beneath them. They were... She stopped just short of letting the "d" word into her mind. Even though that was exactly what they deserved. Then her thoughts shifted to the obvious. Someone had saved her. The vial that Verna had given her was empty on the floor. Had Verna come back? After she'd given her the healing drought and stiffly walked away, she'd never thought she'd see her again.

Quickly, she realized the witch didn't. Her eyes glanced over several bodies until a distinct outline made her heart sink.

Oh no. No, no, no. It was Julius. He was too still. She tapped his shoulder, but he didn't stir.

"Julius." She shook him. Nothing.

"Julius, please wake up." She shook him again. Still, his body remained just as immobile as all the others.

Tears welled in her eyes and fell when he didn't respond to her touch.

A singular hopeful thought repeated in her mind: he wasn't dead. There was no way he could be. He couldn't be because the world needed him in it. His bright smile, his mischievous smirk, his confidence, and generosity were all necessary. She couldn't live in a world where Julius wasn't a part of it. No, she refused to.

"Come on. Please get up." She pushed at him again willing him to move for her. When he didn't, her heart shattered inside her chest, and a darkness threatened to overtake her.

"Please, wake up. Please, It's Erica. Your Erica." She lifted his hand to her face and pressed it against her cheek. "See, it's me. I'm alive, and now you have to be too. Wake up for me. Come on, Julius. You have to wake up. You hear me? You have to. I can't live without you."

When he didn't move, a blast of frustration shot through her and came soaring out of her mouth in a wail. How dare they take him away from her? How could they? It wasn't fair.

She screamed, not caring if she wasn't alone in the warehouse. It would be better if she wasn't. That way they could put her out of her misery.

Then through the warehouse, a buzzing ripped through the air. It vibrated under her hand. She checked through his pocket and found his phone.

Dani was calling.

Her heart nearly came through her spine. When it rang out, Dani called back.

She'd have to be the one to tell her. A golf ball lodged in her throat. Her hands shook as she answered it.

"Julius!" Dani cried. "What the hell?"

"He... he won't wake up," the words choked inside of her throat.

The line on the other side went silent.

"Is he breathing? Is his heart beating?"

"I...I don't know..." She leaned over and pressed her ear to his chest. More of her tears came. "I don't hear it."

"Hey, hey, hey," Dani soothed on the opposite end, "That doesn't mean anything. Human ears are much weaker than ours. Put the phone to him, let me hear it."

Her hand shook more violently as she put the phone to his chest. She wasn't sure how long she should keep it there, but after a short moment, she pulled it back.

"Did... did you hear anything?"

"He's alive," she said. "But very weak. You need to kickstart him, make sure he's awake."

"How?"

"You need to hit him very, very hard. Can you do that for me? Once he's conscious, keep him up."

She wasn't sure it was going to be that easy, but she balled up her fist anyway and slammed it against his chest. Surprisingly, Julius's eyes rolled. Relief released the tension in her gut.

"Oh thank God," she said, clutching at her heart, then laid her head flat against his chest to be sure. He was breathing. They were shallow and slow breaths, but they were there. He was still in there. She scrambled for the phone. "He's awake."

"Okay, keep him up. No matter what. Don't let him go to sleep. I'll be there soon."

The line disconnected and she turned back to Julius. He looked pale and weak. He lay very still.

"Julius? Can you hear me?" She yelled as loud as she could. He blinked several times in rapid succession, but then he went still again. Still like Evan had done back in the hotel suite. Her eyes traced his body, stopping at his arms and legs, then settled on his abdomen. He was cut up bad. Dark red-black resin protruded from his lacerations. He was poisoned.

"Julius! You have to fight," she yelled. His eyes rolled again. That gave her hope. He was fighting. Fighting for her.

That was good. Now she needed to encourage his body to heal. He needed blood. She looked around for something sharp. Several knives littered the floor, she picked one up. No, she looked at Julius then dropped it. It was probably poisoned. She looked at the vial again. It was tiny, but a small glass shard was better than nothing. She smashed it against the ground. Thankfully, it broke apart into something useful. Pressing her teeth together, she raked a shard against the side of her palm until she saw bright red blood bubble up to the cut. Frick, that hurt like hell. But it didn't matter. She looked down at Julius and pressed her hand to his lips.

When he didn't move right away, she rubbed her palm back and forth. More of her blood came out and dripped over the sides of his face.

"Come on Julius, drink," she said, forcing her hand past his lips, hitting his teeth.

She didn't have to wait very long for him to latch on. He drank slowly at first, then he took a few sips. Then he stopped.

She looked at her hand. Fuck. It had healed. She took the shard to it again and put her hand to his mouth. Again, he drank for only a moment, then stopped. When she tried a third time, his head moved to one side.

"Julius?" She craned her head to see if he'd woken. He hadn't.

What the hell? Maybe he'd had enough. When Evan had finished, he'd stopped drinking. She looked down at Julius. Maybe this was the same, but he'd drank so little. She pulled up his shirt to look at his wound.

That wasn't right. It didn't start to close like it had with Evan. He should have been healing faster than that. She pulled his shirt up as high as it would go. The black resin inside his veins had spread much farther.

"Fuck."

It had crawled up to his heart.

"Julius?" she called to him.

Asher's words, from when she'd first tried to revive Evan, played in her head.

He may be too far gone to save.

It was then, as her mind settled on those dooming words, that she realized she'd do anything to keep him alive in this world. The businessman had crawled up under her skin and settled there. She wasn't afraid to admit what was already growing in her heart since the day they met. She loved him. She loved everything about him. How utterly confident he was. How he knew when to rattle her cage and when she needed a gentle stroking. He knew her inside and out. Even with his pleasure venom gone from her system, she felt the pull toward him. Something she'd never felt with anyone else.

Erica shook the voice from her head. She was not going to let him die. Even if he needed every ounce of blood she had, she was not going to see him dead.

She picked up the shard again, then looked from her palm and down to her wrist. He needed more blood. As hard as she could, she jabbed the glass into her wrist, hoping like hell she'd at least get a vein. It hurt worse than with her hand, but when the blood began to spill, she rushed to put it to Julius's lips. It smeared across his face.

"Drink!" she screamed when he didn't respond at first.

His eyes rolled again, but he suckled at her wrist, then took long deep gulps.

"That's it, Julius. Take as much as you need," she whispered. When she felt his fangs push into her skin, she knew he'd latched on this time. She closed her eyes and let him drink. With each gulp, he was going to get stronger.

"Keep going," she encouraged.

He obliged. He pulled blood from her. It never seemed like he had enough. She didn't care. She'd freely give him every last drop of her blood if she could.

By now she realized the warehouse was empty. No one else had come for her, but Dani wouldn't know where they were. They'd have to meet her.

"You have to be strong," she said. "Because we're going to walk out of here. Dani's on her way, but we have to meet her outside so she can see us."

She wasn't sure that was true, but she needed to keep her mind focused on anything other than the lightheadedness she was experiencing. Or the irregular thudding of her heart the that seemed to get wirier the more blood he took.

"She's coming..." She needed to lay down. She curled up with him, leaving her arm craned over her head so he could drink from her. She pressed her ear to his chest. The only thing keeping her from thinking about her blood loss was keeping her mind focused on his breathing. His strengthening breaths were all that separated her from insanity. "You're going to be alright. You have to be. We're mates, remember? That means you're mine too. That means I can't live without you either. Just keep drinking, Julius. You're going to be alright. I promise."

She repeated the words over and over until her voice was raw. She was getting colder. So, so cold. Her body shivered against his. It was getting harder for her to stay awake. Feeling his warmth against her body was soothing.

"I'm so tired." She tried to fight for every bit of consciousness she could muster. She shouldn't go to sleep. She had to fight for Julius. Though, she wasn't sure if she could anymore. Thankfully, she didn't have to. He unlatched and settled back down. She lay on his chest, listening to him breathe.

She was exhausted. Her eyes were heavy. She tried to blink to keep them open, but she didn't have to, not really. She could keep them closed for just a moment. Give them a bit of rest, then open them again in a little while.

"You're going to be okay," she breathed. Then her eyes fluttered closed.

Time was a funny thing. She wasn't sure how long she laid there, but the longer she was there, the stronger she became. Even in her sleep, she could feel the healing drought still working, starting in her feet and working its way up to the rest of her. She could feel herself growing stronger like a well that was being replenished by rain.

"Erica!" Footsteps bounded toward them.

Finally. Her eyes found just enough strength to open. She lifted her head from Julius's chest and saw a girl with a flowing black mane racing toward them. She inwardly slumped with relief.

"Julius, we're okay. The cavalry has arrived."

"Jules!" Dani raced down the long aisle to get to them.

"He was poisoned. I gave him some of my blood."

"Here." Dani pulled her off of Julius and sat her beside him. When she shivered, Dani pulled off her heavy coat and wrapped her in it. She briskly rubbed Erica's arms from the outside creating as much friction heat as she could.

"I'm fine." She wrenched away and pointed at Julius.

Dani was already lifting his blood-soaked shirt. She quickly assessed Julius's wound.

"He's healing," Dani said with relief, then turned to her. "I can't thank you enough." It only took a moment for Dani to assess the dead shifters around them. "I see we've made a bit of a mess. Let's get out of here before housecleaning shows up."

Dani lifted her first, like she weighed no more than a feather, and carried her to the car. Wow, she was strong. How Dani managed to lay her in the back seat without breaking stride was a miracle she couldn't begin to comprehend. Once Dani made sure to blast the heat to get her warm, she raced back for Julius.

When they returned, Erica was surprised to see his eyes were open, even though they were fully black. His vampire was awake. She'd never been so relieved in her life.

"He might be a bit heavy—"

"Let me down." Julius's voice was gruff and thick.

Carefully, she set Julius on his feet. He was in the car in a flash, hovering over her, studying her with concern. Every bit of him checked and rechecked her.

"I'm fine," she assured him.

He wrapped himself around her. He was so warm. Much warmer than he'd been before and gaining heat rapidly. She snuggled into him like she was curling up next to a warm fire.

"You're okay." She smiled and craned her neck to kiss him.

"Yes, thanks to you." He leaned in to kiss her lips. "I love you too, you know."

"You heard me?"

He nodded. "Every word."

"Not to break up a sentimental moment, but you need to move your foot, Jules."

Julius shifted on top of her and gave her a weak smile. He wasn't completely healed, but he was mending quickly. Dani slammed the door behind him and dashed to the other side of the car. In seconds, she was in the front seat and skyrocketing through the warehouse district like Satan's hellhounds were after her. Once they put enough distance between them and the warehouse district, Dani eased off the gas and looked into the backseat.

"When you're done playing sticky faces..." Dani's voice turned deadly calm as she looked at them in the rearview mirror.

Julius paused for a moment, but still hugged her close. "Go on, I'm listening."

"Good, because I'm going to tell you this once and only once. Don't you ever, *ever* send me away again. You almost got yourself killed for real this time!"

"Sorry," was all Julius managed to say before he laid his head on her chest, fingers playing in her hair.

"That's it? Sorry? You're so lame. I can't freaking believe you had Verna send me across town."

"You did *what*?" She sputtered, looking at him in disbelief.

"Yeah, wish you knew that before you saved his ass, don't you? If I wasn't driving, I'd hit him."

She swatted his arm on Dani's behalf. "What were you thinking?"

"Hey!" Julius didn't even flinch. He was definitely

getting better.

"It's dumb to go without back up."

"See? At least you fell in love with someone who's smart. I can worry less about you now." Dani's mouth closed for only a moment before she was muttering under her breath. "You know how long it took me to get back? I probably exposed vampirekind doing it, since I had to *run*. I'm not sorry, either."

"Are you still fussing?"

"I'll fuss until I meet my final sunfall jackass. You better thank the all gods you've even survived to hear it."

The car settled for a while, then she piped up, "All you had to do was come up with two investments. Two. That's it. Me? I've got to come up with enough blood to feed half the province. You had it easy and barely got that to work. Not to mention you almost got yourself killed. Wait until I tell Gustav that his baby brother is a dumbass. To think, I've been defending you for years."

"I said I was sorry."

"Yeah, yeah. I'm still telling Gustav."

So, Julius did have more brothers. Maybe there was hope for Marie after all. Her eyebrow arched as her thoughts turned to her friend. There was never a time in her entire life that she hadn't told her friend every little secret she had. How was she going to explain this? She looked down at the vampire laying against her stomach. She wasn't. Not without exposing vampirekind. This was the one secret she had to keep, for Julius's sake. She'd tell her everything else, though. She'd burst otherwise.

"Erica," Julius said from under her.

"Hmm?"

"I'm feeling weak. Can I have just a tiny bit more of your blood?"

Without hesitation, she offered her arm. He pulled her hand to his lips and sank his fangs in.

"Oh!" She jolted when a flood of pleasure raced through her veins. He was putting his pleasure venom in her. When another wave hit her, she had to stifle a moan. "Julius."

"Ick, Julius!" Dani complained from the front seat.

Frick. She pushed against Julius's head until his fangs retracted and she could rip her hand away. Then her gaze flickered up to his sister. Crap. His sister knew what he was doing. Dani could probably smell her arousal. Erica pinched her eyes shut as tightly as they would go and wished for a sink hole to open up under the tires.

'Sorry,' she mouthed, her voice muted by mortification. Julius, as always, remained cool and level-headed.

"What? My mate and I were hurt. I'm still recovering. It makes me feel good when she feels good. Don't you want me to get better?"

"Not if you're going to do that I don't. Is there ever one second where you can keep it in your pants? Come on! There're other people in the car with you. I knew I should have sent Asher."

"But I'm hurting. Erica's the only one who can make it better," he whined and made a show of clutching at his side. It was the first time she'd ever heard Julius take that tone. It surprised her.

She joined into their banter, stroking his back. "You're such a big baby."

"But I'm your baby."

"Yes, that you are." She chuckled and stroked his hair.

"So, can I bite you again? It'll make me feel better."

"Ugh!" Dani chided from the front seat. "Jules, come on!"

Julius looked at his sister. "One day, Dani. One day, you're going to find your mate, and you'll want to do the exact same thing."

"I won't be as gross as you."

Julius must have made a face at his sister because in return she gave him the finger. He stilled against her stomach.

"He's not going to bite me," she assured her.

"Fine, we'll wait. But I don't want to hear a single complaint when we get back to the hotel. If you don't like it, get your own suite."

"Don't worry, I already have. I refuse to spend the rest of my joyous relaxing vacation with you and Evan. You two are more trouble than you're worth. And, once again, *I* am the one who has to bail everyone out."

"Thank you for that." She met Dani's eyes in the rearview mirror. Thank you wasn't even enough gratitude for what she felt. She was overwhelmed at how easily she'd been accepted into the family. How strangers had come to her rescue. There were no words for how thankful that made her.

"Oh, don't worry about it." She pulled her ponytail over her shoulder and tugged at it, offering her an

261

apologetic look. It was abundantly clear Dani was just busting Julius's chops and didn't mean any offense with her complaining. "I wouldn't let anything happen to you. I actually like you, Erica. There's no question. Jules, on the other hand..." Dani tossed Julius a look of playful scorn. "He's a pain in the ass. He's lucky he's favored by the King. Damian would have sent his army after me if I left him there to rot. I know where not to make enemies. *Unlike some people.* Jules. Jules! Don't you dare feign sleep, Jules. I know you can hear me."

When Julius didn't move an iota, Dani groaned and her gaze flickered back to her. "Are you sure you want to do this? You're going to be stuck with a pain in the ass for a long time."

"I'm sure." She nodded and stroked Julius's hairline while he pretended to sleep. "He's stuck with me for a long time too."

At her words, Julius tightened his arms around her and snuggled in closer, enveloping her in his warmth.

"Hmm... a long time," he murmured and pressed a small kiss where his lips could reach. "I like that."

"Me too."

22

ERICA

"ARE YOU REALLY NOT GOING TO tell me where we're going?" She asked, adjusting the blindfold over her eyes as they drove to the heart of the city. The closer they'd gotten to downtown, the more it reeked like city sewer and congestion.

"Dani would kill me if I said a word," Julius replied.

"You're afraid of your little sister?" She taunted playfully, knowing that based on their competitive streak, it would get a rise out of him.

"You haven't seen her in action. She's dangerous."

"She's just a kid."

"She's a couple of years younger than you."

"Still, I can't believe you're getting bullied by your kid sister."

Julius laughed. "I see what you're trying to do. It won't work."

"What do you mean?" She played innocent, praying her cheeks would stay in check. She couldn't see him, but he very much could see her.

"I'll never tell."

"That's too bad. I was thinking we could ditch it all together."

"You don't want to miss this."

"I'm pretty sure I do." Even blindfolded, she had no trouble finding his muscled thigh. She let her hand travel toward his crotch.

"You don't play fair woman," he chuckled, but made no move to dissuade her touch.

"I play to win." She would have winked, but the blindfold made it impossible. It already felt like her eyelashes were jammed up against the fabric, straining to burst through. Very much like the growing hardness in Julius's pants. She left a flutteringly light touch against him before going for the top button on his pants. He growled.

"You're playing with fire."

"I told you, there were other things I'd rather be doing tonight."

"If you keep that up, I'm going to stop this car on the side of the road and fuck you so hard you won't be able to walk for days. Then, when we're done, I'm going to straighten your pretty little dress and bring you to our destination anyway. Wobbly legs and all."

A flash of pleasure doused her. Frick. If he was trying to dissuade her, he was doing an awful job of it. She popped the button open. Julius groaned.

"Why are you so eager to know anyway?" His voice was strained and guttural.

"I don't like surprises."

"This is technically not a surprise."

She frowned and chewed on her bottom lip. What did that even mean? She paused her pursuit inside of Julius's pants and sat back. "So, I already know what we're going to do?"

"Why'd you stop?"

"Are we going to dinner?" she asked, ignoring his protest. "Please don't tell me we're just going out to eat."

"What's wrong with dinner? Everyone needs sustenance."

"Because the in-room dining is spectacular. We never had to leave the hotel. It fit right in with my plans."

Julius chuckled, but it was tight. From the noise in the seat beside her, she could only guess that he was adjusting himself. He deserved the discomfort. There wouldn't have been any if they'd stayed in for the night.

"Is it really dinner? My scalp is sore from Dani raking my hair for an hour trying to get it into this bun. I will not have angry hair follicles for dinner."

"I have so many questions. Can you eat angry hair follicles? Can follicles even be angry?"

"What?"

"You said you didn't want angry hair follicles for dinner."

"I didn't mean. I meant..." She trailed off as the words twisted into a jumbled mess inside of her mouth.

"I know what you meant. I was teasing. Although, I

265

will have a chat with my sister about putting you through such an excruciating beauty regimen."

"It wasn't that bad." She shrugged a shoulder. It was a ton of effort to get her waist length wavy hair into a sleek bun, that was for sure, but it was worth it in the end. "She's well meaning. It really does look nice."

"You are always exquisite."

"Your flattery knows no bounds."

"Not for my mate, it doesn't."

Her smile broadened. She loved hearing him say that. Even though they hadn't forged the bond yet, just hearing his words claim her made her feel giddy. Tonight, she promised herself. Tonight, she'd tell him she was ready to bond with him. If she found the courage enough to do it. Then she realized what he was doing. "Don't try to change the subject. Is it really dinner?"

"I still don't understand your sudden distaste. Besides, Dani and Evan say that humans need to breathe fresh air every once in a while."

"We could have opened a window or gone up to your private rooftop terrace for fresh air. None of this requires leaving the hotel." She still couldn't believe private rooftop terrace was part of her everyday vocabulary these days.

"You have been refusing to answer your phone. People will begin to think I've stolen you."

"I have been answering. No one's called really. Just my job and Marie..." and Max, but she didn't say the last part aloud. It didn't matter because Julius was already calling her out.

"They are not the only ones who've been calling," the

way Julius's voice lowered into a near growl had her hand stroking his thigh again. This time more soothing than teasing.

To Julius's obvious displeasure, Max had been calling ever since the incident at the warehouse. She just didn't want to deal with him right now. Maybe in a week or two. Or never would suffice if she had it her way.

"I figured he'd get the hint when I changed my voicemail to say, 'This is Erica, leave me a message. If this is Max, don't bother.'"

"If he calls again, I can answer it." Julius's tone verged on possessive.

"No need. I'll do it." She sighed, knowing she should at least talk to him. After the warehouse, she just wanted to enjoy Julius before he had to go back home. She didn't want to get dragged back into Max's bull crap. There was nothing more to say. He was an emotional time suck. "Next time he calls," she assured him, "I'll deal with him."

Julius's fingers twisted with hers and gave them a gentle squeeze. Several shivers erupted from where his hands met hers. She could live with this feeling forever. The car slowed.

"Are we there?"

"We sure are."

When they parked, Erica waited for him to open her door and navigate her to the sidewalk.

"One big step." He said when the nose of her heels hit what she figured was the curb.

"This sounds like a restaurant." She frowned. The sound of laughter and murmured chatter confirmed her suspicions.

"I bet you a hundred kisses it's not." Julius kissed the side of her face and wrapped her in his embrace. "Ready to see it?"

"Yes," she smiled.

She bounced on her toes when he loosened the strings on the blindfold, the anticipation growing too great to keep still. When he pulled the blindfold from her eyes, her mouth unhinged.

"Are you kidding me?"

She looked in surprise at Julius, then back in front of her.

"You owe me a hundred kisses."

"I can't believe you did this. How?"

"Well, we called up many of our contacts. Told them what we were trying to do. There are a lot of people who yearn to give patronage to young budding artists. I handled the logistics of transporting your paintings. Surprisingly, it was not as bad as I thought it would be. It's careful work transporting fine art, but not impossible."

She looked at the packed house inside. It was overwhelming how beautiful it looked from just the small gallery in the front. Her eyes welled with tears.

"You did this for me?"

"You deserve much more than this," he said tucking her shoulder under his chin. "This is a thanks for saving us. Now, two royals are in your debt."

"No, you're not."

"Those are the rules."

By the way he shrugged, she knew there was no

debating him. When she pulled her coat closer to her frame, he motioned to the door.

"Ready for your showcase?"

She nodded and put her hand in his as he led her inside, and she tried to keep herself from squealing. Her cheeks were already hurting from smiling so much.

It was much more than she could have ever imagined. Every finished piece was meticulously hung. Even her work from her classes made an appearance. Each one of them looked so good up against a wall instead of in stacks across her studio. They looked so professional. Against the cream walls and exposed brick in the back, it looked like a real artist presented here. Then the realization hit her, she *was* a real artist. By some miracle, this was her debut.

She turned to Julius again, "I can't believe this is for me."

"Let's take a look around," Julius said. She nodded.

Everything was so elegant. She'd only dreamed of a concept like this, but to implement it would have taken an army of people she didn't have. Well, she guessed she did now, she glanced at Julius wondering how he was able to pull it off without her knowing.

"Eri! You're finally here," her best friend squealed when she'd walked through the front gallery.

"Marie! You're here too!" She hugged her friend tightly in amazement, matching her enthusiasm.

"Heck yeah I am! You'd think I'd miss this?" Marie smiled.

"How did you know?"

"Someone worth your time called me and said he

wanted to make your dreams come true."

She must have looked ready to cry because her friend pulled her into another hug. They both looked at Julius who was greeting a few people he knew. Then, she looked around the room for the second time. This wasn't just pulling out his list of contacts, but hers as well. The faces of her classmates and her coworkers were all sprinkled into the mix of people, all set against a backdrop of her artwork. More tears started to come.

"He did that?"

"See what happens when you open yourself up to the right person?"

She kept her gaze fixed on the side of Julius's face. She did, she absolutely did.

"He makes you happy, I see."

"I can't even begin to tell you how much."

"Aww, see he's worth it," Marie pulled her into another hug before patting her shoulders. "Now, go on. Get back to him."

Erica chuckled when her friend shooed her away and went to talk to some of the other guests. She turned back around amazed at what Julius was able to pull together.

"Jules, what did you do to her?" Dani said after parting her way through the front gallery and stopping in front of her. Dani turned toward Julius who was already coming their way with a look of equal concern.

"Nothing, I'm just so happy," Erica blotted her eyes with the back of her hand. Thankfully the tears stopped. "This was so sweet."

Dani beamed. "It's our honor. I'm just glad you made

it without looking too disheveled. You two have barely been able to pry yourselves out of bed for the past few days," she plucked at her brother's suitcoat. Erica's cheeks tingled in embarrassment.

"Danica," Julius warned.

"What? It's the truth!"

"You could use more tact," Julius chided his sister.

"Where is Evan?" She changed the subject, gaze flickering through the crowd, too embarrassed to look either of them in the face at the moment.

"Around here somewhere, probably figuring out a way to cheat."

"At what?"

"We have a bet going," Dani animated, then grabbed a glass of wine from a waiter walking around with a tray filled with flutes. They'd even hired waiters for this.

"A bet?" she asked curiously.

"To see who can sell the most paintings."

"Sell the most?"

"Well, technically they're selling themselves. We're going for optimal bid before the last one sells. So far I'm winning."

Her head swiveled around to her hanging art. Next to each one, lay an elegant golden plaque engraved with her name, piece title, and year of debut. Directly under the engravings were colorful dots. Nearly every painting in her sightlines had one.

"Wow." Her brain was stuck on overwhelm. So overwhelmed that she didn't notice her mother enter the gallery until they were met with a disturbance from the front. Instantly, Dani and Julius straightened and looked at her.

"Oh, Erica!" Her mother waved and came rushing toward her, bumping into people along the way, not bothering to excuse herself as she forced her way through the crowd.

"Who is she? Did we invite her?" Dani asked from the corner of her mouth.

"No, I will take care of her," Julius straightened the lapels on his suitcoat and began to make his way toward her mother.

"No." She grabbed his arm to stop him. "We're not going to kick my mother out."

"She doesn't have to be here. Just say the word and she's gone." He settled back on his feet and put on a very charming smile. If she hadn't seen the frown at the corner of his eyes, she would have thought he was genuinely happy to see her.

"We'll be fine," She said and meant it. As her mother came up to her, she no longer felt the frantic energy she usually did. Or the eagerness to please her. "Mother, how are you?"

"Delightful. I hadn't realized your art thing was tonight. It was so kind of Melissa Novak to remind me. I would have been here sooner but, you know how your father is..." She trailed off. Yes, they both knew. He didn't come because they weren't invited. It was unfortunate that her mother decided to invite herself along to save face with her friends. She wasn't there for her. Not with the way her gaze swiped every corner of the room looking for fault. Her scrutinizing look even swept her frame. When she could find nothing to criticize, her lips puckered into a tight smile.

"Well, please feel free to have a look around." Her heart was pounding in her ears as she motioned to the rest of the room.

"Where's Max?" Her mother searched the crowd for him as if she hadn't been dismissed.

"You know Max and I aren't a thing," She said, her hand finding Julius's by her side. Her mother noticed, but intentionally ignored it.

"So, I've heard. You know he loves you to death."

Maybe her mother misunderstood. "Max and I aren't together anymore. We haven't been for a while."

"Nonsense, dear." Her mother scrunched up her face as if she smelled something unpleasant. "He's the best thing that has ever happened to you."

She stiffened and despite Julius's thumb gently stroking over her hand, the anger built inside of her. Before she had the chance to speak, her mother was already talking again.

"Well lucky for you, you still have a chance. He should be here any moment. Let go of your... benefactor's hand and try not to ruin this for us."

"You invited him? You weren't even invited, but you invited him?"

"Oh, nonsense dear, of course I was invited," she said loud enough for anyone within radius to hear.

"No, you weren't."

When Julius took a half step forward, she squeezed his

hand and pulled him back. She had this. She smiled calmly.

"I think it's time for you to leave."

But her mother wasn't paying attention. Her attention was focused on the front door, her eyes brightening when Max walked through it. "Oh, Max!"

Julius growled beside her. Dani quickly called for Asher. Erica turned to them quickly, when she sensed the tension building.

"Don't. I'll handle this." Erica let go of Julius's hand and went to intercept Max before he'd come in any further. Thankfully, her mother stayed behind.

Of course, Julius didn't let her get far. A quick glance over her shoulder confirmed he stood right behind her. Close enough to support her if necessary, but far enough to let her handle it on her own.

Erica tried to smile, but it didn't form even after she saw Max's face light up with relief.

"Eri!" Max fiercely pulled her shoulders so she stumbled into his chest. He squashed her arms at her side and pulled her into the most awkward hug of her life.

"Off," Julius's voice was gruff behind her. In true Max fashion, he didn't let go right away. Julius growled.

"Max," she stepped away from him. "Don't."

"I'm just so happy you're alive," Max softened. There was a flicker of guilt and apology in his sharp brown eyes.

"Of course, I'm alive," She stopped short of saying 'no thanks to you,' and settled on stiffly backing away instead.

"When I got to the warehouse—" Max began, but she cut him off.

"You came to the warehouse?"

"Of course, I did. He had you. He threatened your life. I know I haven't been perfect, but I would never want you hurt. You know that, right?"

She nodded. Max was a lot of things, namely a cheating lying bastard, but he wasn't heartless.

"When I got there, I saw you were gone and they were dead. I figured he got there before I did…" he nodded towards Julius. "I should have been there. You deserve at least that much. Especially after everything I put you through."

For the first time in a long time, there was honesty in his eyes. He'd meant what he said.

"I couldn't leave town before apologizing."

"Leave town?"

"Splinters has a dead man's switch. He always gets what he is owed. Even in death."

"Explain," Julius was right at her back, concern blotting his face.

"Splinters keeps a ledger of names of people indebted to him. If he dies before the debt is paid, each name will be picked off one by one until the ledger is cleared."

Her stomach turned inside out.

"Is Erica's name in his ledger?"

"No," Max shook his head. "Just mine. I am the one who owes him. Eri was a means to an end. He latched onto her because he knew she was innocent." Max couldn't look at either of them.

"What are you going to do?" She asked.

"The only thing I can. Run. Lay low for as long as it

takes."

"Where are you going to go?"

"Far away from here," he checked his watch. "I have to leave. I shouldn't have stayed in town as long as I have. I just had to see you. I needed to tell you I was sorry. For everything... I wish I could have done things differently by you. I know that now."

He turned to leave.

"Max, keep yourself safe."

He nodded, but she knew once he walked out of that door, she'd never see him again.

"Goodbye Eri," he said and walked out of the gallery.

"Bye Max." She watched him until she couldn't see him anymore. As he walked away, it felt like a door had finally closed on that chapter of her life. Freeing her to move on with hers. She said a silent prayer for Max. She knew him too well to know he wouldn't run forever. He was already formulating a plan. He'd find his way through it and he was going to be a better man for it.

"Where did he go? What did you do?" Her mother huffed then settled in a constant state of sighing as she fretted over Max. "Get him back here."

"Mother," Erica called to her mother who was craning her neck to see out of the window onto the darkened street. "I told you, Max and I are over. He just wanted to say goodbye."

"Goodbye? *Goodbye*," she looked more and more distraught as she said it. Then she turned to Julius. "It was *you* wasn't it?"

That was a big mistake. She moved between them and

looked her mother directly in the eye. "Mother, it is time for you to leave."

"Leave?" her voice turned shrill.

"Tonight, is a night for celebration. You're making it very clear that you're not here to celebrate with me. So, I am asking you to leave."

Julius made a simple hand gesture and Asher was already at their side. He whispered something into his ear then turned back to her mother.

"Mrs. Wallace, I believe Erica has said it's time for you to go," Julius's voice was calm but everything about him remained rigid.

Asher moved forward. Her mother's eye's bulged when she took in the sight of Asher's stocky frame, then clutched her purse tighter to her and turned on her heel.

"Well, I never. Wait until I tell your father about this!"

She rolled her eyes as Asher escorted her out. Her mother would never change. At least she no longer felt awful for being in the fire of her disapproval. As soon as the door closed behind her mother, the only emotion she felt was relief.

Looking around, most people hadn't even noticed their tryst. The very few that did all seemed to relax as if a dark storm cloud had passed and only sunny skies were ahead. That was what she felt, at least. A weight she didn't know was there lifted from her shoulders and she felt light and able to breathe.

"Are you okay?" Julius asked, wrapping his arms around her.

"Surprisingly... yeah," she turned to face him, keeping

in the circle of his arms. She nearly gasped in awe. He was truly breathtaking. When he looked at her like that—like she was the only person in the room—he dazzled her. His emerald eyes seemed to sparkle every time their gaze met. She loved his expression, a teasing mix of mischief and love. Especially when it settled into a smirk.

"Good, because you owe me a bet."

"A hundred kisses?"

"We should start now."

He didn't wait for her to respond. His lips were on hers and he was kissing her like he had ever since they'd left the warehouse, like he'd never wanted to stop.

Cheers rang out around them forcing them to come up for air.

"Don't you wish we stayed in?"

"Well, I sure don't," Evan cut into their moment.

"Evan!" Her enthusiasm returned and she pulled him into a hug. "Thank-you for coming."

"Of course, I'm here. Did you think this bozo would have been able to do this by himself?"

"Julius?!" Dani screeched from behind them causing them all to turn. "You took all the credit *again*?"

"Dani, you only helped a little."

Dani stayed dubiously silent for a moment, daggers shooting from her eyes. "Jules! Take that back."

He didn't, but Erica was already breaking away from Julius and wrapping Dani into a tight hug. "Thank you," she said, then her voice dropped to a whisper with a teasing smile, "I knew your brother couldn't have pulled this off by himself."

"Ah! I knew you were the smart one!"

"Hey! You're supposed to side with me."

She broke apart from Dani and stepped up to Julius and kissed his chin. "That makes two and I'm always on your side."

Forever. She should tell him that right now. This was the best moment. Instantly, her heart began to race when her gorgeous vampire stared into her eyes, then let another smirk up onto his face.

"Dani, we need to run the tallies," Evan tapped his sister on the shoulder.

"Right now?"

"Yes, it's imperative," Evan offered her a knowing smile before he ushered his little sister away.

She looked at Evan. Did he know what she was going to do? Before she could think of it more, Julius grabbed both of her hands.

"There is something I wanted to ask you." She felt the urge to pick at her dress, but Julius's hands stopped her.

All the air in the room seemed to rush out. Wow, this must have been what it felt like for a guy to propose. It took guts. Even when she knew the answer, there was still a tiny doubt that he changed his mind. What if he said no? Frick, she was going to throw up.

"Are you okay?" Julius asked cocking his head to one side.

Get yourself together. He already loves you. He's going to say yes. She gathered as much courage as she could into her lungs. "I was doing some thinking. I know you leave in a few days."

"I'm coming back."

"Yes, I know."

"In six weeks, that's as long as I'll need. I'd come sooner but the transportation is a bit slow... I can try to make other arrangements—"

Since when did he become so chatty?

"No, it's fine."

"I was thinking, when I do arrive—"

"Could you let me finish before I lose the nerve?"

Immediately, Julius hushed. His body stilled. He waited. She took another breath as she looked into his eyes.

"I was thinking, when you come back... I-I want to bond with—"

She didn't get to finished the words. His mouth was already on hers. Many cheers erupted from the crowd. Giggling, she didn't take her eyes off of Julius when they broke apart.

"Yes," he smiled and kissed her again. "A thousand times, yes."

EPILOGUE

ERICA

SIX WEEKS LATER

Erica was antsy. Her leg bounced as she tried her hardest to focus on finishing Julius's painting. She was dangerously close and wanted to finish it before he arrived into town late that night. She was running out of time. The sun had already set and she was well into the evening. His plane was due in an hour and all she could think about was being in his arms again. It was almost painful how much she missed him. Without him things felt off. Abnormal.

"Alright, Erica, just focus," she coached herself and picked up her brush. She tried to mix the right shade for his skin, but it was either too dark or too light. Nothing seemed to be cooperating with her today.

Knock. Knock.

She looked at the time on her phone. Too early for

Julius. Her eyebrows scrunched together as she looked toward the door. It couldn't have been her landlord. He and Mr. Hinkley had been eerily silent for quite some time. She speculated that it was probably Julius's doing. She'd speculated that he purchased the building, but a quick internet search confirmed otherwise. Not that she couldn't have just bought the building herself.

The money she made at her art show would covered art school and living expenses while she studied. She didn't have to work while going to school if she didn't want to. Of course, she kept her job tending bar at night. She really did have a blast there. Plus, the extra cash could be socked away for after she graduated. She'd offered to use the proceeds to help Julius pay for blood for his kingdom, but he refused. He said they would have plenty.

She put her brush in the rinsing cup and made her way to the door and looked through the peep hole.

She screamed and flung the door open.

"You're early!" Erica launched herself at Julius.

He took a step back before finding his balance and carried her back into the apartment.

"I'm back," he looked like he was trying to keep his own smile contained. She was glad he was failing. She loved his smile.

She kissed him. "That's seventy-three. I haven't lost count."

He returned it. "Seventy-four."

Then kissed her again and again.

"You even smell the same." She cuddled close to his neck and breathed deeply. "I missed you so much."

"I've been dying without you."

"You don't look it." Thankfully. She never wanted to see him on the brink again. "Are you hungry? Thirsty?"

"No, I ate on the plane and fed in the car." He replied, then the look he gave her was filled with desperation. "I hope you're not hungry because I've been, what did you call it, jonesing for you since I left."

Even though there was not a drop of his pleasure venom in her system, his words still held the magic to make her wet.

"Well, I could go for something." She played coy while he put his hands on her hips.

"Please say sex. I don't think I can hold my vampire back any longer."

"For sex or for bonding?"

"Both."

"You're ready to bond with me?"

"I'm ready for it all."

Unable to hold back any longer, she flossed her fingers in his hair and pulled him down for another kiss. "I'm ready too."

"There's no going back."

"I don't want to."

"Things will change. You'll be able to read my mind."

"I'm pretty sure I know half of what's in that dirty mind of yours already."

"Ouch. I thought you missed me," he tickled her.

"Stop it." She giggled and swatted him playfully. "You know I did. I'm so glad you're home."

"Home, I like that." His playful smile turned serious.

"Are you sure you're ready for this?"

"Absolutely." Was he? Was he having second thoughts? She should just ask, even if the thought started to break her heart into two. There was no rush. They could wait if he wanted to. "Julius, if you want to wait."

"No, there's no more waiting for me. I've been waiting a lifetime for this."

Immediate relief washed over her.

"Okay, now how do we do it again?"

"First, we share blood," he said.

She'd never drank blood before. Well, that was not true. She did when she had a busted lip from a rogue basketball on the playground when she was in middle school. It tasted like rust and copper. She wondered if vampire blood tasted the same. He must have sensed her uneasiness.

"It won't be bad. Try it," he said then pressed his index finger against his fangs. Dark red blood bubbled at the tip. He offered it to her.

Hesitantly, she put it to her lips and glided her tongue over his finger. She wasn't sure what she was expecting. It was like a cross between cherries and something she couldn't quite name.

"It's not so bad," she said. It was actually pleasant.

When Julius dipped his fangs into his own wrist and offered it to her, she took it without hesitation. She drank until it healed.

"Is that it?" She looked up to him.

He looked at her with a reverence she didn't expect. "A taste is all we need."

"Your turn," she inhaled. The blood in her stomach started to make her insides tingle. Not an unpleasant feeling. Just different.

Julius lifted her chin, then kissed her. "Eighty."

Then he tilted her head to one side and sunk his fangs into her neck and pulled just a small amount of blood from her. When he finished, he pulled back and left a gentle kiss behind.

"Eighty-one. I love you."

"I love you too."

Then, she saw them, a swirl of images floated around them all basked in a golden light. She was hallucinating. Julius's blood was making her hallucinate. Until she realized, those floating images weren't just pictures. They were things familiar, like her art show and the first time they met. She reached up.

"Do you see them too?"

"What are they?"

"My memories," he smiled and looked up with her.

"Will we see mine?"

"Eventually," he turned to face her. He was completely open. Drinking from a vampire was the most intimate experience she'd had by far. It required absolute trust. Because when they did, they opened up their entire soul to you. That's what she felt, Julius giving his soul to her. She accepted it without question and gave hers right back.

"Do you feel that yet?" He asked, his voice not carrying above a whisper. As if in confirmation, a new sensation started to form. It was powerful, much more powerful than she'd ever experienced. It felt like raw electricity flowed through her body, leaving her more enamored with him than she could have dreamed possible. Then it was followed by ecstasy.

If she thought his pleasure venom was potent. It had nothing on the power of his blood. This time she couldn't tell where the pleasure began and ended. It just was. And it was everywhere he touched and everywhere he didn't.

"Now, what do we do?"

"We need to close the bond," his voice was hoarse.

"How?"

"We fuck," the words were raw and throaty. There was nothing gentle about them nor what came next. And she didn't want it to be.

There was a burning need inside of her that agreed with him. They needed to fuck. The images dampened down when he pulled at her clothes. In quick order, their clothes became a pool at their feet as she tried to touch every inch of bare skin she could reach. Even touching him was pure bliss.

He flipped her around, bent her over so she was gripping the couch back with her hands.

"Ready?"

She could only nod as the power of his hips met her from behind, driving him deep inside of her.

Her insides relaxed and she groaned.

"I will never get used to that," her head lulled when he drove into her again.

His fingers dug into her hips and he pulled her back against him harder. "By the gods, I missed this."

"This is amazing," she moaned when he thrust inside

of her over and over. They were never going to last long. Not with the bond heightening everything to the point where it was hard not to see stars. Frick, if he kept it up, she might pass out.

His vampire seemed to growl in agreement.

"Tell me your mine," he demanded, quickening his pace. The world was slipping, she was barely able to hold on.

"I'm yours. Always yours." She whimpered, reveling in each wave of pleasure that jolted through her when his hips met her ass.

A sudden, savage orgasm ripped through her. Her legs shook, her back arched and her body clenched down onto him as he drove into her.

She'd never get used to the blinding pleasure he gave her. But at least she'd have an eternity to try.

"I'm yours." She panted as another orgasm hit her as he took several last hard strokes before he too went over the edge.

"I love when you say that," he eased himself out of her and pulled her onto the couch with him.

"S-say it back," she said between breaths.

"I'm yours, Erica."

"Say it again." She cuddled up to his chest and listened to his erratic breaths settle alongside hers.

Julius wrapped his arms around her and kissed the top of her head.

"I'm all yours," he said. "Forever."

LOVE BITTEN

VAMPIRE BLOOD ROYALS BOOK 1

DELETED SCENES

4

JULIUS

Erica's sweet scent was like honey to a bear. Delectable. But her touch was more addicting. He could care less what Erica was drawing, but he could have her ink him all day. The beast inside of Julius crooned at the velvety soft feel of her skin against his.

Her sure hands steadied against his and raced against the clock to sketch something that would delight him. It wouldn't take much for her to impress him. He was already delighted. So, he sat in the VIP booth in a trance and watched as the cacophony of thick lines converged on his pale hand.

With her warm sun kissed skin against his, her pulse raced, thrumming from her wrist and through his. It radiated in his body and throbbed in his chest as if her heart beat for his.

"A Raven." He blinked. Awe settled his cheeks into a smile.

It's just a coincidence. Evan's voice appeared in his mind as if he were sitting in the booth beside him instead of dancing in the tangle of humans down in the pit.

Or instinct. Of course, the girl in front of him would draw his house insignia. Julius was never a believer in fate, but when she began to shade in the bird's feathers, he knew that it's what drew them together.

When her phone buzzed, he wanted to wretch it from her pocket and crush it. Erica's hand clutched onto his harder as the pen moved quicker. Their time was running out. Why did he wager a ten-minute bet?

Fine strands of her wavy blonde hair tickled his forearm as she leaned in closer. She pulled her lip into her mouth and bit on it pensively. The pen moved feverishly, the pressure digging into him harder. It built an equal intensity inside of him.

Her phone buzzed again. One minute.

Not enough time. Erica's nails dug into him as her concentration surged forth. Ink splotched across his hand

and the warmth of her intensified next to him. She radiated like a fireball as she worked.

The minute dwindled down to nothing.

"That's time."

"Five more seconds," she pleaded, but her hand didn't slow its frantic pace. The concentration on her brow was adorable. His heart warmed.

"I see what you're trying to do," he murmured against her ear.

In an instant, she'd broken apart from him. Julius frowned. She was supposed to chuckle and keep hold of his hands as she inked him. Not back away. Oblivious to the distance, Erica kept her keen gaze on the raven on the back of his hand. He watched her eyes dart around it for several seconds before a slight frown took its place. She didn't like it. Then, her brow crinkled in worry as she glanced at him, then looked back at her creation. Was she upset? Afraid that she didn't please him?

By the gods, he wanted to claim her.

The beast inside of him agreed and let his fangs drop. Julius pinched his mouth closed. He needed to will them away. Focus on something else. For a moment his eyes closed trying to evoke a calm over him. Erica set his nerves on fire. With her so close, it was near impossible to separate the beast from the man.

Look at her drawing. Evan's somber voice tapped into his thoughts.

He'd try anything that would keep the beast in him from launching himself at the girl beside him and fucking her into the floor. So, he did. He focused on his pale hand and took in the drawing.

With a blotchy pen and an impossible time constraint, Julius was starstruck. Amazement blanched his thoughts at how it looked so much like the insignia of his house. Right down to the feather's intricate crisscrossed pattern that beveled in long elongated diamonds. It was not finished, but what was visible passed for a perfect replica of what adorned the breastplate of the armor he wore back home.

It worked. His fangs retracted and his beast settled.

Then, Erica stood up, pulling at the hem of her shirt and steadied herself.

"S-so," she cleared her throat, her voice tight with desire as his eyes raked over her frame. He should be less lewd, but the beast inside of him wanted her to know every inch of her would be his even if he couldn't touch her. Yet. But, if he kept on, he was going to make her uncomfortable. Stiffening his shoulders, he forced his eyes to meet hers.

"Do we have a deal?" She asked.

No. Evan's voice was clear in his head. You need to focus on the mission. Not this girl.

Despite his brother's protests, Julius plucked a white business card from his wallet and handed it to her.

"Call me. We'll set something up in the next day or two."

For fuck's sake. If you blow this for us, let it be on your head.

Let it be on your head? You're even starting to sound like them, Julius teased but was diverted when Erica's entire body came alive. She smiled wide and bounced on her toes in excitement as if the realization of what he'd said just dawned on her

Before he said anything else, footsteps bounded up the metal staircase toward them.

Erica put more distance between them. His beast let out a low growl but stopped short when he caught sight of the dragon. The owner of the club let off an encouraging smile.

"Mr. Craul," the dragon greeted him after he made his way past the burly bouncer at the edge of his section.

"Please, call me Julius," he returned Stick's smile with one of his own, hoping he'd say whatever he needed to and left him to Erica.

"Julius." The word was so light, like a feather on the air, that no one else would have heard it but him. His eyes popped to hers and held them for a moment. Please say it again, he pleaded. Wanting to hear it sung over and over to him.

"Julius," her boss moved between them. Julius forced himself to focus on the man with the spiky hair and scale patterned tattoos that cascaded down his arms. "Let me show you the wares of the club. We have several music areas, six bars and even a performance stage," Stick said in excitement.

This was the last thing Julius wanted to do. He wanted to stay with Erica.

Go. Evan's voice crept up inside of his mind, even though at quick glance, he didn't slow in his movements on the floor. We're here for the club, not the girl.

-End

Author's Note:

Sometimes characters don't always cooperate when you want them to. This scene desperately wanted to be written, even though it had no place to go and didn't fit. My serial voters wanted Julius to apologize to Max, because in the original version Julius was a little out of line and Max was perceived as innocent, but I knew Max was not the good guy and this scene came out instead.

Spoiler Alert: I used the first part of this scene in the first chapter of Love Game. I loved it too much to get rid of. Haha.

(alternate scene)

10

JULIUS

"IT'S COLD AS BALLS OUT HERE!" Dani drew her coat closer to her frame when the wind picked up, blowing his sister's jet-black mane into the wind as she deboarded a private plane. Julius's brows raised in amusement.

"You say I need to be less conspicuous," Julius gave his younger sister a wry smile before lifting her into a hug.

"You're going to squeeze me to pieces," Dani made a show of grunting. "It's good to see you too. Now let me down. I can't feel my arms."

To her credit, her arms were pinned at her side. With a chuckle, he let her go.

"By the gods, you look the same. I see you still have that mouth on you."

She made a face.

"And you've matured," Evan moved to greet their sister with a hug of his own.

"How was your flight?"

"You have no idea how hard it is to refrain from draining the pilot when you're thirty thousand feet in the air."

"I'm glad you didn't," Julius said watching ten other passengers descend the same flight of stairs his sister had.

"Do you have the goods? I'm starving," her exasperation was a little more dramatic than he remembered, but completely welcomed. He'd never admit it allowed, but he missed his pain in the ass sister.

"There's plenty in the car," Evan said, taking a small duffel bag from his sister.

Julius tossed him a look. Liar.

Evan merely shrugged, then looked around toward the plane. "Where are your bags?"

"They are being shipped. I couldn't very well lug those heavy things around."

"You do realize those aren't heavy to us," Evan mused.

"I have to blend in! Unlike some of you, I take my inconspicuousness seriously." She pulled her sunglasses off her face and slide them up into her hair like a makeshift headband.

"By taking a private flight?" Julius laughed.

"That's my part. I'm a rich kid, going to boarding school abroad, while I look for opportunities for our brother. We all have our parts to play. Speaking of, Evan tells me you're getting ready to screw this all up."

Julius turned to her teasing smile and softened. The distance from the tarmac to their waiting car was short.

"Evan lies," Julius replied with a hard laugh, watching Dani hop into the back seat, her eyes were on the black box on the floor behind the front passenger seat. "You'll see."

"When do I get to meet her?"

"I'll have to warm her up to you first."

"I'm no worse than Evan," Dani feigned indignation.

"Hey! I thought I was your favorite brother."

"And I love you just as you are," she teased before pushing the combination to the box and rifling through it. "Where's the blood?"

"That is the blood," Evan said, starting the engine.

"No, the real blood."

"I told you," Julius's voice turned sing-song. "Evan lies."

Just as Dani began to fuss, the phone in his pocket rang. Erica.

"Hello, love," he smiled despite himself.

"He-he's after me," her voice was small, but the stress was clear. She was in danger.

He sat up in his seat and leaned forward trying to hear her better.

"Who? Who's after you? What happened?" The car was too noisy. He couldn't hear her. Julius plugged one of his ears. "Can you two stop bickering for a second? Erica, where are you?"

"A-at my school."

"What school? I'm coming to get you."

Immediately, the car stalled for half a second as every set of ears listened intently to the girl on the phone.

"Lincoln Graves."

"Got it," Dani said beside him, her fingers flew over her phone. Less than a moment later, her phone was talking, giving them directions. Evan stepped on the gas hard.

"Erica, what happened?" Julius said, panic rising in his throat.

"He-he just came out of nowhere."

"Is he still there?"

The longest silence of his life stretched between them. When she didn't answer right away, ice shot threw his veins.

"Erica? Is he still there?"

"N-no. He's gone."

"Are you safe?"

"Y-yes," she said.

"Where are you right now?"

"I'm hiding in a classroom. I didn't know where else to go."

Relief washed over him. "Is there a lock on the door?"

"Yes."

"Lock it. I'm on my way."

"Don't hang up. Please," she begged.

He didn't have any intention to. "Drive faster, Evan."

For once, his brother didn't complain. He gunned it, weaving in and out of traffic. Horns of all kinds blared as they whipped in back and forth, barely pausing at the red lights before racing through the intersections. He needed his brother to go faster. Just as the thought left his mind, Evan pressed the gas pedal harder when they met a stretch of open road.

"Erica, what happened?"

"There was a guy... He—He was going to kill me."

She was in tears. He could hear her breaking over the phone. His insides crumbled. Julius tried to soothe her. "It's all right. You're safe now."

"Did she call the police?" His sister asked from the backseat.

"Erica, did you call the police?"

"N-no. I should—"

"No," Julius cut in, he needed to hear her voice now. If he lost connection, he'd lose control. "We'll handle everything."

Dani's gentle squeeze made his vampire hurt worse. She was shooting for comfort, but he'd only felt helpless. Erica was in trouble and he could do nothing but wait in the car until they arrived.

"We're almost there. The phone says we're five minutes out," Evan reassured him.

Five minutes was too long.

"Get there," Julius said, calculating how long it would take him to run on foot. Longer than five minutes, so he stayed put.

"Get her mind off of things," Evan murmured from beside her. Julius nodded.

"Erica, are you still there?"

"Yeah," this time her voice was a whisper.

"How's the painting of me going?" Julius asked.

"What?"

"My painting," he said again. "The one of me. Are you almost done with it?"

"Not yet?"

"What do you still have to do?"

She was silent for a while, but when she spoke her voice was louder, like it was gaining strength. "Well, I finished the color blocking. I've set your eyes. I still have to get the angles of your face right."

"So, you need a live model?" He offered. His chest felt less tight as she talked. Over the phone, she managed to soothe his beast. The most beautiful sound met his ears. She chuckled.

"I guess you're offering your services."

"Always."

-Fin

(DELETED SCENE)

12

ERICA

"Can I trouble you for a ride back to the studio?" Erica asked once they were outside. "I really don't want to ride the bus smelling like last night."

"I kind of prefer how we smell."

"Like sex?"

"With a hint of dragon breath," he teased. "It's utterly intoxicating."

Erica tucked in a laugh and a playful eyeroll. "How do you do it?"

"Do what?"

"You always know what to say. Me? I'm a bumbling fool, but you can just come off the cuff with the exact words. How do you do that?"

"It takes many years of practice... and the best damn speech coach my parents could buy."

"A coach?"

"My family is often in the public eye. Growing up, we all had speech and etiquette coaches."

"What does your family do?"

"They are into politics." Julius's answer was vague.

"Have I heard of them?"

"No, not quite that famous," he said.

"So, what does a speech coach do exactly?"

"Well, I was taught how to use the proper words at the proper time. She also taught me how to flirt and—"

"*She?*"

"Do I detect a hint of jealousy?"

She was most certainly not jealous. Alright, she was a tiny bit jealous. But she was never going to admit that to Julius's smirking face. "No, of course, I'm not."

"Are you sure?"

"What's there to be jealous of? That you needed someone to teach you how to flirt? Some of us have natural charm."

"Ouch."

Julius was such a faker. That didn't hurt his feelings in the slightest.

"Hush, you," Erica chided playfully. "Do I get a ride or are you going to force me to take the ride of shame?"

"Of course I can give you a ride. You rode me, I can return the favor," he threaded his fingers with hers and gave a gentle squeeze.

-End.

LOVE BITTEN

VAMPIRE BLOOD ROYALS BOOK 1

THE ORIGINAL OUTLINE

Author's Note:

Before I ran Love Bitten as a Love Serial, where voters got to decide what happened in the story as we went along, I plotted out an outline of where I thought it would go.

To say the least: The outline version of Love Bitten is waaaay different than the finished product. Admittedly, I loved what the voters have come up with and couldn't be happier with the final story.

Chapter 1

Erica thinks Max is cheating on her. And she's on her way to his office building to confirm this. Erica decides to destroy Max's car, but it turns out to be Julius's car.

Chapter 2

Julius blows up when he realizes his car has gone up in smoke (literally). But he also realizes that there's something distinctly different about Erica that he's attracted to. When she gets away, he mopes. But, we learn there is no time for moping because he and his brother needs to find an investment opportunity to help his kingdom. Evan convinces him to take his mind off of things and they go to the next investment location. A nightclub.

Plot twist: Julius goes to the night club and he finds Erica there.

Chapter 3 & 4-

Julius essentially blackmails Erica into going out with him (painting a commission). She has ten minutes to prove herself and she does her best. She hopes.

Chapter 5 & 6

Me: A few days after, Erica invites him to her art studio after class on a night she doesn't have to go to school.

Chapter 7

Me: They get to know each other, talk and things start to change. They open up with one other. She mentions the art showcase and how she's under so much pressure to perform well. Julius feels guilty that he's been adding to the pressure? (Maybe Max is not the villain we thought he was?)

Chapter 8

After not coming home that night, Evan calls him endlessly reminding him that they have to meet with Max in the morning and he's late. He scrambles over to Max's office building that he's wanting them to invest in. Evan reminds Julius of their goal: Get the money out of the alter realm not to fall in love. Julius is reminded of the stakes. Max is an asshat to his girlfriend. He sends her texts about wanting to explain everything and they read her responses (Julius doesn't know this is Erica).

Chapter 9

Julius convinces her that one night of fun is exactly what she needs. She convinces him to go on a real date. Marie is singing that night at the pre-opening for her gallery show. She invites Julius as her plus 1 since she and Max are on a break. At the pre-show, Julius does everything right. Erica delivers the commission (paints him- sexy times?).

Chapter 10

On the day of the art show, her art installation is sent to the wrong address and is in ruins. Julius comes to the rescue with an old dusty pick-up truck he clearly doesn't own to help her deliver her installation to the correct venue and helps her put the pieces back together again

Chapter 11

At the art show, Max showed up to surprise her for her big event and Julius is there. Dun. Dun. Dun!

Chapter 12

Julius drowns his sorrows in a pretty girls at Savu. Evan shows up and tells him that Erica is not really into Max, she just needs someone to show her that she's worth it. She was planning on breaking it off with him.

Chapter 13

After several missed calls, Julius tracks her down at her job. Evan coaches him through it?

Chapter 14

They have a blow out when Julius tells her that she's making a big mistake. She calls him out for the "one night of fun" they were supposed to be. Julius tells her that she knows it's not true. That they're deeper than that. She's firm in the fact that nothing else can happen between them. Erica announces that Max has proposed to her again, and wants to marry her.

Chapter 15

Erica goes over to see Max. When she gets there, she sees the white sports SUV. Everyone sees her coming, Max is in a "private meeting". She barges into his office and there on her knees is the bimbo from the night she wrecked Julius's car on her knees.

Chapter 16

Julius is drinking at her bar (some kind of masochist) and decides that he doesn't care that he's going to blow the business deal with Max. He goes over to Erica's house, then her art studio. She's throwing things all over the place. And she's heated that she ever thought about taking him back. Max shows up at her studio. Julius and he have a mini showdown, but he backs down. Max can't take a vamp alone. Not without his pack. Erica finally confronts him & tells him that it's over. For good this time and gives her engagement ring back.

Chapter 17

Julius goes back home, but he vows he's going to come back. He can't be away from her for too long.

LOVE BITTEN

VAMPIRE BLOOD ROYALS BOOK 1

AUTHOR INTERVIEW

What are your biggest inspirations?

In terms of writing? Getting lost in the world. Wow, that was lame. Hmmm... let's see. Sassy characters, a working laptop (which is tough when electronics malfunction around me), and a blank page have always inspired me.

What's your writing process look like?

I start at the beginning, but as soon I reach the tipping point, I write the last five chapters backwards. I hadn't even realized I did it until I was writing Love Game. I guess it's because I need to know it's going t turn out alright before I put our heroes in perilous danger.

Outline or Go with the flow?

Hahaha. Seriously, did you see the outline above? I try to stick with one, I swear, but through discovering more about my characters, things fall by the wayside.

Tea or Coffee?

Am I weird for loving the smell of coffee but hating the taste? It's too bitter! But I love tea. Strawberry Oolong or Iced Chai with almond milk if you're going.

Best book of all time?

Harry Potter Series (I know it's 7 books, but still). But I will say, the book that I have read more than once is one called The Last Days of Summer by Steve Kluger. It's a coming of age story that's completely hilarious from the first page and heartwarming until the last.

Do you like writing comedy or drama?

Both! Mostly because I'm secretly driven to prove my oldest brother wrong. He said I couldn't be funny if I tried. Well... you be the judge of that. Did this book make you laugh? I'm secretly taking a tally so I can throw it in his face at Thanksgiving dinner.

Book or Movie?

The book's always better! Although, there was one instance in my life was the opposite. Want to know the book? Hunger Games. I detested Katniss in the book. I didn't even get past the first in the series. But I thought the movie series was better.

What's the best thing someone's said about your book?

"Wow, that's a real book." – Mom (when my paperback proof copies came in.) I wonder what she thought I was doing when I said I self-published my first book. It will remain one of the great mysteries.

You write Vampire Love Serials. Why?

I have an addiction to them. Seriously, I'm hooked on the challenge of writing a story based on what my readers want because each week it's something new. My goal is always to try to blow their expectations out of the water. If I can do that, that would be the ultimate of ultimates.

Julius has brothers, who's your favorite?

Them all! For different reasons. My favorite brother is Gustav, because he really will make a bet out of everything. But my favorite sibling to write so far, is Dani. She can be outrageous sometimes and it's a ball of fun. Her sass knows no bounds.

So, what's next?

LOVE GAME!!!!!!!!!! Oh my gosh. Each story that I write always has a different feel to it. While Love Bitten is more light hearted and sassy, Love Game is a bit edgier but still a fun read. I can't wait for you to get your hands on it. In the meantime, I've included the first few chapters for you on the next pages!

LOVE GAME

VAMPIRE BLOOD ROYALS BOOK 2

EXCLUSIVE PREVIEW

PROLOGUE

DANICA

Text Conversation between Dani & Julius

Dani: Uh, could you two keep it down? By the gods, it's like a freaking woodpecker lives up there. Must this go on all day?

Julius: We're not even doing anything... anymore.

Dani: Next time get a hotel to yourself.

Julius: When are you going back to school again?

Dani: As soon as Gustav gets back into town. Which reminds me.

Gustav has been added to the chat.

Dani: Gustav.

Dani: Gustav.

Dani: Gustav.

Dani: Gustav.

Julius: He's not going to answer.

Dani: He's due home today. Of course, he'll answer.

Dani: Gustav.

Dani: Gustav.

Dani: Gustav.

Julius: Can you remove me from this?

Dani: No.

Dani: Gustav.

Dani: Gustav.

Dani: Gustav.

Gustav: Jesus, Dani, it's 2:00 in the morning.

Dani: Not here, it's not. Wakey, wakey.

Gustav: I hate you.

Dani: I'm glad you're back in town too! I have loads to tell you.

Gustav: We're not having this conversation until a decent hour.

Dani: But it's important. It's about Julius.

Gustav: What's happened to Julius?

Julius: Nothing's wrong with me. Dani, let him sleep in peace.

Dani: Oh, you have a lot of nerve talking about let someone sleep in peace with the way you two have been going at it.

Gustav: Who two?

Dani: Awake now?

Julius: Dani please.

Dani: Him and his forever love have been making a terrible racket.

Gustav: Who and whose love interest?

Dani: Julius's, of course!

Gustav: Whose?

Dani: Julius.

Gustav: Alright, I'm going back to sleep. It's clear you're trying to get one over on me.

Dani: I'm serious! You should see the way he looks at her. He has hearts in his eyes. <3 <3

Gustav: Goodnight Danica.

Dani: Gussy, stop.

Gustav: Call me Gussy again and I'm flying out to kick you in the pants.

Dani: You'd treat your sister that way?

Gustav: Call me Gussy again and find out.

Dani: I'm telling mother.

Gustav: Go ahead. She'll tell me to kick you in the pants too.

Dani: Hmph. ANYWAY—We're talking about Julius.

Julius: No, we're not.

Gustav: Which Julius?

Dani: Our brother, fool. He's met his one true love.

Gustav: True love—Wait a minute, is she crazy?

Julius: I DO nOT LIkE the CRAZY ONES

Gustav: Last time you talked true love, you'd just come off a weekend binger with a vampire who carved your names in hearts all over the castle.

Julius: It's not so bad.

Gustav: She carved them in stone.

Julius: Still not bad.

Gustav: With her fingernails.

Julius: This one's different.

Dani: I'll say, he's mated to her.

Gustav: ~~Fuck me sideways and put a flower in my hair. What do you mean mated?~~

Gustav: ~~Julius doesn't do serious~~

Gustav: ~~I had my money on Damian finding another mate (which is virtually impossible btw) before Julius would even~~

~~consider it.~~

Gustav: ~~Can I borrow six hundred chelets? I owe Evan. Did he have something to do with this? Tell him, that's cheating and I won't pay.~~

Gustav: ~~This isn't true.~~

Dani: Hello? Did you drop dead of shock?

Gustav: Let us be clear here, this is *our* Julius who has a mate?

Julius: Why is it so hard to believe?

Dani: Yep, it's him alright.

Gustav: Wow. Our Julius, huh? When did this happen?

Dani: Just before he went back to Elder.

Gustav: Why didn't anyone tell me?

Dani: You've been off the grid for almost three months jackass. What the hell were we supposed to do? Send word by carrier pigeon?

Gustav: Fair enough. A real-life mate, huh? Is she a hag or what? I wagered that she'd probably be like the Hunchback of Notre Dame. Pure soul but ugly as sin. Lucian thinks our brother is too vain for that nonsense.

Dani: OMG, that sounds like Lucian.

Julius: Why are we betting on my love life anyway?

Gustav: It's what we do.

Dani: What did Damian bet?

Gustav: You know Damian. "A king sides with no one." So, which is it? Her looks a flaming dumpster fire or what? I've got 100 chelets on this.

Julius: You lot are appalling.

Dani: Stop, Gussy. He's really pissed. I think I hear him throwing something. Besides, looks don't matter. She's good to him.

Gustav: She's hideous, isn't she? Victory is in hand.

Gustav: You're not going to tell me?

Gustav: Fine, keep your secrets. I'll fly out to see for myself.

Julius: No.

Gustav: Come on, if you're tethering yourself to her for the rest of your existence, she'll have to meet your siblings eventually.

Julius: I don't want to overwhelm her.

Gustav: So, it's really true. You have tied your life to someone else instead of being a selfish son-of-a-bitch. There has to be a story behind this.

Julius: A long story.

Dani: Not really. She bashed his car, they fell in love, here we are.

Gustav: Didn't you say she wasn't crazy?

Julius: SHE's noT CRAxuy!

Gustav: I'll leave that until I meet her, but is she human? I've got fifty chelets on her being human.

Dani: I think he broke his phone up there. Not that it matters, but yes, she is. They are talking about the change in a few years.

Gustav: I'm stunned. Well, tell him I send my congratulations. We'll feast in his honor when we return to Elder. How are you getting on?

Dani: You know, the usual. Trying to find blood for an entire kingdom of people, no big deal.

Gustav: Need help?

Dani: Thank you but I have everything under control. Make sure you're ready with a route.

Gustav: Will do. Are you sure you don't need anything? I told Damian it was too much to put on you.

Dani: ~~I'm not a baby.~~ I can handle it.

Gustav: You sure?

Dani: Of course, I'm sure!!! I'm getting human blood from the human realm. It's going to be easy freaking peasy.

1

DANICA

"IT'S COLD AS BALLS OUT HERE!" Danica stepped onto the tarmac, drawing her coat close to her frame. The wind whipped around the car, blowing through her hair. Jumping back inside of the car where it was warm and toasty was way more appealing than catching a flight back to school. Too bad her brothers were already scrambling behind her.

"Evan, I'm telling you we're in the wrong place. Dani, wait, get back in the car," Julius said in a flurry from inside. He tried to pry his seatbelt off without ripping the entire mechanism out again.

"We're in the right place." Evan paid their older brother no mind as he jumped out of the driver's seat.

"We have to go through the terminal thing then sit in the lounge until the plane is called. Come on, I don't want Dani to miss her flight. I have a mate to get back to. She'll wake soon." Julius stared pointedly at the watch on his wrist.

Like he could read the time. She rolled her eyes.

He'd probably seen his mate do it when he dragged ass to go anyplace that didn't involve a bed. Well, at least she found one reason to go back to school. She'd no longer have to be around their mate-fest anymore. Yuck, really.

"Chill out, Erica will still be there. Not that I'd blame her if she wasn't. She's way too good for you, you know," she quipped.

"Drop dead." Julius his lips flattened into a line when he finally emerged from the car. She fought a snicker.

"Ooh, I think you've touched a nerve," Evan grinned, fiddling behind the trunk.

She scrunched her nose in agreement, then raised a challenging brow at Julius. "He knows when someone's out of his league."

"No, I don't want to be stuck at the airport with you while you try to wrangle another plane. I'll leave you here alone."

"What's your rush? It's not even dawn yet. Eri won't be up until the sun is well within the sky," she assured him, looking at the brightening sky. Streaks of blues and oranges blossomed on the horizon of the airfield, but the sun wasn't out yet.

"Is it a crime to want to be there when my mate wakes up, maybe with a little hot breakfast?"

Evan paused to stare at their brother in disbelief. "That's actually thoughtful of you."

Yeah, she had to agree, Julius with a mate was a changed vampire.

"Very sweet," she nodded. "Now, grab me a paper bag so I can hurl in it."

"You wait until you find your mate," he grumbled.

"Don't put that in my path!"

The last thing she needed was to get caught up in a mating situation. She glanced sideways at Julius who bounced on his toes then looked at the watch he couldn't read again. Mating made you do crazy things.

He'd faced a warehouse full of shifters for his mate. Dumb ass. Not that he wasn't supposed to save his mate—of course he was—but going off alone was the dumbest thing he'd ever done. Good thing he lived through it or she would have figured out a way to resurrect his dead body so she could kill him herself.

If that was the kind of trouble a mate would bring into her life, she'd rather not have one at all. She had enough to deal with already. Her eyes darted to Evan, a reminder that she needed to be careful of her thoughts around him.

Why? Do you have something to hide? He pushed the thought into her mind, then fiddled with the trunk again.

Yeah, my own business. What the hell are you doing?

Trying to get this damned thing open.

Danica huffed, then crossed the few feet it took to grab the keys dangling from her brother's pinky and push the button to open the trunk.

"Ah, that's what that does," he said, crunching his brow. "Can I push it again to make it go back down?"

"No."

Evan pushed the key fob anyway, then waited for the trunk to have a reaction. He frowned when the trunk didn't move. When would they realize she knew more about the human realm than either of them combined?

"Well, that's stupid. Why do humans create things that only half work?"

"Don't blame them for your inadequacies."

"Are you sure we're in the right place? I don't see anyone," Julius said impatiently, flipping up the collar of his thick black peacoat around his ears.

"This is the right place, dear brother. That's my ride right there." Danica motioned to a private plane debarking from a hangar and moving its way toward them. Julius's eyebrows hit his hairline.

"Weren't you on me about being inconspicuous as the King demanded?"

"This is!"

"I believe a private jet is the definition of conspicuous," Julius laughed.

"Semi-private," she corrected, then explained that she'd have to share the plane with a few other passengers.

"Then, why not take a regular plane? We do it all the time."

"I don't fly commercial," she snorted. When that pill didn't go down well, she explained, "Damian's forcing me to do it."

Her brothers tossed her twin disbelieving looks.

"I'm serious! While you get to be businessmen, I get to be a socialite turned university student while I look for opportunities for our brother. That means, I don't ride commercial." Although, quite frankly, taking a semi-private jet was hardly a hardship.

"You're taking this role a bit too seriously," Evan said, leaning inside of the trunk.

"*No*, I cannot afford to screw this all up like you have."

"Excuse me?" Julius turned to her, offense lining his eyes.

She waved him off. He knew he'd failed to get the two investments their brother needed to buy blood for their kingdom. Sure, the dragon's bar was going to be a cash cow, but having one investment was risky. Just as she was going to point it out *again*, and how it was now up to her to procure the real thing to have it hauled back home, Evan's head popped up around the lid of the trunk.

"Uh, Dani, where are your bags?"

"They are being shipped. I couldn't very well lug those heavy things around."

"You do realize they aren't heavy to us."

She groaned in frustration. "Blending in, remember?"

"You never cease to amaze me," Julius scoffed playfully.

"You're just jealous because I'm better at this than you are."

"Better at being a spoiled socialite? That's hardly a stretch for a vampire princess," Evan chuckled.

"Hush before I demote you."

"From what?" His chuckle turned into an all-out laugh.

"Being my favorite brother."

"Yeah, it's a coveted spot you know," Julius butted in with a wiggle of his brow.

She frowned. "Quiet Jules. You're only jealous because you could never earn the spot."

"Ouch," he laughed.

"True is true," she shrugged, glancing around the tarmac.

A few of the other passengers had pulled up beside them and waited for the flight crew to open the plane. Five so far. Not bad, five humans in cramped quarters she could handle.

"How is he your favorite anyway?" Julius cut into her thoughts. "Evan lies."

"No, I don't."

"Evan is more honest than you are," she protested. "Plus, *he* wouldn't have sent me across town when his mate's life was in danger."

"You're never going to let me live that down, are you?"

"No, because I should've been there helping you fend off those damned shifters."

More cars pulled up to the lot. A lot more humans than she'd originally thought were going to be on her flight. Sure, five or six she could do. She counted the number of luxury cars. Ten. Not good. Just to tease her, the sound of their heartbeats grew stronger. Her throat became suddenly too dry to swallow.

She knew she should've had a blood bag as soon as she woke up. Going too long without sustenance was a danger to everyone. It already took a mountain of energy to keep her thirst under control when she wasn't desensitized.

There's blood in the car.

Thanks be to the all gods. A sigh of relief escaped her. At least one of them had enough smarts to scratch two brain cells together to come prepared. She definitely needed to placate her thirst before boarding. Otherwise, her control would slip.

It'll get better with time. Evan's reassuring thoughts invaded her own. Yeah, sure. She'd heard that song and dance before. The thirst would diminish as she got older, or so, every one of her siblings had said.

That was easy for them to say. They weren't the surprise child who had to learn everything fifty years behind everyone else. Of course, to them, controlling their carnal urges was easy. How long it would take for her to not want to open a human vein on sight was anyone's guess. For now, she'd been relegated to regular feedings to calm her thirst.

"It's in the box in the back," Evan pointed at the car.

Opening the back door, she reached into the box on the floor, rifling through several black packages looking for the few clear ones that she'd kept at the hotel.

"Evan, where's the blood?"

"That's it," Evan said, leaning against the car, nodding at the packages in her hands.

"No, the real blood."

"Hmph," Julius's voice turned sing-song. "Are you sure Evan's your favorite?"

"That's not funny Jules," she cut him a glare then looked over her shoulder at her lanky brother who'd better have an explanation.

"I am not lanky."

"Where's the blood?" Her voice came out low in a near growl.

"We're back on rations. Vacation's over."

"I can't drink this," she looked at the black bag of synthetic blood in disdain.

"Why not?" It was a simple question, but from the gleam in his eyes she could tell he was trying to get into her head. Not going to happen.

"Synth blood is disgusting."

"Tell me about it," Julius grumbled in agreement.

"You have no idea how hard it's going to be to refrain from draining the pilot when we're thirty thousand feet in the air with only synth blood in my stomach."

"Well I hope you do. Bone mending is nasty business for vampires. Not to mention, it'll be extremely difficult to explain how you're the only survivor in a plane crash that left those on board without any blood in their veins," Evan watched several people walk toward the gathering area.

"I will try my best not to expose vampirekind, but if I don't succeed, tell Damian it was your fault," she slammed the box closed after grabbing a few bags.

Evan bit the inside of his cheek; his unnaturally azure eyes bore into the side of her face in concern.

What's wrong?

Nothing.

Then, why are you avoiding your thoughts.

Because they're mine and I can do whatever I want with them. You know, by definition, you shouldn't be reading them at all. It's rude.

What are you hiding?

Besides, I'm not hiding anything.

Let me see, then.

No. Nosey ass.

There was no way she was going to open up her mind to him. She didn't need to. She wasn't a baby anymore.

I worry about you.

"I'm fine. Really."

He let out a reluctant sigh then pulled out his phone. "I'll make sure Asher is there when you land with provisions. Maybe you should take another bag just in case."

She groaned. "I'm not going to lose control. I don't need my babysitter to pick me up."

Asher was her bodyguard who'd gone ahead of her to run security checks and to probably sneak in a visit with his mate. This would have been the first time in months since he'd been able to take a few days off. Being her personal body guard didn't allow him much free time. She didn't want to disturb him.

Evan said something that she dutifully ignored and turned to Julius.

"Tell Erica I'm going to miss her dearly. You should work on convincing her to come to the castle. You know mother would love to meet her."

"I am not throwing her to *those* wolves."

"Well, maybe not to Magest, but what about Elder. She'd love Elder castle. Damian would let her stay."

"We're permanent here."

"You're no fun."

"Why do you want us back there? It's not like you're going back any time soon."

"I will when school's out. Mother insists. For the games," she groaned.

She hated everything about the courting games. Any eligible vampire of age gathered to court each other in an attempt to find their "love match." Severe air quotes intended.

Contrary to its name, the love games had no love in them. Just political social climbing that was more of a contract between countries than marriage between lovers. Matches made in the love game were a guaranteed lifetime of misery. But as an unmated princess, she was primed to be brought to the auction and married off to the highest bidder. Royal life was a total douche.

Evan snickered. "Mom's trying to marry you off too?"

"It's Julius's fault. If he hadn't gotten himself mated, mother wouldn't be in such a rush to marry the rest of us off to increase her political alliances."

The flight crew opened the plane. Several passengers in the gathering area made their way to the open door. Dani adjusted her purse. "Looks like it's time for me to go."

"Have a safe flight," Evan wrapped her into a hug. *Are you sure you can handle it? We can always get you on another flight.*

I'm fine. She let an easy smile play on her lips, returning his hug. "Don't miss me too much."

"I, for one, won't," Julius chuckled when she gave him a scathing look. "I'm only kidding. Come here, you."

Julius pulled her into a bear hug.

"You're going to squeeze me to pieces. I'm going to miss you too. Now let me down. I can't feel my arms."

With a chuckle, Julius let her go. "When's your next break? I want to be prepared for when you come barging in where you're not welcomed."

"Fuck off, you love it." The boarding line quickly. She needed to get going. "Time for me to go or get left behind."

Pulling her sunglasses from the small purse at her side, she slid them onto her face just in case her eyes went all vampire on her. Having them pool to black and scaring the hell out of the humans on board was not her idea of a good time. Neither was being on a crowded flight for the next six hours with nothing but nasty ass synth blood to keep her satiated.

"Make sure you drink it. It'll help," Evan said, glancing down at the black bag clutched so tight in her hands it might burst over her fingers.

Gritting her teeth, she nodded and bid her last goodbyes, then went to join the line. All the while, making sure to keep her thoughts clear of everything except the smell of fresh air instead of the sweet smell of the passengers gathering on the plane.

The flight attendant grabbed her ticket with a smile. Danica recognized her immediately. She'd been the rock star who took care of her on the flight in.

"Stacy. Good to see you again."

"Welcome back Miss Craul," the woman brightened instantly, "If there's anything you require on your flight, please let me know."

Your vein, she thought with equal cheerfulness, but instead, she gave the astute woman a small smile and made her way up the stairs with one final look over her shoulder.

Evan and Julius were back in the car and pulling away from the tarmac. She let her shoulders slump.

How in the hell was she going to survive this flight without blood?

Her body didn't tolerate synth blood the way theirs had. Whenever she had more than a mouthful without real blood in equal measure, it would come back up on her. She would've mentioned it, but everyone else had taken their rations so well. Then once again, she'd be the odd man out. *The baby.*

A lot of good that secret did her now. Now, she was stuck in an airplane with the most delicious smelling humans alive with nothing but her self-control stopping her from tearing the entire place apart.

Pushing those thoughts from her mind, she forced herself to her seat. She could do this. It was only six hours. Once the cabin was saturated enough, she'd become nose blind to the scent of blood and be fine.

She hoped.

2

DANICA

WHAT THE HELL WAS TAKING the pilot so long? She'd chosen this airline for their promptness, which it delivered on in spades on her flight into town. It ran like clockwork. Everything from boarding and takeoff to in-flight services and landing could be calculated to the minute.

Today, not so much.

Danica looked around the cabin. Everyone else was buckled in. All too busy to notice they hadn't taken off at 6:00 A.M like their boarding tickets promised.

Hmph. It wasn't like checking one's financial stats or taking a last-minute phone call was more important than getting to their destination on time. Didn't they realize they could be in mortal danger with a teetering vampire on their flight?

She glanced at the time again. 6:15. She looked for the flight crew who should've been preparing them for takeoff.

Stacy distributed extra blankets while her colleague, a tall, skinny, overly cheerful man whose red tie was a tiny bit crooked, handed out breakfast cocktails and snacks.

You've got to be kidding me. They should have been off the ground already. She held in an exasperated sigh.

Patience had never been her strong suit. When she wanted something done, she wanted it done immediately. Not in a second, not after distributing a warm blanket and a mimosa to the woman in the floppy hat in the back.

She needed the flight crew to hurry the hell up already. The least they could do is pretend they were the premiere avionics company they touted to be on their website and close the freaking door.

Trying to go nose blind was ridiculously hard when new air reset her olfactory nerve ever few minutes. To spite her, another gust of wind whirled through the cabin.

Great. Just freaking great.

She clenched every muscle she had to keep a tight rein on her vampire who itched like a fiend to come to the surface. There was not a gods' chance in hell was she going to allow that to happen. If she did, mayhem and murder would spew all over the jetliner.

She fought with her base instincts until the antsy feeling of wanting to open a vein disappeared.

There, another crisis averted. Well, until another gust of wind would rip all of her hard work away again.

Look on the bright side. At least the seat in front of you is vacant.

That was a small victory. Every other seat had been filled, but somehow, by some miracle, the one opposite of her had no one. Thanks be to the all gods.

Because keeping a voracious vampire at bay with a walking blood bank sitting in front of her would have been nearly impossible.

Instead of looking at her phone again, she rummaged in her purse for something to do. Pushing a useless black package of synth blood to the side, she grabbed hold of her compact.

She probably looked like hell. A glance in the tiny mirror confirmed she wasn't far off. Her skin was paler than usual, her lips dry and starting to crack. She should have taken a cue from floppy hat in the back and wore a sun hat that covered half her face. That way she'd look like an incognito movie star instead of a pale, dry faced broken down heiress.

She hadn't realized how much more human she looked when she had their blood in her system. Now, she looked every bit a stereotypical vampire. Pale-faced, gloomy, and tragic as hell.

She couldn't have that now, could she? The whole point was to blend in. She rifled around in her purse for her makeup bag and pulled out her blush pallet, praying it wouldn't make her look like a porcelain doll with clown circles painted on its cheeks. That would be a thousand times worse.

Thank the gods for moisturizer, blush, and concealer. In the right proportions it could even make Frankenstein look like a beauty queen, which was exactly what she needed right now.

After an overhaul, a lip gloss application and a quick comb through her hair, she could almost pass for human.

Satisfied with her handywork, she put her compact away. At least she would look good while she sat in suffering for six hours. That's if the plane ever took off. She checked the time again.

6:30 and no sign of any gumption to get the hell out of there.

She should probably try to muster up some of that patience her mother had always told her she should practice every once in a while. She was going to be fine. The wind seemed to have calmed down, she didn't look like the depths of the underworld had come for a reckoning, and the scent of blood wasn't quite so potent.

She settled back in her wide leather seat and stared out the window until her phone beeped with a text message. Gustav.

Of all her siblings, he'd been the closest one to knowing the truth about her blood problem. He knew firsthand how bad her cravings were when she'd gone too long without blood.

Gustav: How are...things?
Dani: ~~Things are shitty seeing as my meal's still at the hotel.~~

Her finger hovered over the onscreen keyboard in hesitation when she read back her response.

No, then he'd ask about the synth blood and the truth would make him worry.

Dani: Evan got to you, didn't he?
Gustav: He's worried.
Dani: Evan needs to mind his own damn business.
Gustav: I'll be sure to tell him ☐.
Dani: Good that way he can stop poking his head in where it doesn't belong.

Gustav: It's nothing to be ashamed of. We've all had problems with the bloodlust. Just drink the synth and find your place of Zen, like we practiced. Remember?

Dani: Yep, I remember.

Gustav: Have you left yet?

Dani: Getting ready to take off now. Have to go.

She exited the app and put the phone under her thigh.

Gustav was a last resort. She had to practice by finding her Zen like he taught her, that's all. If she focused on her vampire's desires too long, she'd be apt to give into them. So, she needed to find her happy place.

Every picture of tranquility she'd ever seen included a person in front of a sun with a serene look on their face and closed eyes. She couldn't do much about the sun since it was coming up behind an overcast, but she could do everything else while she trained her brain to ignore the smell of blood.

Especially the businessman in the back. Short sandy hair and a racing pulse that was probably due to pre-flight nerves. She needed to ignore the loud thudding of his heart. And not focus on how it would be easy to flirt with him and convince him to join the mile-high club while she opened a vein. Just a tiny one, he'd be healed before he'd stopped shaking from his orgasm.

Now, that was Zen. She could get what she needed. And maybe she wouldn't have to hurt anyone. It was better to satiate the cravings now. If they got any worse, she'd want more and more blood. Now, a few mouthfuls would tide her over.

She shifted in her seat to get a better look at him. His booth partner, a pretty middle-aged woman with a killer sense in shoe fashion, was reading a book on leadership in the workplace in front of him. Were they together?

She didn't remember them boarding together. Then again, she was too busy trying to find blood to notice much of anything.

Their body language didn't give her a read on whether they were acquainted.

She should risk it. Ask the woman to trade seats with her. If they were married, she'd tell her to fuck off. If they weren't, she'd probably rejoice in an empty booth.

Easy peasy.

She rose from her seat.

"Ms. Craul, can I help you with something?"

The flight attendant's sudden voice behind her thwarted her back to reality. Adrenaline made her legs unsteady as she realized what she was planning to do. Orgasms wouldn't make him oblivious to the fact that she was a freaking vampire who'd just fed on him.

"Uh, no," she gave Stacy a small smile before thinking of an excuse. "I'm sorry my legs are cramped from sitting so long. How long before we takeoff?"

"We have a final passenger to board, then we will make our departure."

A man in a dark grey suit beside them crumpled the corner of his newspaper to check the gleaming watch on his left wrist before making a sound of disapproval.

"We were supposed to leave at 6," he complained. "I have a meeting to get to this afternoon, we can't wait."

"I understand your concerns," Stacy kept her voice gentle. "We'll only be a moment."

"I paid for timeliness," the man crumpled the newspaper in the cubby beside him and stood up even though his suit jacket made it difficult.

"And you'll have that. We will land on time. The pilot will make up the time in the air," Stacy explained, then offered him a warm smile. "Would you like me to bring you anything while we waited?"

Talk about a customer service personality. Stacy managed to remain collected when he refused to sit in his seat. She also didn't back away when he approached her.

She must've been used to dealing with his type. The kind of businessman who thought just because he could afford to ride private, that gave him the right to step on anyone he deemed beneath him. Anger curled inside of her, but Stacy's calm reassuring voice was already on the case.

"Sir, take your seat. We'll take off shortly."

"No, we should take off *now*," he ordered. "It's already half-past the hour."

"Do we have a problem here?" Stacy's skinny flight attendant companion came from the front of the aircraft to stand right behind her.

"I do have a problem. I demand to speak to the pilot."

The man's voice awoken the rest of the plane. Too many pulses raced at the growing tension between the man and the flight crew.

"No," Stacy emphasized, remaining level and calm. "You will take your seat."

The man turned a brilliant shade of red, his anger highlighting the veins in his neck to perfection. Sputtering he looked around the cabin. A rather thick vein in his neck pulsed. Dani's mouth went dry. After a second pulse, her vampire surged forward. Her fangs drew down into spires against her lips.

In an instant, airplanes had become her worst enemy. There she was, sandwiched between several meals. Two equally delicious flight attendants on one side and an angry stumpy businessman on the other. And businessman was standing much too close for his own good.

All it would take was a swipe of her left arm to grab him by the middle and sink her fangs into his thick neck. It would take less than a quarter of a minute for anyone else to react. By then, she wouldn't be able to stop until she'd drank her fill. Once she'd polished him off, she'd take on the others, leaving the business man with the sandy hair for dessert.

Then for ha-has she'd even suck down that nasty ass synthetic blood in her purse while she figured out how to get her name off the manifest and...

For the all gods.

She wrenched herself back and forced herself to think of the atrocity she was contemplating.

What was wrong with her? Her thirst was not worth fourteen innocent lives. No one deserved to die. She needed to remove herself from the buffet.

"Excuse me," she said through barely opened lips as she pushed past the flight attendants and into a narrow hallway in search of a bathroom.

Three doors on the left led her into her temporary sanctuary. If everything wasn't crumbling against her ears, she'd take time to enjoy the fact that she didn't have to be a contortionist to turn around in it. But she did enjoy the tan leather chair that promptly became her ass's new home as she threw her head in her hands and screamed into her palms.

She was completely losing it.

She'd tried doing what Gustav taught her. Kept her focus on the consequences of losing control. Fourteen innocent people didn't deserve to die because she'd lost it. There was no way she'd ever be able to look at herself in the mirror again if she went through with it.

She breathed through the tension. The scent of human blood was still strong.

She needed to clear the smell and start over.

Good thing she was locked inside of a bathroom—a place notorious for its smell. Starting with the more pleasant pursuits, she grabbed at the metal soap dispenser and yanked it from the wall. She squeezed a palm full and put it up to her nose and took a whiff.

Lemon was a good scent. It was especially pleasing on the woman who wore dark sunglasses and a big floppy hat in the back of the plane. The lingering aroma mixing with the scent of her blood had left her wondering if a hint of it would end up in the taste.

Not helping.

Dani grabbed a soft white towel from the basket bolted next to the sink and scraped off as much soap as she could before rinsing the rest.

She needed something else to clear the scent of blood. Her eyes glazed over the toilet room door.

Desperate times called for desperate measures.

Her face scrunched up into a frown when she opened the door that housed the bowl of destruction.

The bathroom may have looked like five-star accommodations, the toilet room did not. Consisting of only a toilet seat in the center of a metal bench, it looked like they'd run out of budget by the time they'd gone to design it. And it smelled like it looked.

"Eww," she whispered, then gagged.

Just do it, it'll be over before you know it.

This was definitely worse than synth blood. Trying desperately not to touch the lid any more than she had to, she pinched it between two fingers and lifted it.

She dry-heaved, but took in a deep breath despite it. A second was all it took.

If there had been anything in her stomach, she would have upchucked it exorcist style all over the restroom at just the thought. It definitely hadn't been cleaned out between flights.

As disgusting as it was, it did the job. It got her vampire's mind off the scent of blood. She took in a cautious breath. It wasn't gone, but more manageable now.

"Are you alright in there Ms. Craul?" Stacy gently knocked on the door.

"Yes," she said, but the words came out like she'd been caught swallowing knives.

"The captain's ordering everyone to take their seats."

Apparently, their mystery passenger had arrived. She took another breath to steady herself. As long as no one triggered her, she could keep her vampire at bay.

"I'm coming out now," she replied swinging the door open. They both jumped back when they realized they were inches apart.

"Oh!" Stacy said brightly, "Let me move out of your way."

The flight attendant flattened against the panel so she could scoot by and into the main cabin.

"We'll be ready to take off shortly," she announced to the rest of the passengers through a phone tethered to the wall.

While everyone murmured their appreciation, her vampire went stalk still, frozen like a caveman encased in ice.

A deep cologne wrapped around her and weaved its way into her consciousness, its earthy notes made her close her eyes to revel in it. Business man with the sandy hair in the back had nothing on the sheer delightful sweetness that emanated now. Forget about focusing on anything but its earthy notes.

The blood sung to her. A low rhythmic thud pulsed from the owner's veins to her ears.

The dryness in her mouth increased tenfold. She wanted to taste it. No, she *needed* to taste it.

There was no stopping her fangs this time.

Or the vampire inside of her clawing to get out.

LOVE GAME

Her mission should've been easy, they said.

Masquerade in the human realm as a rich socialite turned college student, secure blood for her kingdom, and don't get caught in the love game. Easy freaking peasy. Right?

Ha!

Not with *him* at the center of the game board.

Sebastian Wade held her kingdom's fate hostage.

If he wanted to wager her kingdom, then she'd raise him his heart. Then, crush it. All she had to do was resist his devilish charm. Easy freaking peasy.

Because after all, all is fair in the love game.

ABOUT THE AUTHOR

Sabrina C Rose lives in the dry heat of Arizona, where she spends her days retreating from the sun and her nights cooking up fairy tales that include oodles of paranormal goodness.

When she's not plotting against the vampire king, she's kicking back and watching all the Netflix. Current line-up: Agents of Shield, the Originals, Sense8, and Stranger Things.

Ask her why Eric Northman is one of the greatest vampire boyfriends ever created and you may unearth the secrets to the universe (no promises, though).

Join her on her website:

www.sabrinacrose.com

Join the fun on her newsletter:

sabrinacrose.com/newsletter/

Printed in Poland
by Amazon Fulfillment
Poland Sp. z o.o., Wrocław

59948184R00211